A
Disappearance
in Fiji

Nilima Rao is a Fijian Indian Australian who has always referred to herself as 'culturally confused'. She has since learned that we are all confused in some way (and has been published on the topic by Australia's Special Broadcasting Service as part of the SBS Emerging Writers Competition, so now feels better about the whole thing). When she isn't writing, Nilima can be found wrangling data (the dreaded day job) or wandering around Melbourne laneways in search of the next new wine bar.

A Disappearance in Fiji is her first novel, and she is currently working on the second in the series.

A Disappearance *in* Fiji

NILIMA RAO

ZAFFRE

PRAISE FOR *A DISAPPEARANCE IN FIJI*

'This is an utterly charming novel. The setting is exotic and the characters are intriguing. Nilima Rao is an author well worth discovering.'
—Alexander McCall Smith, bestselling author of the *No. 1 Ladies' Detective Agency* series

'Meet Sergeant Akal Singh, the complex and charming hero of a thoroughly original mystery set in 1914 Fiji. Fans of Golden Age mysteries will relish this debut novel by a compelling new talent, Nilima Rao. More, please!'
—Sujata Massey, Agatha Award–winning author of *The Widows of Malabar Hill*

'A poignant and entertaining read … Sergeant Akal Singh is a charmingly imperfect and captivating protagonist. I love Akal and hope we'll be seeing a lot more of him!'
—Ovidia Yu, author of the *Aunty Lee Singaporean Mysteries*

'A marvellous debut that beautifully paints life in a part of the world that few of us have a chance to visit. The highlight of Nilima Rao's well-crafted novel set in Fiji in the days of British colonial rule is the collision of cultures and class and how one man is charged with the task of unlocking the mysteries they create. A pleasure to read.'

—Colin Cotterill, author of the *Dr. Siri Paiboun Mysteries*

'A gripping, authentic and brilliantly told mystery story that brings to life colonial era Fiji with a wealth of intriguing characters and underlying tensions. I have found a new favourite mystery series!'

—A.M. Stuart, author of the *Harriet Gordon Mysteries*

First published in the US by Soho Press, Inc.

First published in the UK in 2023 by
ZAFFRE
An imprint of Bonnier Books UK
4th Floor, Victoria House, Bloomsbury Square, London WC1B 4DA
Owned by Bonnier Books
Sveavägen 56, Stockholm, Sweden

Published by arrangement with Rights People, London.

A CIP catalogue record for this book is
available from the British Library.

ISBN: 978–1–80418–300–7

Also available as an ebook and an audiobook

1 3 5 7 9 10 8 6 4 2

Typeset by IDSUK (Data Connection) Ltd
Printed and bound in Great Britain by Clays Ltd, Elcograf S.p.A.

Zaffre is an imprint of Bonnier Books UK
www.bonnierbooks.co.uk

For Aaji and Nani and those who came before them

THE FIJI TIMES,
MONDAY, OCTOBER 5, 1914.

Chop Chop

... No, no, Mr Editor. Mr Crompton, speaking at the 'Night Prowlers' meeting didn't say we want 'bodies', we've got quite enough 'busy' ones in Fiji, he said 'bobbies', good old common or garden peelers, Rogers, Cops or John Hops!

CHAPTER ONE

'The Night Prowler was out again last night.'

This portent of doom first thing in the morning made Sergeant Akal Singh once again forget to duck as he walked through the door of the Totogo Police Station in central Suva.

'*Arre yaar*,' he muttered with feeling. In the six months he had been in Fiji, Akal had knocked his head on that very door any number of times. It wasn't a particularly low door, but his turban added inches to his already formidable height.

Akal smoothed his hands over the turban, cursing the lack of mirror in the sparsely furnished front room of the station, or indeed any of the police buildings. One had been ordered for the European officers' barracks, but the ship from Sydney had been delayed. There was no talk of ordering one for the Indian and Fijian barracks.

'Is my turban correct?' he asked Taviti. The Fijian constable was manning the front desk, and had been the one to deliver the news about Akal's current nemesis.

'Um, I think it's alright, sir. I don't know much about turbans.'

'Is it straight? Is any hair falling out? Are there lumps and bumps?'

'Yes, sir, straight, sir, no hair falling out, sir. Seems like a lot of work.'

Akal continued to smooth his hands over the sides of his turban, checking everything was in place despite Taviti's reassurances. 'It's a bloody bugger in this heat, I tell you. But the ladies love it.'

He waited for Taviti to scoff at this, given the dearth of women in Akal's life, but instead the Fijian man mirrored Akal, his hand running thoughtfully over his tight wiry curls. 'You think I should try it?'

'Do you think you can handle all the women?'

'Probably not. But my wife could!' Taviti shot back as he slapped the counter, resulting in a satisfyingly meaty echo throughout the room. Both men roared with laughter until they ran out of breath.

Akal had never in his life laughed as hard as he did with Taviti. No matter whether something was actually funny or not, Akal found himself convulsing in breathless spasms, Taviti's laughter rolling over him, while not really knowing why. Still chuckling, Akal dropped down into the spindly wooden visitor's chair and started to inspect the dust on his shoes.

Akal and Taviti's fledgling friendship was unique in the Suva police force. They were of an age, Akal twenty-five to Taviti's twenty-six, but many of their colleagues were a similar age so this alone didn't explain their rapport. There were other Indians in the police force and plenty of Fijians. The language barrier left them all at arm's distance, making themselves understood with a garbled mixture of English, Hindi and Fijian when they had to, but never really trusting one another.

Even without the language barrier, Akal had not broken through with any of the other Indian officers. None of them were Punjabi Sikhs, so they did not have the immediate bond of home and religion. In fact, they all regarded him with a mixture of resentment and contempt. They were constables to his sergeant, and they had not seen him earn his stripes, so they had no idea whether he was capable or not. Add to that the rumours about the reasons behind his abrupt departure from Hong Kong, and it was no wonder that they gave Akal a wide berth.

When Akal had disembarked from the ship that brought him from Hong Kong to Fiji six months ago, Taviti had been waiting for him, having been sent to collect Akal and take him to the police station. Taviti had approached Akal as he stood swaying on the dock, trying to adjust to solid ground. A few minutes into their walk to the station, Akal and Taviti had adjusted to their vastly different accents and discovered in each other a reasonable grasp of English. Taviti immediately started teasing Akal about his inability to walk a straight line, and their friendship had been quickly cemented.

'I cannot believe we have all started calling this bugger the "Night Prowler". Bloody *Fiji Times* and their stupid names,' Akal grumbled.

'What would you rather call him? He prowls around at night. Seems like a good name to me,' Taviti responded with a shrug.

'Whatever we call him, I need to find him, or I will never get a decent case again.'

'What do you mean, "again"?' Taviti said, cocking his head at Akal quizzically. 'You have not had a decent case since you got here. The inspector-general hated you on sight.'

'So, who was our wonderful Night Prowler bothering this time?' Akal said, focusing on his shoes and not making eye contact with Taviti. He had managed thus far to avoid explaining to Taviti the reasons he was in disfavour with the inspector-general, and he hoped to keep it that way, though Taviti almost certainly had an inkling of the truth. Everyone in the colony talked to Taviti.

'Too much to ask that they got a look at him, I suppose?'

'No, usual story. It was the Wishbournes up on Knolly Street, you know, with the two daughters. Eleven o'clock. Mr Wishbourne was at the governor's party. The Night Prowler was naked at the youngest girl's window. She woke up and saw him, started screaming, and he bolted. By the time the mother arrived, all she saw was his behind bouncing down the hill. But she definitely could tell it was a black behind.'

'Could she tell what kind of black?'

'My kind, not your kind. A good round Fijian behind, not one of your scrawny Indian arses.' Taviti flashed his teeth, each roughly the size of a small shovelhead. Akal was always astounded that Taviti managed to talk around all those teeth and mourned the day he would start losing them, as seemed to be the fate of all the older Fijian men.

'I'm off to Knolly Street, then. Maybe he will have left us a clue this time. His calling card, perhaps?' Akal looked up with a grin for Taviti, then jumped to his feet when he saw the inspector-general glowering at him from the door to the back rooms of the station.

'Singh. My office.' The inspector-general didn't wait for a response, and disappeared back down the corridor, his footsteps echoing through the room. Akal hurried to follow him.

'What did you do now?' Taviti asked.

Akal shrugged and muttered as he passed Taviti: 'I'm still breathing. I think that might be enough.'

Akal approached the door to the inspector-general's office with some trepidation. He had been in this office only once before, when he had first arrived in the colony. As soon as he had walked in, it had become apparent to Akal just how far he had fallen. The concrete room with its grimy louvres was a hovel compared to his previous commander's office in Hong Kong, which had been all high ceilings and polished wood. He had spent countless hours in that elegant space, consulting with his commander as his star rapidly rose with the British administration in Hong Kong. In his first meeting with Thurstrom, it had been made crystal clear that he would not enjoy that same elevated status here.

The reception desk outside the inspector-general's office, which had been full of neatly piled stacks of paperwork on his last visit, was now bare. This had been the desk of Sub-Inspector Marks, who had left the colony a couple of months ago, causing much consternation. Against the wishes of the colonial administration, the young inspector had managed to secure a commission to serve in the war being waged in Europe, leaving Suva without a European sub-inspector and the inspector-general without his right-hand man.

Akal knocked on the open door of the inspector-general's office. Without looking up, the inspector-general waved him in.

Inspector-General Jonathon Thurstrom, head of the police force for the fledgling colony, was seated behind his large desk, which was littered with papers, as was every chair. He was an imposing man, tall and robust with a shock of greying red hair that illuminated the dim room. Akal stood to attention before the desk.

'Inspector-General, sir,' Akal rattled off with crisp precision, to no response.

Akal maintained his military bearing as Thurstrom continued to ignore him. The room was quiet but for the scratching of the inspector-general's pen and the sounds of the trainees learning how to march outside. Thurstrom finished with his piece of paperwork and put his pen down, finally focusing on Akal.

'Singh, I have a problem.' Thurstrom jabbed his finger in Akal's direction with vigour. 'And I am making it your problem.'

'Yes, Inspector-General, sir?' Akal rattled off again, with slightly less precision.

'We've got a missing coolie out at the Parkins plantation in Nakavu. A woman. We have taken a report, and the plan was that whoever goes out that way next would do the usual checks. But some busybody missionary has gone and told the newspaper that there is no way she ran away. Went out to print this morning.' He stood up and leaned over the table, brandishing a copy of the *Fiji Times* like a pace stick. 'He is saying she must have been kidnapped. It's a bloody mess. And the Indian delegation arrived yesterday.'

The vaguely named Delegation for India's Relations with Fiji was visiting to review the Indian indentured servitude program. Until now, nobody had seemed overly concerned about this. The *Fiji Times'* reporting on the delegation had focused on who was attending the gala reception planned that night, and, crucially, what they would be wearing. The delegation's actual purpose had been relegated to a single sentence towards the end of the article.

'I've heard rumblings that the Indian government are

keeping an eye out for situations like this,' Thurstrom continued, beginning to pace the office and slapping the newspaper into his hand. 'They want to see how we treat a crime against an indentured worker. I tried to get Keane involved to head off the political mess, but do you think he's paying any attention?'

David Keane was the agent-general of Immigration. He had arrived six months ago, having never laid eyes on an indentured worker before, and had since lived in an uneasy sort of ignorant bliss. He had done nothing thus far to investigate the abuses that were alleged to be rife against the Indian labourers, male and female. Akal had arrived on the same ship as David Keane and he also had yet to make it out to a plantation. This was something he was glad of, in a quiet, selfish corner of his heart.

'I wish there were somebody else I could send,' the inspector-general said, pausing mid-pace to give Akal a sideways glance. Akal gritted his teeth. 'But having a senior Indian officer involved might just get the Indian government off all our backs. Go see this idiot missionary and report back to me post-haste. Try to get him to calm down and see reason. If we can get him to stop screaming that she has been 'kidnapped' maybe this whole thing will go away.'

Akal hesitated before reluctantly raising the topic of his current unresolved, frustrating case.

'Sir, what about the Night Prowler investigation? I don't know if you have heard, but he struck again last night.'

'Hmmm ... the Night Prowler,' Thurstrom muttered, sitting heavily back down in his chair. 'Do you know what I think, Singh? We just should not have women in the colony. Bloody headache.'

'The Night Prowler targets children, sir.'

9

Thurstrom glared at him. 'Well, if there are no women there will be no children, will there, Singh? You do know how children are made, don't you?'

'Ah, yes, sir.' Akal tried not to squirm.

Thurstrom's glare turned even sharper. 'The Night Prowler investigation, it hasn't been going well for you, has it, Singh? Haven't caught the bugger, have you?'

'No, sir.' Akal struggled to keep the resentment off his face but failed to keep it out of his voice. Thurstrom knew very well that he had not 'caught the bugger'.

'It seems my first impression of you was accurate.'

Akal could feel the warmth creeping up his neck. The Night Prowler had been peeping into the windows of the children of Suva for months before Akal had arrived. He had been handed the case with no description of the perpetrator, no pattern to the night-time excursions and no leads whatsoever.

In the six months since Akal's arrival into this backwater colony, the Night Prowler had made six more appearances. Akal's achievements to date had been to coax descriptions out of the children, something the previous investigators had not managed. Six different descriptions of six entirely different men, as far as he could tell. Frightened children did not make good witnesses. Thurstrom knew perfectly well how difficult the case was. After all, he had assigned the case to Akal to demonstrate how unwelcome he was in Thurstrom's police force.

Thurstrom leaned back in his chair, steepling his fingers in front of him. 'This is an important case, Singh, and you are my only option. If I could send one of the Indian constables, I would, but then I'd be in hot water for sending a constable when a sergeant was available. Perhaps this is an opportunity for you to show me what you can do. Make this go away without upsetting the Indian government, and perhaps some other, more solvable cases will start coming your way.'

'Yes, sir,' Akal replied, working hard to keep his excitement down. He had been getting nowhere with the Night Prowler; at least this case might give him another chance to redeem himself.

'Now, get moving. Oh, and go see Mrs Parkins as well, see if she knows anything about this coolie woman. We have been trying to call Henry Parkins on the telephone out at the plantation, but nobody has answered. Go carefully with her, though. Her father is an important man in Australia.'

Akal had never met Susan Parkins, but had seen her around Suva. Despite his short tenure in Fiji, Akal already knew all the Europeans on sight. Another reason to miss Hong Kong. 'Yes, sir!' Akal saluted and smartly marched out of the office. Back downstairs, he collected a copy of the newspaper from Taviti and they spread the paper over the counter, turban and wiry curls almost colliding as they leaned over to read the small print.

Coolie Kidnap

Planter calls it Run Away, Missionary calls it Kidnap!

A coolie has disappeared, this time a female on the Nabanigei plantation in Nasinu. The woman, named Kunti, was last seen two days ago when she reported sick from work and stayed in the coolie line for the day. It was reported by Mr Parkins, the plantation proprietor, that she had run away. However Father David Hughes, a Catholic missionary, has come directly to the *Fiji Times*, alleging she must have been kidnapped!

'Run away, rubbish,' the good missionary has told us. 'I have met this young lady a few times and she would never run away and leave her daughter behind. If she has gone, it is against her will.'

A mystery is afoot! As reported in this newspaper two weeks ago, the high rate of coolie suicides has sparked outrage in India. How will the Indian government respond to this latest situation? Could we see an end to the indentured system anon? In the face of all this interest from India and from our planters here, what will our worthy colonial administration do?

_____

Taviti frowned. 'That seems weak. Some missionary met the woman a few times and thinks she wouldn't run away. And this is the case the inspector-general is worried about?'

Akal nodded. Whether the woman had run away or had indeed been kidnapped, however unlikely, if the colonial administration were seen not to investigate, a whole new cause would be created to add to the pressure for the end of the indenture system. The end of the indenture system would likely lead to the end of the sugar plantations, which were the backbone of the economy of the colony.

'I suppose I'd better go find out what the good Father has to say.'

'Looks like you are going to church,' Taviti said with a grin.

The walk from the station to the Sacred Heart Cathedral was all uphill and distinctly lacking in shade. The saving grace was that it was mercifully short. Despite this, by the time Akal was standing on the steps of the grey stone church, he was a sweaty mess. Standing in the shadow cast by the spire, Akal stopped to take a closer look at the church. It was an impressive building. The stone, brought over from Australia, provided a feeling of permanence that the wooden buildings which were the standard in Suva could not match. But even this solid edifice wasn't impervious to the environment. The steps were mossy in places, with grass growing out of any available crack.

Akal held his sticky shirt away from his body and fanned his face with his free hand, trying to cool down the flush blooming all over his face. A trickle of sweat escaped his turban and ran down his back. Akal would not dream of attending the *gurdwara*, the Sikh temple, in such a sweaty mess, and the thought of entering a Christian church this way felt equally disrespectful. He wiped his forehead and flicked the perspiration off his hand in disgust. Nothing to be done about it. Perhaps Father Hughes would overlook his dishevelled state. He must be used to it, after all.

As soon as Akal walked through the stately wooden door of the Sacred Heart Cathedral, he felt a sense of calming, cooling peace. When the door closed behind him, the room was quiet, far away from the dirt and noise and heat of Suva. The only sound was a rhythmic sweeping, gently echoing up to the high wooden ceiling. Akal paused at the first pew and closed his eyes, absorbing the serenity.

He hadn't been to a *gurdwara* since Hong Kong, and even then he was never at the temple on his own. Akal was used to religious places being of colour and noise, drumming and movement. Of the ghee and sugar in the desserts offered to *Waheguru*, to God. Of feeling immersed, overwhelmed by the presence of *Waheguru*. It was a very communal thing, worshipping at the temple. He always left with a deep sense of connection, not only to *Waheguru* but to everyone he worshipped with.

This was different. This was sweetly, piercingly peaceful but a little lonely. Akal had glimpses of the English God here, but he thought if he wanted to know Him, he would have to work for it. He wondered if it would be different if he attended a service. Would he even be welcome?

'Can I help you?'

Akal's reverie was broken by this enquiry, made in a suspicious voice. He looked around to find a tiny woman with a mop of curly blonde hair. She was looking at him with an air of puzzlement and clutching a broom.

'Can I help you?' she repeated, a little louder and slower this time.

'I am looking for Father David Hughes.' Akal, fighting the urge to respond in kind, replied at his regular speed and volume.

'A policeman,' the diminutive woman said, relaxing her grip on the broom. 'You will be here about the Indian woman. Father Hughes will be pleased.' She turned towards the door and gestured for Akal to follow her. 'Please do help him. He has not stopped talking about this. I need him to focus on his sermon for next Sunday.'

Akal followed her a little reluctantly to another door at the side of the church. He hesitated at the doorway, taking a long breath, trying to instil the sanctity of the place deep within his body. This peaceful state fled when the woman popped her head back inside the door, urging him along. Akal emerged from the cool haven into a small garden, blinking in the blinding sunlight.

When his eyes adjusted, Akal found the priest kneeling in a small vegetable garden and muttering to himself while vigorously digging out weeds from between rows of carrots. The weeds seemed to be winning the war, while the carrot tops languished in a torpor with which Akal could sympathise. Father Hughes was, as promised, exceptionally pleased to see him.

'Yes, yes, hello,' Father Hughes exclaimed, leaping up and offering Akal his hand, still clad in a dirt-covered glove.

When Akal hesitated, the priest looked down and snatched his hand back, grabbing the glove off his hand before offering the hand again.

'Good to meet you, wonderful,' Father Hughes said, pumping Akal's hand and not letting him get a word in edgewise. 'Come in, this way, let me get you some tea. Hetty!'

In a flurry, Akal was ushered up the garden path and into the sitting room of a modest residence on the church grounds. The priest all but pushed him into a seat before disappearing off to procure the promised refreshments. In Akal's short time in the colony, nobody else – European, Indian, Fijian alike – had offered him a simple cup of tea. The Europeans always wanted a European officer and the Indians resented him for not being more like them. The warmest reception he got was from the Fijians, who seemed to consider him, with his turban and his police uniform, a curiosity. This was a welcome change.

Akal sat for a few minutes, drumming his fingers on the arm of the chair, before standing to look around the small, sparsely furnished sitting room. The room had a lived-in feel to it, floorboards polished by decades of familiar footsteps. Akal stopped in front of a picture of Jesus, the Christian holy man he had heard much about. Jesus was holding his heart in his hands, hands which were faded by time, with rays of light escaping through the fingers. He seemed to be looking at Akal with a compassion and wisdom that was both comforting and eerie. Akal turned his back to the picture and hastily returned to the sturdy wicker chairs.

Akal sat back down in one of them and immediately stood again, removing the lumpy cushion. There was a proverb stitched into it in blue cotton, frayed strands draping limply across the coarse beige linen. *Give, and it shall be given unto you; Luke 6:38*. He was contemplating this adage, cushion in hand, when Father Hughes returned.

Akal rushed his introduction in before the priest could open his mouth, concerned that he might never get the opportunity otherwise. 'Father, I am Sergeant Akal Singh of the Fijian Constabulary, Suva Division.'

'Of course, yes, very pleased to meet you,' Father Hughes replied. 'Please take a seat. Hetty is bringing tea.'

Akal sat once more, moving the cushion out of the way.

'So, *somebody* is paying some attention. Who sent you? The governor?' the priest asked, triumph evident in each word.

'No, Father, Inspector-General Thurstrom sent me.'

'That will do, I suppose. I had hoped to get the governor's attention.'

'Well, yes, you certainly did get his attention. This has become extremely sensitive ...' Akal paused for emphasis. 'As you went to the newspaper rather than the police.'

The priest glared at him in disbelief. 'I *did* go to the police first. All you did was call Henry Parkins and accept his story that she had run away. That is when I went to the newspaper. This way you could not just ignore it.'

Father Hughes had stoked the political fires and now it was up to Akal to put them out with a thimbleful of water while trying not to get too severely burnt himself. He had not heard that the priest had initially approached the police with his concerns, but it did not surprise him that those concerns were ignored, given the dismissive way the inspector-general had spoken about the case.

'Please tell me what you know of the alleged victim.'

'Kunti. Her name was Kunti.'

Father Hughes looked at Akal, eyebrows raised. He waited. Akal realised the priest was not going to continue until he acknowledged her name. What difference her name made to Father Hughes, Akal did not know.

'Yes. Kunti.'

The priest's narrowed eyes caused a cascade of wrinkles to appear across his face. 'Just ... wait here a moment please, Sergeant.'

Father Hughes went into another room while Akal waited, his right knee starting to restlessly bounce up and down. Meanwhile, Hetty, the woman who had been sweeping in the church, arrived with the tea.

'Chewing your ear off, I suppose?' she said with a wry smile, as she put the tray down and poured both cups full of strong milky tea.

Akal looked at her blankly.

'Going on about the coolies,' she clarified. 'He has responsibilities here in Suva, you know, but no, he is always gallivanting around the country.' She tutted as she handed Akal his cup and passed the sugar bowl.

Father Hughes returned holding an album before she could elaborate. Hetty gave the priest his cup of tea and bustled out, admonishing him to not take too long and to remember his unfinished sermon. Father Hughes waved her away. He balanced the album on his knees and flipped the thick brown cardboard pages, stopping about halfway through. He turned the book around to show Akal a black-and-white photograph of an Indian woman.

'This is Kunti. She is a real person, Sergeant Singh.'

'Yes, sir.' Akal kept his tone respectful, though he thought perhaps his one eyebrow creeping towards his turban may have negated the effect. He reached out and took the album for a closer look.

The photograph was of Kunti's head and shoulders, sari draped over her hair. Elongated eyes tipped up at the ends dominated her face, drawing him in. She was not actually smiling, but there was something about her eyes which spoke of joy. It certainly did not look as though Kunti was imminently running away, though what that might look like Akal didn't know.

'How did you get this photograph?'

'I took it the first time I met Kunti, at the plantation. I was travelling around the colony, gathering information for my report for the Church. I'm trying to show how the terrible conditions the Indians are living in are resulting in their moral decline. The Church is deciding on its position on the indentured servitude program, and when the bishops see my report, I think the conclusion will be unavoidable. The situation on the plantations is an indictment of the indenture system, and it is incumbent on all good Christians to –'

'You said you met Kunti on the plantation?' Akal interrupted, putting his hand up to stem the torrent of words. The priest started and then nodded, climbing down from atop his soapbox and back to the present.

'Hmm, yes. It was towards the end of my trip; the Parkins plantation was one of my last stops. I was tired, a little numb. The visit started with the usual hostile conversation with Henry Parkins. "What's the problem?" he said. "They all signed their contracts." *Hmph*. Put their thumbprints on a contract they could not even read, more like. They were told all sorts of stories. Do you know, one of the common lies was that Fiji was just south of Calcutta! Told that the work was easy when really the daily "task" defined in the contract was only achievable by the strongest. Never told that if they didn't complete the full task in a day, that day didn't count towards the contract. Never knowing that they had sold themselves into slavery for five years.'

Akal had heard some of these claims before, but he had never known how much to believe. Father Hughes's passionate recital gave him the uneasy sense that perhaps he should have paid more attention in the past. He rubbed his forehead and said, resigned, 'Yes, sir. Please continue.'

The priest took a deep breath, chest swelling in his fervour. 'None of the plantation owners want reform of the system. They are all much more concerned about the state of their pockets than the state of their souls, you see. None of them are happy to see me. But Parkins knew better than to bar me from the plantation altogether. He would have, if he thought he could get away with it. But the man has some political ambitions, and he wants to stay on the right side of the Church.'

He waved his finger at Akal and nodded with grim satisfaction. 'After reminding Parkins of his Christian duty, I went to visit some of the women where they were working. They were removing weeds from a field of young sugar cane. They were spread out across the field and they couldn't stop working, of course, so I was walking from one to the next, seeing if anybody would talk to me.'

'Do they speak English?' Akal asked, surprised. The people desperate enough to sign the *girmit*, the indentured servitude contract, were the poorest of the poor.

'No, of course not. I speak enough Hindi to communicate simple things. The thing is, even if nobody will speak to me, I can learn enough just by observing. They were a sad looking bunch. One woman had her baby with her, and the baby started crying at one point. It was pitiful, Sergeant, even the cry sounded thin. As usual, the women were reluctant to speak to me, so I went down to the coolie line to see what the conditions there were like. Have you seen a coolie line before, Sergeant Singh?'

Akal shook his head. What he'd heard of the accommodations provided to the indentured servants had given him a fair idea that he didn't want to spend any time there. A sentiment Akal didn't want to share with this crusading clergyman.

'Well, this one was about average, which is to say it was a dire place. Parkins has followed the regulations to the letter and not a single thing more. The rooms are exactly the minimum size allowed, scarcely enough to swing a cat. The internal walls run to the mandated height and use chicken wire at the top for ventilation, which means that there is no privacy whatsoever. Families in a room with singles right next door. How is anyone supposed to maintain a moral family life in these conditions? My report –'

'And Kunti?' Akal prompted.

'Yes, yes, Kunti, of course. So, there I was, too tired to be angry about the state of the coolie line, frustrated that nobody would speak to me. I was having a very low moment – until I walked around the corner and there she was. Kunti. It was like the sun came out. She was shy, but not scared like the other women. I asked her if she would sit for this photograph, through gesture, of course, and she nodded. I took the photograph and left. A few months later I came back through and gave her a copy.'

'And you say that was a few months ago?' Akal asked. 'Do you think she may have just worn down and run away?'

Father Hughes did not even consider the possibility. 'No, no, no. Impossible. She was three years into her contract. Why would she suddenly wear down now, unless something happened? But I can't imagine what would be so dreadful that she'd leave her daughter. No, I stand by my statement – if she has disappeared, it is against her will.'

'Sir, with respect, this doesn't seem enough to call it a kidnapping. We don't know what has happened to this woman since you saw her.'

The priest seemed truly taken aback for the first time in the conversation. 'It would be exceedingly foolish to ignore this,' he warned, as if surprised at Akal's matter-of-fact demeanour. 'The Indian people will demand justice, here and in India.'

'I will report your concerns to the inspector-general,' Akal reassured him, inching forward in his chair, eager to depart.

'When you do, make sure he understands that I won't be quiet about this. The church will continue to fight for justice for Kunti.' Father Hughes took a deep breath, visibly calming himself, then proceeded in a less threatening tone: 'Sergeant Singh, please tell me that you care enough to find out the truth, even if she has run away. I know that to the planters and to the administration, these Indians are beasts of burden more than people. But for you, Kunti is your countrywoman.'

'I'll do what I can, sir,' Akal responded in a clipped tone. The priest's words had him a little restless, perhaps even a little angry. He did not want to look too deeply at the problems in the *girmit* scheme. What did Father Hughes think Akal could do about any of it? He had not created the situation, and it had nothing to do with him, really. The Indians being brought over as *girmityas* were not the kind he would have ever dealt with in India. They were not his people, even if they were his countrymen.

Akal's second interview for the day was with Mrs Henry Parkins. The Parkins house was on Cakobau Road, alongside the homes of all the other well-heeled plantation owners. Akal and Taviti slogged their way up the hill, walking past the newly reorganised Suva Botanical Gardens, where the cicadas sang of their love of the sun.

'Watch out,' Taviti said, putting a hand out to steer Akal around a small crater in the road that Akal had missed while he was looking longingly at the cooling green of the gardens, which provided a lush counterpoint to the dusty road.

'These bloody potholes,' Akal grumbled.

'You just have to learn to walk properly. Wouldn't want you to snap your chicken legs.'

Akal shot him a sideways glare, always sensitive about his gangly legs, and said, 'Remind me why I asked you to join me for this interview?'

Taviti chuckled but wisely stopped his teasing at this reminder of the opportunity Akal had given him.

Akal had stopped back at the station after the visit with the priest, and asked Taviti to join him while he questioned Mrs Parkins. He had had no problem interviewing a clergyman on his own, but with a European lady, he preferred to have a witness. Taviti had leapt at the opportunity.

'Why are they so big?' Akal asked, swerving to avoid a rather large example of what he was complaining about. 'I walked up here two days ago, but I am sure the potholes have gotten worse.'

Taviti shrugged. 'It rains every day. The rain comes down

the hill and takes half the road with it. You think you have it bad? Think of the cyclists.'

What remained of the road following the afternoon rain was often a sodden mire in which cyclists got stuck and had to dismount, with varying levels of grace but consistent degrees of irritation. Sometimes the potholes joined forces and grew big enough to swallow a cyclist whole.

'Seriously, thank you for bringing me along,' Taviti said, ducking his head down and looking at the road. 'I really want to learn.'

Akal looked at his friend with sympathy. Despite the inspector-general's low regard for Akal, at least he was assigned real cases, albeit painful ones. Taviti had so much that Akal didn't – a wife and children, a position in Fijian society – but those very things were putting something Taviti craved out of his reach: to truly maintain law and order in Fiji. Akal was determined to help him where he could.

'Well, you can start earning your keep. What do you know about Mrs Parkins?'

'I have met her a few times at parties. She is invited to everything.'

'So are you,' Akal shot back with a sly half-smile.

'That is different. I have to go, to represent my uncle.'

Taviti was the nephew of a prominent chief who lived too far away from Suva to regularly attend the important social events of the colony. As far as his family were concerned, Taviti's true purpose in Suva was to represent the clan. Policing was something Taviti did over his family's objections.

'She is going to all of these events to drum up support for her husband,' Taviti continued. 'He is running for chairman of the Planters' Association in a couple of months.'

'Planters' Association? That will make him one of the most powerful men in the colony,' Akal moaned. 'And I have to investigate his runaway coolie.'

The Planters' Association represented the plantation owners' interests and was the only body which tried to stand up to Colonial Sugar Refining, the Australian company that bought all the cane in Fiji. CSR was both the biggest contributor to the Fijian economy and the biggest bully.

'If it helps, I've heard it is really her who will end up running the association. He's not that interested.'

'If he isn't interested, why is he running for chairman?'

'I've only got rumours,' Taviti said, giving Akal a questioning look. On Akal's nod, he continued. 'From what I hear, Susan Parkins comes from a political family in Australia. An only child, so her parents did not have a son to carry on the family traditions in politics. Henry Parkins comes from money. Their parents arranged their meeting. They were supposed to be a powerful force in Sydney – and he was supposed to be climbing the political ladder there. But somehow, they ended up in Fiji.

'She was not happy when she first got here. Turned her nose up at all of the social events, wouldn't talk to the other planters' wives. Until the Planters' Association election came up. Now she's suddenly charming everyone in Suva: the planters, their wives, the administration. Meanwhile, Henry Parkins never leaves his plantation. So, everyone knows that if he is elected, she will be running the show. But the planters are happy with that. They are hoping her family's influence will help when they are negotiating with CSR.'

They reached the Parkins house towards the top of the hill. It was a typical house for well-to-do Europeans in the colony. Wooden and raised on stilts, it was designed to make the most of the breeze that flowed over the top of the hill. The front garden was in full bloom, festooned with flowers. The family must have a Fijian gardener, Akal thought. It was cared for but not ruthlessly tamed, like some of the others on the street.

He brushed past a row of hibiscus bushes, causing the blooms with their wide red petals to wave their improbably large stamens at him indignantly. The bougainvillea got into the act, its spindly branches heavily burdened with clusters of deep purple triangles swaying in the light breeze and breaking away to dust his shoulders with gossamer petals.

The front of the house boasted a wide verandah, with four wooden chairs arranged around a matching table, a perfect spot for sipping gin and tonics as the sun went down over the Pacific Ocean. Akal and Taviti proceeded up the shallow wooden steps leading up to the verandah and knocked on the front door. Taviti charmed the shy house girl who answered the door into fetching her mistress for them.

When Susan Parkins arrived, opening the door just enough so that she could see him, and he could see her, the bottom fell out of Akal's stomach. He felt as though he had been transported back to Hong Kong, to another small, blonde woman who had turned his life upside down. He stared at her in a reverie until she snapped him back to the here and now by speaking.

'Yes?'

Akal blinked rapidly and squared his shoulders, putting the past behind him, at least for the moment. 'I am Sergeant Akal Singh of the Fijian Constabulary, Suva Division. Are you Mrs Henry Parkins?'

'Yes.' She arched an elegant brow at him.

'May I come in?'

She frowned. 'What is this about?'

They stood at an impasse for a moment, before she brusquely said, 'You can ask me your questions outside.'

She yanked the door open, and Akal got a glimpse into the front room of the house. The room was elegantly appointed with furniture that must have come in on ships from elsewhere in the British Empire. Wooden shutters had been propped open at the many windows and the morning light flooded through the room. That was all he saw before the door was abruptly slammed shut in his face.

When she stepped out onto the verandah, Mrs Parkins's delicate appearance was incongruous with her actions. She was slight and small, the top of her head well below Akal's shoulder. A fluttery floral dress and blonde curls elegantly pinned up completed the picture of a genteel lady. She did not appear to have the strength to slam the door shut with sufficient force to make the house shudder, and yet she just had.

Then there was the narrow-eyed glare she gave Akal. He could feel the heat of her anger directed towards him, and he was puzzled by it. Irritation, disdain, even discomfort he would have accepted without question. These were not unusual reactions from a European woman when dealing with an Indian police officer, and he had learned to suppress his feelings at these reactions. In Hong Kong, it had been easier. There, he was valued by his superiors and his peers. Here, with no external validation, he was struggling to rise above the everyday bumps and bruises of being an Indian officer within the Raj. Nonetheless, Mrs Parkins's outright anger did not make sense. Akal wondered if she knew why he was there.

When she saw Taviti, Susan Parkins's demeanour changed

entirely, the glare replaced with a welcoming smile. So that was how it was, Akal thought. It wasn't about the colour of his skin – not entirely, anyway. It was that he had no power here, whereas Taviti had influence through his uncle. Akal didn't know whether that made it better or worse. He watched as she approached Taviti, ignoring Akal altogether.

'Is that you, Taviti?'

'Yes, ma'am,' Taviti responded, stepping forward with a respectful nod of his head.

'And in uniform. I forgot that you also dabble in police work.'

'I am a constable, ma'am,' Taviti replied evenly.

'I saw your uncle at the Christmas ball. He did not seem pleased about your "career",' she replied with a smirk.

'Did you know that your husband has reported that one of your coolie women has run away?' Akal asked, intervening before she could needle Taviti further.

Mrs Parkins stiffened again. She walked slowly away from the door towards the right side of the verandah, going to stand behind a wooden chair and putting all the furniture between them. Akal did not move, allowing her the space that she seemed to need.

'I do not get involved in the operations at the plantation,' she eventually replied, with a sniff. 'I take care of our affairs in Suva.'

'Her name was Kunti. Can you tell me anything about her?'

Mrs Parkins laughed at this. 'Why would I know the coolies on the plantation by name? Don't be ridiculous.'

'So, you have no information about when she ran away?'

'My husband mentioned something about our overseer,

Brown, taking a coolie woman with him when he left. Perhaps it was her.'

'Why would he take Kunti?' Akal asked.

'They were probably having an affair. These coolie women all do it. I think they are trying to get out of work. Morals of alley cats.'

'Where would they go?' Akal asked in clipped tones.

'Well, Brown said he had secured a commission with the British Army and he was leaving for the war in Europe. The coolie woman disappeared when he left. My husband and I drew our own conclusions. Who knows where he actually went, though. I can't imagine the army would want him with a slatternly low-caste Indian woman in tow.'

The ensuing silence on the verandah was broken only by the distant sound of the cicadas and the creaking of the nearby coconut palm as it languorously swayed in the breeze. Akal struggled to hold back a retort, suppressing a desire to defend the woman whose photograph he had seen just that morning. This was an unexpected and unwanted change in attitude. He cursed Father Hughes for making this case more personal. Taviti hesitantly stepped forward.

'So, ah, you don't know where Mr Brown is?' Taviti asked, his usual booming voice quiet in the tense little bubble they had formed on the verandah.

'No idea. On a ship? Fighting in Europe?' Mrs Parkins suggested dispassionately, as though she was speculating on the field positions of a cricket match. Despite her nonchalant tone, she was holding onto the back of the chair, her knuckles showing white.

'And you believe she ran away?' Taviti asked, his voice getting louder as he found his footing.

Mrs Parkins gave a short nod.

'Have you seen the newspaper this morning?' Akal said and turned to Taviti, who passed him the newspaper. He tried to hand it to her, the headline regarding the priest's allegations face-up. Mrs Parkins kept her arms crossed and her eyes slid away from the article. Akal lowered the paper.

'Again ... I do not know anything about this.'

Akal mentally raised an eyebrow at the steel in her voice, but his face remained impassive. 'You don't know why Father Hughes has alleged that she was kidnapped?'

She huffed again. 'Father Hughes. What a nuisance. He is trying to make a name for himself, I think. I am really not sure why he has made this his crusade. I mean, how many runaway coolie women are there in the colony?'

'Yours is the only one that has been reported, madam.'

Akal regarded the newspaper for a minute, allowing the uncomfortable silence to lengthen. When he looked back at Mrs Parkins, she was looking away, arms still crossed.

'Do you know if the telephone to the plantation is working? We have been unable to reach your husband to clarify some of these details.'

'I spoke with him yesterday on the telephone. He called me. It was late. He often works late, especially since Brown left.'

'Can you remember the time your husband called yesterday?' he asked. 'It is important that we speak with him.'

'Oh, I don't know. I told you it was late,' she said dismissively. 'Look, I don't know anything more, and I really must be getting on with my day. I've got to get ready for the gala tonight.'

Mrs Parkins paused at the doorway and, without looking

back, said, 'Tell the inspector-general that if there are any other questions, he can ask me himself. He should not send his coolie officer to this house.'

THE FIJI TIMES,
MONDAY, OCTOBER 5, 1914.

Wedding Bells

Swinbourne-Wishart

... The bride was given away by her father and looked very pretty in a beautiful dress of white chiffon satin draped skirt with fish-tail train and bodice of honiton lace over chiffon tulle. She also wore the conventional veil and orange blossom and carried an exquisite bridal bouquet.

CHAPTER TWO

'You will have to go out to the plantation in the morning.'

Thurstrom scowled at Akal as though this turn of events was somehow his fault. When he had returned to the station, Akal had reported directly to the inspector-general to ensure that his superior understood that Father Hughes was not going to drop the matter. The message was not well-received.

'Sir, may I take Taviti with me? His local knowledge may help. And I don't know the way,' Akal admitted.

'For God's sake, Singh,' Thurstrom snapped. 'Go see Dr Holmes. He goes out that way sometimes. He can tell you the route.'

'Yes, sir,' Akal replied with resignation.

The inspector-general leaned back in his chair and steepled his fingers in front of him, a sure sign that he was going to bring up something that Akal did not want to hear. 'Tonight, at the gala, there is going to be an Indian chap who is with the delegation. I need you to make sure he is comfortable. No matter what I think of you, you are my ranking Indian officer.'

'Yes, sir,' Akal said, thinking that it was a small mercy that the inspector-general had remembered this fact for once.

'Mr Choudry is his name. Keep it simple. Keep him happy. We need the delegation's visit to be uneventful.'

'Yes, sir.'

Thurstrom picked up a piece of paper and inspected it. 'It may not seem like it, but I am giving you a chance here, Singh,' he said, without looking up. 'I suggest you make something of it.'

Pen in hand, he returned to his paperwork.

A chance, certainly, Akal thought bitterly as he turned to the leave the room. A chance to be a scapegoat.

Akal trudged up the incline towards the Colonial Hospital. He had seen the hospital on top of the hill from a distance and had not realised how steep it was until he was too far away from the station to return to the stables and get a horse. Akal wondered how the infirm managed to make it up for treatment.

He paused for a moment to catch his breath and look back down the hill. Below him, Walu Bay flowed out to the ocean, a horseshoe of sparkling blue ringed by deep green foliage. The tranquillity worsened Akal's mood. It was a beautiful scene, but not the one he wanted. He wanted the view from the tram in Hong Kong as it climbed up Victoria Peak, wires running overhead, looking down to the harbour, full of ships transporting the wealth of the British Empire all over the world.

Akal sighed and, after looking around for the least dusty spot to sit, carefully manoeuvred himself down to sit on the ground, stretching his legs down the hill. His thoughts turned to home. He put the notepad he was carrying on the ground next to him, peeling the fingers of his hand away and leaving behind four damp fingerprints. Akal scowled at the offending marks and gingerly pulled a letter out of his pocket. It was a little worn at the creases, the paper rough and full of imperfections. It was the best his father could afford, unlike the smooth, perfectly white paper that Akal had become used to handling in his time with the Raj across two colonial administrations.

Akal's father was the teacher in the village in which Akal had grown up, and he valued the written word in a way Akal had never really appreciated until he left India for Hong Kong. Since then, he and his father had gradually built up a regular correspondence, awkwardly at first, and then with greater grace as the years went on. Akal found these letters more comforting than he could ever have anticipated. He looked at the letter, feeling the words rather than seeing them as he read the letter yet again.

Beta,

How are you, my son? Your mother and I are both well, as are your sisters. Anoopma is now married as well. The wedding was lovely, as such things generally are. You were greatly missed. Your mother has found good matches for all of her daughters, so she is euphoric right now. I am happy for the girls, but also hugely relieved that I do not need to find any more dowries. Of course, that means that once your mother recovers from organising Anoopma's wedding, you will become her focus, no matter how far away you might be.

I am sorry to hear that you have not had any success with your case. Be patient, Beta, you will solve it. I know how important it is to make a good showing after the mistakes of last year. But I trust in the plan Waheguru has for you. If you are meant to return to Hong Kong, you will.

I hope you will consider coming home for a visit. I know it would fill your mother with joy. Rest assured, I have not given her the reasons for your transfer to Fiji. She is still boasting about you to all the mothers in the village in the hope of securing you a beautiful bride when you come home. Be patient with her. This is her very reason for being. I know she has always been sad that she provided me with only one son. I have never managed to convince her that you and your sisters were enough for me.

Know that I am proud of you. In my mind's eye, I can see you shaking your head as you read this sentence. For now, I will be just a little bit more proud of you than usual, while you cannot be proud of yourself.

Baba

Akal refolded the letter and returned it to his pocket with care. He looked back out to the water, able to appreciate the beauty now, with his father's familiar words centring him once more.

The hospital loomed at the top of the hill, two floors of solid concrete. The architect had tried to add a touch of elegance with arches and a grand circular driveway, but these seemed incongruent on a building that had a serious mission to fulfil under difficult conditions. Blinds were drawn in the arches on the second floor to provide some respite from the heat, giving the appearance that the building was shut to visitors.

Akal wearily pushed the front door open to reveal a hum of ordered activity. A Fijian nurse strode past him, her brisk pace echoing through the reception. Akal approached another nurse seated behind a wooden desk, reading from a textbook.

Enquiries of this nurse yielded directions to Dr Robert Holmes's office on the ground floor, and Akal arrived there in short order.

The door to the office was open and the doctor was standing by a desk at the side of the room, gathering paperwork and instruments. He was a tall man, with blond hair gradually silvering, highlighted by the sun shining through the nearby window. Akal had always found the doctor's face rather soothing, his calm demeanour hiding implacable rigour around his medical practice. Akal knocked on the frame of the open door, and the doctor turned around, seeming surprised at this disruption to his routine.

'Singh! Where were you last Sunday?'

'I'm sorry I missed the match, sir.'

'Not as sorry as your team. We thrashed them!' Dr Holmes grinned, unrepentant in his gloating.

Akal reflexively rotated his shoulder through some bowling motions. While his fall from grace had preceded his arrival to Fiji, resulting in a frosty reception from his fellow police officers, his reputation as a bowler had also preceded him, with altogether different results. The few Britishers in the police force were all cricket-mad and had immediately conscripted him to join the police team.

It was one of the few arenas in which he felt he was making inroads. His teammates had unbent enough to deign to greet and farewell him at matches, rather than ignoring him until he was bowling. Akal had even received a congratulatory nod from the team captain after Akal had bowled out two batters for ducks in a row. He still was not invited to any post-match drinks, but he lived in hope.

The cricket matches were hotly contested, with rivalries

abounding in the young colony. He regretted missing the match last week, losing his chance to don the crisp white uniform and perform in front of the well-turned-out crowd, who spanned the strata of the colony's racial and social divides. Whenever Akal was on the bench awaiting his turn to bat, he would take the opportunity to observe the spectators in their Sunday best. Replete with straw hats and ribbons fluttering against a backdrop of coconut palms and the ocean, the crowd were as much spectacle as the cricket match they were there to see.

'It's this Peeping Tom case, sir. The inspector-general has us working on it all hours.'

'Oh, yes, the elusive Night Prowler. What's going on there?'

Akal suppressed a sigh. Even a serious man like Dr Holmes was calling the perpetrator 'the Night Prowler'.

'We just can't catch the bugger, sir. Not enough men to patrol every night. Only the children see him, and all they see is a Fijian man. We just keep waiting to be lucky, really.'

'I hope you get lucky soon. I worry about the day he stops just looking.'

'As do I, Doctor.'

'Now, what can I do for you, Singh? I need to get going on my rounds in a minute.'

'I just need to get some directions. I have to go to the Parkins plantation and the inspector-general says you know the way.'

'Oh, is this about the woman who has disappeared? Read about it in the newspaper.' Dr Holmes gave an approving sort of nod. 'I bet Father Hughes has set the cat among the pigeons, hasn't he?'

'I'm not sure, sir,' Akal replied hesitantly. The doctor's colourful turns of phrase often flew straight over his head.

'But he has certainly caused us all sorts of problems. I must go straight out there, but I have not been out of Suva before. What are the roads like?'

'Roads?' The doctor barked a short laugh. 'You *are* new here, aren't you? Not sure if you should be let out on your own, Singh. Your team needs that bowling arm too much to lose you to the wilds of the Fijian jungle.'

'Is it really that bad?' Akal's heart sank. He mentally shook his fist at Father Hughes once more.

'Come now, don't tell me a Sikh warrior like yourself is worried about a little trip through the jungle?' the doctor teased, then looked thoughtfully at Akal. 'I tell you what, I was due to go out that way soon. Why don't I take you out there? I can meet you at my house in the morning. At Walu Bay, just past the hospital. Think you can get yourself that far on your own?'

'Yes, Doctor. I did manage to get myself from the Punjab to Fiji via Hong Kong on my own.'

Early in the evening, Akal walked to the Grand Pacific Hotel, being careful where he put his feet to avoid the worst of the dust. Resplendent in his emerald-green dress uniform, he ought to have been marching, but had decided to sacrifice that formality to prioritise showing up in the same pristine state in which he'd left the police barracks.

With the dearth of formal events in Fiji, there had been no urgency in procuring a local dress uniform for Akal, so he still retained his dress uniform from Hong Kong. There had always been some delegation or another stopping by Hong

Kong on their way to another more remote outpost of the Empire, and the dress uniform had had a good workout there. He and his fellow Sikh police officers were often put on display in their turbaned glory for ceremonial marches and generally to impress. This delegation to Fiji was the first since Akal's arrival. Fiji was not on the way to anywhere.

That afternoon, Taviti had run him through how these parties generally unfolded, who would be there, when to arrive to avoid attention, who might be friendly with a brown man at a predominantly European party and, more importantly, who definitely wouldn't. It seemed incongruous to Akal that Taviti – who never took anything seriously if he could help it and was only one year older than Akal – knew how to navigate society so seamlessly. For his part, Taviti had been surprised that it was Akal's first time at such an event. Despite his generally favoured position in Hong Kong, Akal had never been invited to receptions there.

Akal approached the hotel, merging in behind the other attendees, couples in their formal best representing the elite of the colony. The Grand Pacific loomed tall and stately, a resolute statement of British colonialism against a backdrop of palm trees and the Pacific Ocean. Planters who didn't own a home in Suva stayed here when visiting from their plantations for a taste of British civility.

Akal walked past the tall white columns and under the arches to the front door, which sported a Fijian constable standing to attention on either side. He eyed the Fijians' dress uniforms, their white *sulus*, with envy. They were much better suited to the humidity than his own woollen suit with full-length trousers.

Inside the hotel lobby, Akal spotted Taviti, also imposing in his dress uniform, which was similar to those of the constables outside. Unsure whether he should approach, Akal positioned himself in Taviti's line of sight. From this vantage point, he could see that Taviti was sitting a little too close to a woman who was not his wife. He was giving the voluptuous red-haired woman everything he had, the charming half-smile, the sleepy eyes, the undivided attention. Akal got a little closer to see who it was, but he did not recognise her. She must be one of the guests of honour, perhaps the wife of one of the delegates.

The woman was blushing prettily and laughing at everything Taviti said. She should really have known better; the grooves that bracketed her mouth betrayed her as being easily twenty years Taviti's senior. Taviti finally looked up and saw Akal. Akal lifted a mocking brow which got the expected response from Taviti: a helpless shrug and a grin that was intended to be sheepish but fell far from the mark. So it was that Akal entered the ballroom chuckling to himself and immediately earned a frown from the inspector-general.

The inspector-general was deep in conversation with the governor and Mrs Parkins. She provided quite a contrast to the gentlemen with her diminutive stature and feminine laughter, floating through the party. Akal noted that her hair was still perfectly pinned, now with the addition of a delicate gold comb, and marvelled that the woman had made it all the way here without a single curl moving. This was a conversation Akal was not welcome to join, and one in which he certainly didn't want to be involved.

He kept walking, starting to circumnavigate the ballroom, in search of the man he was there to entertain, the other token Indian. The next familiar face he spotted, however, was Dr

Robert Holmes, who was leaning against a tall table staring into a cut crystal glass.

'Doctor.'

The doctor started. 'Oh, Singh. Sorry, I was off with the fairies. So, they've trotted you out in your dress uniform, no less. Wouldn't do to greet the Indian delegation with not a single Indian at the party, I suppose.'

'Yes, Doctor. After all, who else would they invite? As the inspector-general reminded me today, I am the ranking Indian officer in the police department. And I look good in this uniform,' Akal finished, preening.

'Hmph. They should invite one of the ex-coolie farmers in his *dhoti*, fresh from his work ploughing the fields that will barely make him a living. Then they'd see the real situation for Indians in Fiji.' The doctor shook his head and glared around the room.

'Not excited about the party?' Akal asked solicitously.

'Bah. I've already tried to talk sense into this delegation. Would they listen? They are going to the Tamavouvou plantation tomorrow. They have come all this way and they are going to visit exactly one plantation: the closest plantation to town and the one which treats its workers the best. I tried to get them to go out to Labasa. The conditions are appalling on the plantations there. "Too far," they said. They aren't interested in reviewing the system. They just want to take a quick look around and get back to Suva so they can slap each other on the back.' The doctor knocked back the rest of his drink and slammed the glass down. 'Seems like the best thing I can do at this party is get drunk.'

'I would join you, but I must maintain the dignity of the administration, I'm afraid.'

The doctor cocked a sceptical eyebrow as Akal looked at him, maintaining a wide-eyed and innocent look for as long as he could.

'But really, I am here to entertain the Indian man on the delegation, Mr Ravendra Choudry. I need to keep my head straight for that,' Akal conceded with a wry smile.

The doctor shook his head again in disgust. 'Well, he shouldn't be too hard to spot. Who decided who would be on this delegation? One of the delegates actually tried to tell me he understood the issues here because he had held an administrative post in India.' He gesticulated around with his empty glass. 'I don't know if he noticed, we aren't in India.'

'Why don't we get you another drink,' Akal said, hoping to placate the agitated man. The doctor looked around and signalled a waiter to come over. With his usual impeccable timing, Taviti joined them just as the waiter arrived.

'Yes, please. Don't mind if I do.' Taviti snagged a gin and tonic from the tray while Akal took a lemonade.

'Oh, have you finished talking to that *memsahib*? That is, the lady with the red hair. Who is not your wife. And not the mother of your three children,' Akal said pointedly.

'Oh, it's fine, don't worry. My wife is very happy back at the village. She sits around with my mother and complains about me. You would fit right in with them.' Taviti thumped Akal on the back while the doctor laughed, and Akal glared at them.

'So ... I hear you are leaving Suva,' Taviti said. 'Do you think you can handle the real Fiji? You know my cousins are cannibals, right?' Taviti nudged Akal with his elbow, almost causing him to spill his drink.

'Hey, watch it. This uniform is a bugger to clean,' Akal chided.

'I'll be going with him, so I'll save the city boy from any cannibals,' Dr Holmes responded.

'Will that work? No cannibal is going to want Akal, all skin and bones, but you don't really have any meat on you either.' Taviti reached over and jiggled Holmes's modest belly. Both men laughed uproariously, as Akal looked on sourly. Taviti was just being his usual self, but the doctor had clearly had a little too much to drink already. His face was beet red and his laughter had him unsteady on his feet. Akal regretted suggesting another drink.

'I'm glad you are all having fun with this. I am from a village in India, you know, so I have been outside the city before. I just prefer a little civilisation, if you do not mind,' Akal ended with a grand flourish and a bow. He arose from his bow to find an Indian gentleman had joined their party.

'Sergeant Singh, I presume?' The man spoke English with a refined accent, the kind one might acquire from the English-style boarding schools gaining popularity among the moneyed in India. It was the same accent that Akal generally affected, learned through observation and practice, though the flaws in his delivery were apparent next to the genuine article.

'Yes, sir. You must be Mr Choudry?'

Akal introduced the doctor and Taviti, and the two Indian men exchanged pleasantries about the journey to Fiji while Dr Holmes visibly grew impatient.

'So, will you be visiting any of the other plantations then?' the doctor interrupted. 'Surely, as the only Indian in the delegation, you would like to see how your people are really being treated?'

Mr Choudry eyed the swaying doctor warily, but responded to the belligerent question with civility. 'Yes, I heard that you were suggesting that we visit Labasa. I wish we could. Unlike my fellow delegates, I do see the value in a more thorough review. Unfortunately, we have limited time here. A ship journey of many days to get to another island is not possible, even if I wanted to get back on another ship, which believe me, I do not. We are going to see a plantation tomorrow, you know.'

'For God's sake, man, you can't assume all plantations are the same. Tell him, Akal.' Robert swung towards Akal, his entire body tense.

Akal shifted, not making eye contact with the doctor. 'I have not been to a plantation. I could not say.'

'Oh, that's right. And why not?' the doctor asked pointedly. 'Aren't you curious to see what it is like?'

Akal shook his head stiffly. 'It is not within my duties. I am needed here in Suva.'

'Well, it is within your duties now. Thank God the priest kicked up a fuss about that missing coolie woman, or that would have been hushed up as well.'

Akal groaned silently. This was just what the situation needed.

'What is this, Sergeant Singh?' Mr Choudry focused his sharp gaze on Akal, cordial demeanour forgotten.

Akal explained the situation as diplomatically as he could with the doctor looking on, with a mounting sense of dread. The inspector-general would inevitably find out about this exchange.

'Well, this is very disturbing,' Mr Choudry muttered, shaking his head. He looked at Akal. 'Do you believe that it would have been swept under the rug without this priest's intervention?'

'Oh, definitely,' Taviti interjected.

'Ah, well, I am sure the inspector-general would have done as much as he deemed appropriate,' Akal said hastily, glaring at Taviti.

'Never mind the inspector-general,' Mr Choudry snapped. 'If I can do nothing else for the indentured labourers, I can at least insist that the inspector-general allows you to investigate this case properly. I will expect a personal report from you on this case and on the conditions at the plantation, a plantation which hasn't been thoroughly vetted and warned of our visit by the governor.'

'Mr Choudry, is there anything I can help you with?' The inspector-general had approached the group unnoticed and had clearly overheard some of what Mr Choudry had said.

Akal had thought his stomach had already sunk to the lowest levels of his abdomen, but it turned out there was still space for it to get lower.

'Well, I am not sure, Inspector-General,' Mr Choudry replied, words clipped. 'Sergeant Singh was explaining to me how he is about to investigate a case of a missing indentured woman. I presume he will be given every resource to help with his investigation?' The question did not sound very much like a question at all.

'Yes. Of course, Mr Choudry.' The inspector-general's words were equally clipped.

'Excellent. I have requested a personal report from Sergeant Singh. That should not be a problem, should it, Inspector-General?'

'No, not at all.' The inspector-general's teeth were so tightly clenched that Akal had a mental image of them exploding outwards and taking Mr Choudry's eye out.

'Very well. I look forward to a speedy resolution. Thank you, gentlemen, this has been enlightening.' Mr Choudry nodded to each of them and swiftly moved away to talk to other members of the delegation.

The inspector-general turned to Akal, rigid with rage.

'You could not keep your mouth shut for one night? What are you trying to do here?' Thurstrom managed to convey a roar in a whisper, a talent that Akal had not witnessed before.

'No, no,' the doctor slurred. 'I was the one who told that chap what was going on.'

Thurstrom continued to glare at Akal. 'You had better hope you can get this wrapped up neatly and quickly, because, so help me, if there are any other mistakes, you are going to be demoted so far back down the chain you will be manning the front desk for the rest of your days.' He straightened his jacket, fixed a smile on his face, and moved off to shake the hand of one of the prominent plantation owners.

Akal glared at both the doctor, who was swaying in place, and Taviti, who was unsuccessfully trying to hold his laughter in with his fist. 'You idiots. I am never going to get off this godforsaken island.'

Chop Chop

There you are, you see! We take the
Public's advice, get a man who knows
all about coolies as agent-general of
Immigration, and soon he has to leave
us (a Cadet would have stayed forever).
The government have now brought in
a pet, who has never seen a coolie, to
succeed Mr Smith. Mr Keane might be
useless, but he is 'one of us'!

CHAPTER THREE

The following morning, Akal approached his horse with anticipation. As a teacher in the Punjab, his father had neither the income to maintain a horse, nor the need, despite a horse-mad young Akal's best efforts to convince him otherwise. Luckily for Akal, Heminder, the son of the wealthiest family in the vicinity, had been a dunce at his numbers, so Akal's father was employed to tutor the boy. Akal had always joined his father in the tutoring sessions and had struck up a firm friendship with similarly horse-mad Heminder, whose family maintained an extensive stable.

Through his teenage years, he had spent every moment he could with Heminder, learning how to ride like the wind and how to care for horses. Heminder's family's stablemaster had been encouraging Akal to apprentice with him, and Akal had been torn. His father had been gently encouraging him to see the world and utilise his brain by taking the civil service exam. Unable to make a decision, Akal had been pursuing both courses, apprenticing with the stablemaster and studying for the civil service exam when he could, when his father had ailed.

With his father no longer teaching, and with six mouths to feed and three dowries to provide for Akal's sisters, the family was in urgent need of money, more money than either of Akal's original options would provide. His best option for an immediate well-paid job was to go overseas as a police officer, Sikh police officers being highly valued throughout the British colonies. Over his father's objections, which were heavily tinged with guilt, Akal had joined the police force and left for Hong Kong.

Since coming to Fiji, he had had scant opportunity to be on the back of a horse. The police department maintained several horses for excursions such as this. Akal had spent some of his leisure time getting to know the horses and had snuck in the occasional ride under the guise of exercising them. This particular horse was a favourite of his, calm and obedient but eager for a run when the chance presented itself. He lingered as he adjusted the reins and stirrups, relishing the feel of the leather on his palms and the warm prickly skin underneath, crooning to the patient, disinterested horse and making sure the buckles were tightened just so.

It had been such a long time since he'd had the peace and solitude of a journey with only the undemanding presence of a horse for company. The last journey Akal had taken had been the long sea voyage from Hong Kong to Suva, during which he had been lost in a haze of seasickness and shame. There had been no opportunity for quiet contemplation on that journey. Perhaps today he would find some time with his own thoughts.

Unfortunately, he couldn't keep the doctor waiting – nor the inspector-general and the impending fury of the Indian government, for that matter. Akal led his horse along the lane leading out from the police station and paused to mount at the end where the lane met the street, swinging his long leg over with an athletic ease that was the envy of his shorter colleagues. The horse jumped abruptly to clear the deep ruts torn into the side of the street and Akal turned her to start up the hill, away from town.

He dodged around the usual mix of dapper pedestrians, cyclists, horses and buggies. Behind him, Akal heard a motor vehicle being inexpertly driven in jerking, shuddering spurts. He warily edged the horse to the side and stopped to let the car pass. They were a menace, these motors, but luckily there were only a few of them in the colony. At best, they left dusty pedestrians shaking their fists in their wake, and on occasion a cyclist in a ditch on the side of the road. Once the car had made its way up the hill, despite stalling every few metres, Akal and his horse resumed their climb.

When he reached the top of the hill, Akal looked back over his shoulder down the dust-choked street, down towards the town that was stirring into action for the day. He was not keen on leaving this safe haven with its veneer of civility. Never mind that Suva's façade of civility showed as many cracks as its roads had potholes. He kicked his horse into a trot and made his way into the wilderness.

Akal left the noise and dust of Suva behind in about ten minutes, after he passed the hospital on top of the hill. The track was quieter after that, and Akal started to relax. But as the sounds of Suva waned, Akal started to hear the sounds of Fiji. Unfamiliar birds trilled overhead. Occasionally, an ominous rustling sound came from the underbrush by the track. Akal nervously glanced around, ostensibly looking for the turnoff to the doctor's house, but also keeping an eye out for predators. He was startled to see small eyes on a tree branch, distressingly close to his face, but the iguana ignored his presence and continued to soak up the sun which dappled across its back.

Akal took the left turn at the fork in the track, per the directions the doctor had given him the day before. The soft sounds of the ocean came closer until the track abruptly ended at a clearing with a ramshackle wooden house in the middle of it. The forest had been cut back to the front and sides of the house at some point, but it must have been a long time ago, as nature was now inching its way back towards the house. Behind the structure, Akal could see where the grass tapered off and the sand took over, the ever-present coconut palms providing shade. A horse was tied up at the front of the house, nose down and munching the grass. The doctor was nowhere in sight.

Akal dismounted and tied up his horse next to the other one. He climbed the few steps to the front door and knocked to no response. Coming back down, Akal walked back over to the other horse.

'You're already packed up, aren't you, boy?' he asked, rubbing his knuckles against the horse's nose. The horse pushed back against his hand, as if nodding in agreement. 'I wonder where your master has gone.'

In search of Robert, Akal moved towards the sound of the water coming around the house. He found himself on a small beach, opening out to a sheltered cove, wavelets lapping the sand. The doctor was standing motionless by the water, staring out to the sea. Akal started picking his way over to him, trying to avoid getting sand in his shoes. As he approached, he saw the doctor push the dented leather brim of his hat back and tip his face upwards.

'Doctor,' Akal called out, to no response. He kept going, waiting until he was closer to repeat, 'Doctor?' more loudly.

The doctor whirled around. 'Oh, Singh, I didn't see you there.'

'Doctor. Are you well?'

'Yes, yes, of course,' Robert replied, somewhat distractedly. 'Just lost in thought.'

He resumed staring up at the sky for another moment before reluctantly dragging his gaze back to Akal.

'I suppose we should go.'

'What were you looking at?' Akal blurted, curiosity overcoming his natural reticence. He hastily added a 'Doctor *sahib*' at the end, in an attempt to make the question sound more respectful, though Robert didn't seem to notice the disrespect or the attempt to repair it.

'Oh ... just the sky,' he replied. 'My wife, Samantha – she passed away a few years ago – she would always look at the sky. We travelled a little, went to Egypt for our honeymoon. The sky seemed endless there. I was wondering what she would make of it here, about as far away as one could get from Old Blighty in every way.'

Robert returned to his introspective sky-gazing, as Akal stood awkwardly by him, unsure how to respond to this insight into the doctor's past. In their few interactions thus far, Akal had felt a growing rapport, but this was the first personal detail either one of them had disclosed to the other. After a few moments, Robert gave himself a small shake and turned to Akal, brisk and businesslike.

'We had better get a move on. It's a few hours to the Parkins plantation. We should make it around noon. What do you think you'll find out there?'

Akal summarised the situation and his interview with Mrs Parkins. 'I am still not sure whether Father Hughes is just causing trouble because he has problems with the indenture program, or if he really thinks the woman has run away,' he concluded.

'Well, I happen to be in sympathy with the priest. If some reforms come about because of your investigation, then I don't think that would be a bad thing.' Akal glared at him, and the doctor chuckled. 'Yes, I can see that is not helping you. Well, at least I have always found Parkins to be reasonable, so you have got that in your favour. Not so much his wife, but she is safely back in Suva. Henry himself should cooperate.'

Akal nodded slowly. This did not match what Father Hughes had told him about Henry Parkins, though it certainly matched his experience in meeting Susan.

They were soon mounted and travelling down the track, single file, with the doctor leading. They proceeded in silence, conversation difficult from horseback. The quiet was broken by the gentle rushing of the river to their left, the drone of ever-present flies investigating the nostrils of horse and man alike, and the sucking sound of the horses' hooves pulling away from the mud of the track. Akal could see the pink of the doctor's skin through his white cotton shirt, rendered translucent by sweat and clinging to his back. When they turned away from the river an hour later, the track narrowed further and became increasingly overgrown, so they were fully occupied pushing branches out of the way. After a few hours, just as Akal was starting to question the doctor's knowledge of the way, the track opened out and the plantation sprawled ahead of them.

Akal's first glimpse of a Fijian plantation roused him out of the fog that had descended after hours of wrestling with overhanging branches as they rode. To the left, a low hill with two houses on it. At the crest was a house on low stilts with a wide verandah, not dissimilar to some of the houses in Suva. On the slope below was a second, smaller structure, which the doctor identified as the overseer's house. To the right and as far as the eye could see, fields of sugar cane closely planted, leaves occasionally managing a half-hearted wave in whatever breeze made a token appearance.

Straight ahead were two long, low buildings, running parallel to each other. The swollen wooden boards of these blunt rectangles were scarred by stains of mildew crawling up the walls. They seemed to suck away the sunlight. Looking at them raised the hairs on Akal's arms, despite the oppressive midday heat.

'Coolie lines,' said Dr Holmes, shaking his head. 'Dire, aren't they? They're worse inside.'

'Worse?' Akal grimaced.

'Police barracks don't seem too bad now, eh? Let's head up to the house and see if we can find Parkins.'

The two men rode up the hill and dismounted with some relief. Akal shook out his nerveless legs and rolled his shoulders, wincing at the sound of his bones popping. As they approached the house, Akal was struck by the forlorn air of the place. It looked as though nobody lived there; everything in the flower bed at the front had withered with neglect. The cracked wooden stairs leading to the verandah bowed under Akal's feet. The doctor knocked on the door to no response.

'I suppose we should wait a while.' Dr Holmes rapped on the door one more futile time. 'He might come home for lunch.'

As they waited on the wooden chairs on the verandah, Akal could feel his eyes drooping as the early morning, long ride, and midday heat took their inevitable toll. The creaking of the verandah steps roused him to alertness. A stocky European man approached them, taking his hat off and wiping his right hand on his pants before offering it to the doctor.

'Dr Holmes, good to see you.'

'Hello, Henry.'

Henry Parkins approached Akal with a cynical grin twisting his face. 'And you must be the crack investigator Thurstrom has sent out to find my missing coolie.'

'Yes, sir. I am Sergeant Akal Singh of the Fijian Constabulary, Suva Division,' Akal said.

'There is a first for everything. Never seen a coolie runaway generate this much interest from the police. Or any part of the administration. I guess I should thank Father Hughes.' This last statement was uttered in a slow, sarcastic drawl.

'Yes, sir. His interview with the newspaper has caused many problems.'

'Effective, though. Maybe I'll get my coolie back. But a kidnapping? What nonsense. I suspect she has run off with my overseer.'

'Your wife said the same thing,' Akal replied.

'In any case, where is Marks?' Parkins asked, quickly changing the topic. 'If the administration is so concerned about this, they should have a sub-inspector on it.'

'Sir, Sub-Inspector Marks has left Fiji to join the British Army. He is fighting in the European war.'

Parkins rolled his eyes. 'Hmph. My overseer went off to the blasted war as well. Idiot boys playing at being hero. So, Sergeant Singh, what do you need from me? I want this thing wrapped up quickly, before my wife starts politicking in earnest. Whether you find the woman or not, I just need the good Father to stop saying she has been kidnapped!'

'That is the inspector-general's desire also,' Akal confirmed. 'I will need to interview the coolies, especially the family of the alleged runaway.'

'Her husband will be back from the fields later this evening. But somebody will be down at the lines.'

'Where is he working? I will go and interview him there,' Akal replied.

'I don't know where every single worker is at every minute,' scoffed Henry Parkins. 'Besides, I won't have work disrupted for this wild-goose chase. You will just have to wait for tonight.'

'Very well. I will see whom I *can* find to interview.' Akal tried to maintain an even tone despite his impatience.

'I am going to set up a clinic for your Indians tonight and do my rounds for everyone else tomorrow. Can you put us up somewhere, Henry?' the doctor asked.

'Doctor, of course you are welcome in the guest room. Sergeant Singh, there should be an open room at the coolie lines.'

The world shrank until there was only the three men on the verandah and the blood pounding through Akal's skull, one thudding heartbeat at a time, like the *tabla* being played, drumbeats speeding up into a crescendo. When he heard the doctor's voice, it sounded like it was a lifetime away.

'I'll stay in the coolie lines as well, then. Don't want to disrupt your routine.'

The doctor's words were deceptively mild.

'No, Doctor!' Henry Parkins and Akal replied simultaneously.

'You must stay here,' Parkins insisted. 'I can't let you stay in the coolie lines. It just wouldn't be right.'

'I will be staying wherever Sergeant Singh stays.' The look the doctor gave Parkins was implacable.

'No, no, Doctor,' Akal interjected emphatically. 'You cannot stay there.'

'Henry?' The doctor's steely gaze had not moved from the plantation owner.

'The overseer's house. Brown's house. I don't know what shape it is in since he left, but it will be a roof over your heads,' Parkins offered with an air of panic. 'There is only one bed, though.'

Robert's gaze finally moved to Akal, who flinched at the fury he saw on the doctor's face.

'That will be fine. Thank you,' Akal replied hastily. The doctor nodded.

'Well, that's settled,' Parkins said with a relieved sigh. He stepped through the door and hastily retrieved a key from the sideboard at the entrance.

Akal and the doctor exchanged a loaded glance, Akal's full of both curiosity at the doctor's staunch defence of him and gratitude for it. He thought Robert looked disgusted and apologetic, though surely not at his own behaviour. Perhaps the doctor was taking on some guilt for the way Parkins was treating Akal? Akal hoped that wasn't the case. He enjoyed his growing rapport with the doctor. He didn't want misplaced guilt ruining that.

'Will you at least join me for dinner, Robert?' Henry asked

as he handed Dr Holmes the key. 'I would like to get caught up on the happenings in Suva. I'm sure Sergeant Singh can manage on his own for the night.' Henry Parkins's genial tone rang hollow.

'Dinner. I would like that,' the doctor conceded, unbending a little. 'Perhaps tomorrow. I would like to set up the clinic tonight. Might have to go through to tomorrow night if there are a lot of patients.'

The doctor and Parkins spoke for a few more minutes, organising the best time and place for the doctor's clinic. Akal listened with interest. Mr Parkins seemed to be knowledgeable about his indentured servants after all, providing the doctor with information about who had been sick and who he thought was just malingering.

Akal and Dr Holmes took their leave and moved their horses into the stables that Parkins had directed them to. They then headed towards the overseer's house, to drop their packs off. The doctor insisted the whole way down that they should draw straws to decide who should sleep on the floor. Akal kept politely declining. The doctor finally capitulated when Akal mentioned that he would be ashamed to sleep on the bed when his elder was on the floor. This irritated the doctor enough that he agreed with a huff. Despite the banter, Akal couldn't shake his unease at the atmosphere of the plantation and the demeanour of Mr Parkins. Sleeping on the floor was probably going to be the least of his worries.

After dropping his pack at the overseer's house, Akal went to explore the plantation, hoping to find somebody from the coolie community to interview. As he approached the coolie lines, the same sense of despair arose as it had on his first glimpse of the squat buildings. Akal knocked on the door of the first room in the first building. It creaked inward under his hand and he realised there was no lock to bar his way. Akal pushed the door harder and it opened fully with a shudder, revealing a room with so little light he could not make out what was within.

As he stepped inside, Akal was assaulted by the stale stench of residual smoke from an extinguished ashy fire in a corner of the room. The miasma of layer upon layer of days-old cooking smells, cumin and fenugreek fried in oil, was bitter against the back of his throat. His eyes adjusted to the gloom inside the room, the only light coming from the gaps between the rough planks of the wall. He saw the chaos of a family living in a confined space.

There were three bunks attached to the wall, firewood stacked in a corner next to the fireplace, and pots which looked in need of a good scrub. He turned and hurried back out of the oppressive room and took several deep breaths to clear the unwholesome air from his nostrils. This was the sort of room Parkins had expected him to sleep in. Akal resolved to avoid entering another of those rooms unless he absolutely had to.

After circling the two buildings of the coolie lines, Akal concluded that there was not anyone to interview. He looked for somewhere to wait, and not too far away he found a likely looking mango tree, boughs heavy with lustrous green leaves. Akal sat in the shade with his back against the trunk, long legs sprawled out in front of him, as he plucked at the grass and his eyelids drooped.

It was due to this lazy semiconscious state that he initially dismissed the sound of children yelling and laughing in the distance as a figment of his imagination. Akal couldn't believe anybody would be laughing while living in these conditions, not even children, so he ignored the noise until he felt something nudging his foot.

He cracked one eyelid and started into alertness when he saw a ragged young Indian boy staring at him. Based on his height, Akal guessed the boy's age at around eight or nine, though it was difficult to be sure, as skinny and covered in dirt as he was. His too-large shirt and too-short pants were more hole than cloth and his hair was made brown and stiff with the sheer volume of dirt he was carrying around in it.

They stared at each other for a long moment, the whites of the boy's eyes the only clean-looking thing on his face. Then from the right, another child ran full tilt and barrelled into the first boy, tackling him to the ground. Akal folded his legs out of the line of fire as the two children – he assumed they were both boys, but he couldn't really tell – wrestled furiously in the grass.

'*Bas!* Stop! Get off!' shouted one of the boys, but to no avail as the scrawny brown limbs, patchy with dried mud, continued to thresh about. Finally, the original boy pinned the second to the ground, straddling his torso and holding him down by the shoulders as the other boy continued to try to buck him off.

'Stop it! I want to talk to the policeman,' the boy on top shouted.

At the mention of police, the second boy stilled.

'Policeman?'

He craned over to look at Akal, who nodded at him gravely.

'Is he a real policeman? Why is he here?' the boy on the ground asked in a hushed tone, seemingly unaware that his childish version of a whisper was clearly audible to Akal. They were speaking a garbled version of Hindi, which Akal could only just understand. If this was the standard of Hindi on the plantation, Akal worried about his chances of getting any information out of the coolies.

'I don't know. I want to ask him. Will you be quiet now?'

The other boy nodded and they untangled themselves and sprang up to standing as only the very young can do. Akal remained seated, which left him at close to the same height as the two boys. And they *were* both boys; he could tell now that they were temporarily still. They had a restless tension about them that signalled that they could take off running at any minute.

The boys seemed to not know where to start, so Akal started the conversation for them.

'I am Sergeant Akal Singh of the Fijian Constabulary, Suva Division. What are your names?' he asked, politely inclining his head at each of them in turn.

'I am Zain, and he is Dev,' replied the victorious young wrestler. 'You are really a policeman? Are you going to arrest somebody?'

'Yes, are you really a policeman?' Dev earned a scathing look from Zain at this redundancy. 'And ... where are you from?' he added, triumphant that he had managed to come up with a previously unasked question, but clearly missing the fact that Akal had already told them he had come from Suva.

'Yes, I am really a policeman from Suva,' Akal responded, fishing his warrant card out of his pocket and extending it to show the boys. Zain took the warrant card and inspected it carefully, albeit holding it upside down the whole time. He gravely nodded at his friend before handing the card back to Akal.

'Who are you arresting?' asked Zain.

'Who should I arrest?' asked Akal, keeping the amusement from his face with some effort. While he didn't really expect the boys to wrap the case up for him in a nice, neat banana leaf parcel, these were the first plantation residents he'd met, so there was a chance he might learn something.

'The *sahibs*,' replied Zain without hesitation. 'They beat my father and mother all the time. Everyone, they beat everyone. They are bad men.'

Dev nodded vehemently throughout this pronouncement.

Akal had heard stories about such beatings before. He had found one Indian eatery in Suva, where he ate once a week when his finances allowed; it was run by an ex-coolie man. One night, after finishing work late, he had overheard the owner, deep in his cups, lament the cruelties inflicted during his indenture. Slumped over his whisky in the light of a kerosene lamp he told his stories, unnoticed tears tracing through the lines prematurely formed on his face during those harsh years, a map of all he'd endured.

Akal was surprised that Zain only mentioned the *sahibs*. In the stories he had overheard, the beatings and other indignities had not only been administered by the plantation owners and European overseers, all collectively referred to as *sahibs*, but also by the Indian overseers, known as *sirdars*. Akal had sat unnoticed in the corner and listened to the man's history long after his meal was finished. He had felt a deep revulsion – not only towards the *sahibs* and *sirdars*, but, to his shame, also towards the indentured Indians. When Parkins had suggested he sleep in the coolie lines, he had wanted to howl that he was not one of those wretches.

'I'll see what I can do. Anybody else?'

They both pondered for a moment then shook their heads. 'No, sir,' replied Zain.

'I'm here to ask some questions about the woman who is missing, Kunti. Do you know her?'

Both boys visibly withdrew, shuffling their feet and looking at the ground. Zain nodded but continued to avoid eye contact. Akal hadn't imagined he'd be grateful for the Night Prowler, but the experience he had gained in interviewing young children during that investigation was now going to hold him in good stead.

'I'm sorry. Are you sad she is gone?' he prompted, dropping his voice down to a soothing tone. Zain shrugged. Dev ignored the question, staring into the distance in the direction he had come hurtling from a couple of minutes ago. His whole body tensed up as he got ready to flee. He looked back at Zain, gestured for him to come, and then bounded away without another word.

'He is not very smart,' Zain said, rolling his eyes.

'He's fast, though,' Akal responded wryly.

Zain flashed him a grin. 'So am I, but I'm smart too.'

'I believe you.' Akal grinned back for a moment, then allowed his face to become more serious. 'So, you *did* know Kunti?'

The boy nodded.

'Was she sad here? Did she want to leave?' Akal asked.

'I don't think so. Divya would have told me.'

'And who is Divya?'

'Divya is my friend.' Zain puffed up his chest. 'Kunti is her mother.'

Akal thought about teasing the boy about his girlfriend but, not wanting to lose the tenuous connection that they had made so far, decided to err on the side of caution.

'And Divya didn't say anything to you about her mother?'

'No ... She's just been crying a lot since her mother left. She doesn't play anymore. She just sits and cries.'

'Where is she now?' The priest had made much of the idea that Kunti would not have left her daughter. Perhaps a conversation with Divya would shed some light on Kunti's motivations.

'We went to the creek today because it is so hot. We were on our way back, but Dev and I ran, so the others must be close. Bala Aunty is going to be angry at us for running ahead.' He seemed pleased at the idea of the woman's ire.

'You can tell her that you were assisting in a police investigation,' Akal said, giving the boy a conspiratorial wink. Zain beamed delightedly and nodded with vigour. That seemed to be the limit of his ability to stand still, as he then started to look around restlessly, shifting from foot to foot.

'Will you arrest the *sahibs*?' he asked abruptly, seemingly wanting some assurances before he took off.

'I don't know. I might not arrest anybody. I'm just here to find out what happened to Divya's mother.'

'Oh. Why won't you arrest them? I told you they beat people, even when they are too sick to work. You should arrest them.'

Akal looked away from the boy, whose face was lit with both hope and anger. He felt the shame of his own impotence, a new sensation for him. In Hong Kong, he would have brought this situation to his commanding officer with confidence that he, and the issue, would receive a fair hearing. The inspector-general in Hong Kong had, for a long time, trusted his judgement. Inspector-General Thurstrom had no such history. His view of Akal was entirely formed on one incident. Even if Thurstrom had any interest in crimes against the indentured servants, he wouldn't have time for anything brought to him by Akal.

'They shouldn't do that,' Akal said quietly. 'But unless I see it or the doctor has some proof that people are being mistreated, we can't do anything.'

'Why did you come, then?' Zain looked at him with disgust. 'I thought you were going to help us.'

'I'm sorry.'

The words were inadequate, but Akal didn't want to offer false hope.

'What good does that do anyone?'

The sentiment was too bitter to be coming from such a young boy. Zain turned and started walking away. After a few metres, his natural exuberance reasserted itself and he broke into an unrestrained sprint, arms windmilling as his legs seemed to maintain a pace his body and the laws of physics could not keep up with.

Akal could see that he was pelting towards a group in the distance, presumably the other children returning from the creek with Bala Aunty. He got up and brushed off the assorted twigs and leaves he had accumulated on the back of his trousers, then started to walk towards the group of children and their nanny, eyes squinting as he left the shade of the tree.

Bala Aunty was a plain woman, probably in her late twenties, Akal estimated. She was slim with hunched shoulders, nervous-looking, and her lips were so pinched together that they seemed to have disappeared into her face. At his approach, she shepherded the less active children, mostly girls, closer to her like a fence of small bodies. The other children continued to dart away from her grasping hands and form their own little clusters. The one word he heard over and over again, in childish high-pitched tones, was 'policeman, policeman'.

'*Namaskaram.*' Akal had stopped a few feet away from the agitated woman, giving her some space.

'*Namaskaram.*' She bobbed her head but kept a narrowed eye on him.

'I am Sergeant Akal Singh of the Fijian Constabulary, Suva Division.'

She nodded but did not say anything.

'What is your name?' he prompted.

'Bala.'

'And how are you, Bala? Hot day, isn't it?' he asked casually.

'Why are you here?' She clutched a child from her protective barrier closer to her, the little girl wriggling in protest. Akal noted with relief that she spoke reasonable Hindi. It probably wasn't her native dialect, but at least he could understand her.

'I want to talk to you about the disappearance of Kunti. Did you know her?'

'Of course. We all know each other here.'

'Is one of these girls her daughter?' he asked, inspecting the girls' upturned faces. They were all peering up at him with quiet curiosity, but any girl he made eye contact with looked away – except for one. A slim girl of around eight, hair in twin plaits tied with faded blue ribbons, ragged at the edges.

'Divya?' he asked her, maintaining eye contact.

'Yes, sir.' The reply was quiet but firm.

'Don't you talk to her.' Bala stepped in front of Divya, reversing roles as the human shield. 'She's just a little girl. She doesn't know anything.'

Divya darted out from behind the defensive woman. 'Aunty, I want to talk to him.'

'No, *betee*, your father wouldn't want you to talk to the policeman.'

'Why not?' Divya and Akal asked simultaneously.

Wringing her hands, Bala eventually responded only to Divya. 'It'll upset you. You've only just stopped crying.'

'I don't care if it upsets me. I want to talk to him. You aren't my mother.'

Bala looked set to raise more objections, but at that moment, a high-pitched wail rent the air. As one, Bala, Akal, and the girls swivelled around to see a group of children huddled over a prostrate child in the shade of one of the ubiquitous mango trees. Bala frantically switched her gaze between the fallen child and Akal. She finally shook her finger at Akal and said, 'You leave Divya alone.' Bala then hitched her threadbare cotton sari up and scurried away at pace. The other girls, except for Divya, ran to the action as well, easily outpacing the older woman. All of them sent glances back over their shoulders, curious on the part of the girls, baleful on the part of Bala.

'She wants to marry my father.' Divya scowled at Bala's back disappearing into the distance. 'Her husband, he is dead now, he used to beat her. My father never beats my mother.' Her matter-of-fact tone as she talked of violence and broken marriages horrified Akal even more than what she was saying.

He focused on the least disturbing part of the statement: 'What makes you think Bala is after your father?'

Divya pursed her lips. 'My mother has only been gone for a few days, but Bala Aunty is already coming around every night, making dinner for us. She isn't even a good cook.'

This pithy comment from the little girl startled a smile out of Akal, unexpected after the grim conversation immediately prior. He was loath to upset her anew, but he couldn't avoid the topic. 'Tell me about your mother.'

'My mother did not run away.' Tears sprang up to hover on her bottom eyelids, distorting her eyes, but her jaw and voice were firm.

Divya's voice joined Father Hughes's voice in the same refrain – Kunti had not run away. Hardly an objective view in Divya's case. What daughter would want to believe that her mother would leave her?

'*Acha acha*,' Akal soothed. A pause, then delicately, he asked, 'Why are you so sure she would not leave?'

'She wouldn't leave me! Or Appa! She wouldn't! You don't know anything about her! Why would she leave me?'

Akal bristled. He and Divya glared at each other for a pregnant minute. He wasn't used to being challenged by a female, particularly not a young girl of a lower caste. But he reminded himself that this young girl was worried about her mother. He took a deep breath and continued calmly.

'Had anything unusual happened recently?'

The little girl hesitated before grudgingly admitting, 'She was angry at my father. I heard them fighting the day before she disappeared.'

His previous irritation forgotten, Akal latched onto this fact, leaning forward. 'What were they fighting about?'

'I don't know. They went outside and I couldn't hear them, but I could see them. Amma was crying and she looked mad. Appa just kept looking around to see if anyone could hear.'

Bala was coming back towards them with a determined shuffle that moved her along faster than Akal would have anticipated. He asked Divya with some urgency, 'Anything else?'

'No. Just please find my mother,' Divya said, the tears finally escaping her eyelids and tracing down her face, going ignored by the young girl as she fixed him with a fierce stare.

Father Hughes had suggested he should investigate on account of what he had in common with the indentured servants, an appeal which had left Akal feeling guilty and resentful. He had suspected the missionary was pursuing his own agenda. But this appeal from the little girl with liquid eyes and a suddenly uncertain future was far more compelling. He nodded once, and, seeing the trust in her tear-streaked face, he felt something fall into place. If he ignored all the politics swirling around this case, perhaps he could still do something worthwhile here.

Bala reached them a moment later, slightly out of breath, eyes darting from Akal to Divya and back again. 'What have you said?' she demanded of Divya.

'Nothing helpful,' Akal responded, deflecting attention back to himself.

'*Aree*, for God's sake, how is she going to help you? Her mother is gone and that's it. Nothing more to say.' The woman grabbed Divya by the arm and started pulling her back towards the other children.

Divya looked back at him in a mute appeal for sanctuary, but Akal could only shrug helplessly. He could investigate her mother's disappearance, but unless he found Kunti, he could not stop Divya's father from marrying one of the scarce women on the plantation.

The sunset was a distant memory by the time Akal walked into the kitchen of his temporary home and contemplated the slim pickings available. A quick search unearthed two tins of fish and some solid breakfast crackers, a Fijian staple. The pale blonde squares looked innocuous, but his jaws ached just looking at them. They could break the teeth of the unsuspecting muncher. From the kitchen window, he could make out the coolie lines at the bottom of the hill, faintly aglow with cooking fires, stirring with the movement of a community preparing for the evening.

The smell of smoke from the fires mingled with the heady aroma of frying onions and spices, the freshness of it a welcome contrast to the acrid scents he had encountered earlier in the day. The landscape was completely different from his home in the Punjab, but that smell remained the same, the smell of home. He snagged the tins from the kitchen and headed down the hill, whistling a traditional tune he thought he had forgotten.

As he approached the coolie lines, Akal gradually toned down the jauntiness of the tune until he stopped whistling altogether. There was a subdued air over the entire settlement. Akal's first thought was that the quietness was from worry about the missing woman, but in all honesty, it could be from simply another grindingly hard day at the plantation.

The first person he saw was a man sitting slumped outside

his door. The man lifted his head just enough to glance at Akal as he approached, his interest warring with exhaustion. His head dropped back down again until Akal stopped in front of him.

'Excuse me. I am looking for Venkat.'

The man slowly lifted his gaze again to regard Akal warily. With a small shrug, the man closed his eyes once more, but there was a new tension in his shoulders. Akal moved on.

As he passed by the open doors, Akal sensed movement inside. He glanced into one of the rooms, and through the hazy air he could see a woman cooking a late dinner for her husband, who was sitting outside in a posture of exhaustion. This scene was replicated throughout the coolie lines. Akal wondered where the women found the energy. They had worked full days themselves in the fields, though their contracts stipulated lighter tasks.

All the men were unnervingly still. Akal passed unacknowledged through a landscape of inanimate bodies. He approached one of the men at random but with deliberate purpose, feet stamping a little harder than necessary, looking for a response. At this point he would prefer another shrug than this sensation that he wasn't even there. A look of alarm flashed on the man's face and he suddenly found a reason to duck inside his smoky room.

Akal had thought that a stranger on the plantation would be a cause for curiosity. But this was not curiosity; something had spooked them. Perhaps his uniform? Perhaps his gun, a Webley revolver holstered at his right hip. Had Parkins warned them against speaking to him? But Parkins had not seemed concerned about the presence of a police officer on his plantation. Was it about Kunti's disappearance, or a general warning to keep the happenings on the plantation to themselves? There were myriad things Parkins could threaten them with – his control over them was near-absolute.

As Akal reached the end of the two huts that represented the coolie lines, the level of activity increased. People were queuing at the entrance to an unoccupied room that he had noticed earlier that day. The queue consisted of individuals and small families, sitting quietly, cross-legged on the ground, many with their eyes closed. There were about ten such groups waiting, which took the queue past the edge of the coolie line and into the darkness beyond. It seemed that Dr Holmes had taken his clinic to the people.

Akal hesitated as he neared the room, contemplating whether he should enter. If he worked with the doctor, perhaps he could break down some of the suspicion and people would talk more freely. However, he was not sure whether Dr Holmes would grant him permission. The doctor was protective of his patients, and Akal suspected he would be unceremoniously ejected if there was any possibility that his presence would affect the doctor's work. Still, Akal thought it could hardly hurt to try.

He went to the open door and put his head inside, ignoring the queue of people who shuffled back away from him and looked at the ground to avoid his gaze.

The room had the same arrangement as the one Akal had reluctantly entered earlier in the day, but it was barely recognisable. It had been emptied of any household items and ruthlessly scrubbed clean, and lamps had been brought in, illuminating the room so it almost appeared cosy. The doctor was sitting on a stool, gently manipulating the swollen foot of a man who was lying on the bunk, eyes squeezed shut in pain.

Dr Holmes raised an impatient hand without looking up from what he was doing.

'Just wait your turn,' he said. 'I am going to see everyone.'

There was another Indian man in the room, standing against the wall, and he was the first to realise who had walked in.

'Ahem ... Doctor *sahib*. The policeman is here.'

Dr Holmes looked up and gave Akal a sheepish smirk when he realised his mistake. 'Ah, Akal. I thought you would make your way here eventually. I have somebody here you probably want to talk to.' He nodded towards the man who had spoken. 'Meet Venkat.'

Venkat pushed away from the wall and nodded gravely to Akal. He was a short, dark man with powerful shoulders, and with his masculine version of Divya's soulful eyes, he exuded a quietly commanding presence.

'I need to speak with you about your wife's disappearance,' Akal said. 'Can we talk?'

A look of consternation flashed across Venkat's face before he composed himself. He turned to Dr Holmes. 'Doctor, may I take my dinner break now? I will go find Satish. He will interpret for you while I am gone.'

'Fine. And Sergeant Singh can interpret for me in the meantime. Will that be alright, Akal?' Robert asked.

Akal was surprised by the twinge of excitement he felt at this idea. 'Yes, Doctor. Let me check that I have a language in common with this patient and the next,' he replied.

After exchanging a few words in Hindi with the current patient, Akal stepped outside and confirmed that the next patients, a young couple with the wife heavily pregnant, also spoke enough Hindi that they would be able to manage. He stepped back inside and nodded at Venkat, who quickly broke eye contact to politely take his leave from the doctor, then leave the room without any further interaction with Akal. Akal was now the doctor's interpreter, a role he was looking forward to more than he would have expected.

'In an ideal world, I would say stay off the foot, but I know that isn't possible.' Robert muttered these comments to his patient's foot, as he fastened a wrapping on his heel. The patient was Mr Angtesh, a scrawny man with frazzled, thinning hair and a scrappy look in his eye. Dr Holmes had filled Akal in on the background: Mr Angtesh had come in with an ulcerated foot, probably due to his ill-fitting boots. The muddy conditions in the fields meant the sore never had a chance to heal. Without treatment, he would either lose his foot, or lose his life.

For the instructions, Robert turned to Akal.

'Tell him to change this bandage every night. I'll give him a spare one and an ointment. He needs to apply the ointment exactly as I did today when he changes the bandage. Every night he needs to wash the dirty one with boiling water. It must be fully dry before he puts it on again. Oh, and if the one he is wearing gets wet during the day, take it off. A wet bandage is worse than no bandage. Make sure he understands how important that is.'

Akal relayed this information to Mr Angtesh, who listened carefully, his eyes trained on Akal. He asked some questions to confirm his understanding and nodded his head side to side when he had it. This communication, rooted as it was in caregiving, didn't come easily to Akal. His job normally involved scared or angry victims, so he was capable of soothing, of calming. But the intimacy of dealing with a person's body, with their life, was new to him. And he was starting to see why the doctor was such a crusader for the rights of the coolies. As far as Robert Holmes was concerned, they were all his patients, and he saw their lives were in danger.

Mr Angtesh carefully swung his legs off the bunk and thanked the doctor with clasped hands and a small bow. As the patient started to tie the frayed laces on his tattered boots, Robert went to his satchel and retrieved a small jar of ointment and an extra bandage. He handed it to Mr Angtesh, accepted another bow in thanks, and then went to wash his hands in preparation for the next patient.

A large bowl of clean water had been brought in and placed on one of the emptied bunks, with another bowl available for discarded dirty water. Akal helped pour water over the doctor's soaped hands using a small saucer, and then tidied up as the doctor sat down to write his notes.

'Will he be alright, Doctor?' Akal asked. The usually genial man was quiet, and Akal didn't know whether this was his professional demeanour or if something was amiss.

'I don't know,' Robert responded with a sigh. 'I'm sure you translated well, but did he really understand? Will he be able to keep the bandages clean and dry? Will he have the time and energy? I did what I could, and I have increased his chances of recovery. I'll see by how much next time I come out.'

The next patient through the door was the heavily pregnant woman. She was accompanied by her husband, his hands hovering near her the whole time, as though she could fall imminently. Robert was finishing up his notes from Mr Angtesh and waved them in with a smile. 'Come, come. Get off your feet, take a seat on the bed.'

Everyone in the room looked to Akal, who translated, speaking slowly. The woman sank down on the bed, her husband standing by her. She leaned her head back against the wood planks of the wall and closed her eyes. From his position against the opposite wall, Akal could see the map of veins under the translucent skin of her upper chest and neck. The doctor finished his notes and went over to the couple.

'Hello,' he prompted, and her eyes blinked open slowly. 'I am Dr Robert Holmes. What are your names?'

Their names were Shiri and Anjali, and Anjali was about seven months pregnant, or so they thought. This was their first child, and they were visibly anxious. Robert performed the most thorough examination that he could, given the rudimentary facilities. Akal smiled as the doctor muttered to himself about his lack of scales.

'The baby is in breech,' Robert said as he pressed his hands gently into her abdomen, checking for the position of the foetus's head. He looked up to see Akal's confused frown. 'Upside down. It would come out feet first, which would be bad. But that is not a concern at seven months. Her measurements do back up the timing, but I cannot know for certain without more information and better equipment.'

Akal puzzled his way through the translation, recognising the truth of the doctor's prior comments on the accuracy of translations. He certainly couldn't relay the doctor's message exactly.

'Who will you have to help with the birth?' Robert asked. After some back and forth with the couple, Akal informed the doctor that Anjali would have help from a few women with whom she was close. They had all had their own children and had helped with other women's pregnancies and labours. The

Indian women on these plantations were used to being self-sufficient in bringing new life into the world.

'And how are you feeling, Anjali?' Robert asked, giving her a reassuring smile.

'Too tired, Doctor *sahib*.' It was Shiri who answered.

'Yes, I can see that. Is she normally this pale?'

Shiri shook his head, almost in tears.

'What is her diet like?'

Shiri's response was vehement and accompanied by broad gesticulations, his hands tracing his agitation through the close air of the room. After a flurry of translations, Akal concluded that food had been scarce for the family, with little meat. In fact, Anjali had less food during pregnancy than she normally did. She was not always able to work due to her exhaustion, so her wages had been docked. That had meant less food for them both and greater exhaustion for Anjali. They were on a downward spiral.

'I'll talk to Mr Parkins. I will try to get her some more food or make sure her wages don't get docked,' Robert said flatly, his brow furrowed.

This statement brought a marked change in Shiri. He held his hands up, eyes wide.

'No, no. Please do not bother Mr Parkins,' Akal translated. 'Shiri says they will manage.'

'I certainly *will* bother him. Mr Parkins has a responsibility to the workers on his plantation. I only wish I could do more.'

Shiri's look of alarm increased, and he started to get Anjali up from the bed as he barked a response for Akal to translate. 'No, no, I will make sure she has more food. I will borrow from my friend. He has offered to help. Please do not bother yourself, Doctor *sahib*.'

Shiri hurried Anjali out of the clinic, only stopping when she resisted so she could turn back and nod her thanks. Robert watched with dismay as they departed and turned to look at Akal for some explanation. He gave Robert a shrug. Shiri's reaction to the mention of Henry Parkins was worthy of further investigation.

When the couple departed, Venkat stepped inside with his replacement, Satish. Venkat made the introductions to Dr Holmes, relieving Akal of his brief stint as interpreter, and they departed the clinic.

'Are you a *sirdar*?' asked Akal, as they walked through the coolie lines to find a quiet place to talk. It was a logical assumption. As the Indian overseers who helped run the plantations, the main qualification for the job of *sirdar* was being able to translate the European overseers' orders. It was a coveted position, with better pay and a level of power none of the other coolies could hope for. If Venkat was a *sirdar*, Kunti's life on the plantation should have been better than that of the average coolie woman.

Venkat nodded after a moment, his thoughts clearly elsewhere. 'Do you mind if I eat as we speak?' asked Venkat. 'Have you eaten?' The latter was added with resignation.

Akal had been hoping for an offer to join one of the families for dinner, but had wondered whether this custom, so ingrained in the villages he knew in India, could survive the scarcity on the plantation. He knew that food would be precious, even for a *sirdar*'s family. But now that he had met Venkat, the offer of a meal was unsurprising. Venkat's eyes were red-rimmed and brown where they should have been white, but he maintained a steady gaze, powerful in his sense of place in the world. This man didn't seem to be broken like the ex-coolies Akal had met in the course of his duties in Suva.

'I have not. I have these tins of fish. I would be happy to share them if I could join you for a home-cooked meal.' Akal pulled the tins out of his pockets and showed them to Venkat. Meat was a rare luxury, so even the dubious pleasure of tinned fish was not to be dismissed.

The smile that bloomed over Venkat's face was infectious. 'Of course, that would be wonderful,' Venkat replied with joyous surprise. 'We will be eating with my daughter, Divya, and Bala, who cooked for us tonight. Bala mentioned you met them today.'

Akal nodded. He remembered Divya's comments on Bala's cooking with chagrin. Hopefully Divya's tastebuds had been tainted by the bitterness of her mother being supplanted, and Bala's abilities in the kitchen were better than Divya had suggested.

They walked back through the coolie lines, the other residents satisfying some curiosity with glances their way now that Akal was safely occupied with Venkat.

Venkat broke the silence: 'Thank you for looking for Kunti.'

'I am just doing my job.'

'And is bringing us tinned fish part of the job?'

'No, I just really wanted some *dal bhat*. I could smell the spices all the way up the hill.'

'Well, you and your fish are welcome to join us for dinner. Let me tell Bala.'

Venkat disappeared into the family's room, where Akal could hear some murmured conversation. The tone was terse, but he couldn't make out the words. Divya emerged shortly afterwards. Her thin frame was vibrating with tension, but her face broke out into a beaming grin as she ran the last few metres to Akal.

'*Namaskaram*, Sergeant Singh,' she chirped. 'You are having dinner with us!'

'*Namaskaram*, Divya. I heard your Bala Aunty has made dinner. Is she teaching you how to cook?' Akal asked with a twinkle in his eye. This animated version of Divya reminded him of one of his young cousins at home and teasing her was instinctive. As the words left his mouth, Akal wondered how Divya would react, this little girl who was missing her mother. He was immediately rewarded for taking this risk with a fine show of young girl obstinacy.

'She is not teaching me how to cook! She is *not* my mother!' Divya stomped in place, droplets of muddy water spattering around her feet.

'*Acha acha*, I was just teasing.'

'Well, stop it.'

'Very well, I will treat you as the young lady that you are. Tell me, young lady, do you know your numbers? How high can you count?'

'I can count to twenty!' the little girl told him, stumbling over her words in her excitement. 'But I don't have a teacher anymore. Our previous nanny, Sujula Aunty, she knew how to do sums. She was teaching us.' The girl scowled. 'Bala Aunty doesn't know anything. All she does is take us to the river and let the boys run around. And she is mean to the girls. Appa doesn't know. I tried to tell him, but he thinks I just don't like her.'

'No schooling at all? Can you write? Read?'

Divya looked at him as though he was touched in the head. 'No. What am I going to read? What am I going to write with?'

Akal pondered this. Perhaps there was no point. Perhaps she would never use those skills. But Akal was the son of a teacher. Even before starting at the village school, he had started learning his letters on his father's knee. Akal couldn't imagine a childhood devoid of learning how to read. He couldn't imagine a life without being able to write.

Venkat and Bala emerged with a tin plate in each hand, a modest portion of rice and lentils steaming from each. They all walked over to the communal eating area that had been crudely set up on top of a hillock nearby. Hessian sacks had been laid to soak up the afternoon rain, the worst of the water having run off the elevated point. Finally, mats woven from coconut palm leaves were layered on top.

Divya slipped her hand into Akal's as they walked. He hadn't held a child's hand like this since he said goodbye to his family and left India. The delicate bones of her hand filled him with unease. How could anything this fragile survive in such a hostile place?

They found a spot by the fire, which sparked and sputtered its way through wet twigs and branches, providing light for the various families who were sitting around eating their dinners. There wasn't the *halchal*, the clamour of boisterous children and friendly chatter that Akal would have seen in India, but despite the subdued atmosphere, Akal felt more at home than he had since he left his own village.

'Sergeant Singh, the fish?' Venkat enquired politely.

Akal retrieved the tins from his pockets and deftly opened them with his pocketknife. They shared the fish out between the four plates and made short work of their meals. With the fingers of his right hand, Akal deftly mixed the rice and lentils and fish into perfectly portioned mouthfuls, the grains of rice firm against his fingers while the lentils lost their cohesion and became silk and velvet. The fish provided a salty burst of flavour, without which the meal would have been quite bland. Akal suspected that salt may have been a luxury these families rarely had access to.

The meal finished, Venkat sent Divya and Bala off to wash the dishes. Divya didn't want to go and trailed along behind Bala, mournfully looking back at them over her shoulder.

'She's a good girl. She just needs to learn to talk a little less.'

'She seems very bright. It is a shame there is no schooling here for her.'

Venkat frowned at him. 'Do you think she would have been better off back home? She would not have had schooling in India either. We were moving from place to place trying to find work, scraping to find food. Why do you think we came to Fiji? In this country, once we are through the indenture, we can give her so much more than we ever could have in India.' He belatedly amended his statement: '*I* can give her so much more. Kunti thought the same way. That's why we came.'

'So what went wrong? Why did Kunti run away?'

Venkat looked at Akal, eyebrows lifted. 'You *do* think she ran away. You were just telling my daughter what she wanted to hear?'

'No. Not at all,' Akal reassured him, hands out in a placating gesture. He wasn't sure if Venkat would believe him, given that Akal did still think it most likely that Kunti had just run away. 'I am not sure of anything yet. But I will investigate, I promise. Tell me, what do you think has happened to her?'

'Look around you, Sergeant.' Venkat's hand swept around the hill, encompassing the families huddled together eating their meals by gasoline lamps and farther down the sodden hill to the coolie lines.

Akal saw anew the squalor and meanness, and he nodded. 'You think she ran away?'

'I wouldn't hate her for it, except she broke Divya's heart.' He shook his head, bewildered. 'I knew she could leave me without a second thought, but how could she leave our daughter?'

'Leave you? Where could she have gone? A woman on her own in Fiji?'

'She is not on her own.' Venkat scoffed. 'And I doubt she is still in Fiji. Do you think it is a coincidence that she disappeared at the exact same time that the overseer left?'

'Brown?'

'Yes. Brown.' Venkat spat the name out. 'She had been having an affair with him for some time.'

'The priest who took this to the newspapers ... he gave a very different description of Kunti. He seemed convinced that she would not leave your daughter. He certainly did not mention anything about an affair,' Akal responded, puzzled.

Venkat barked a short sharp laugh. 'The priest? Another man in love with my wife.'

'If she ran away, then she must have taken things with her,' Akal suggested. 'What did she take?'

Venkat frowned. 'Nothing, really. Just a photograph that the priest took of her. Divya noticed it was missing, she keeps asking where it could be. I don't know why Kunti did not take anything else. Maybe wherever they were going she couldn't take anything with her.'

Akal looked at him dubiously. 'Nothing? That does not seem likely.'

'Perhaps they didn't have time.'

'It would be a big risk for Brown to take. Stealing a woman away when she was under contract. Do you really believe he would take the risk?'

'You never met my wife.' Venkat shook his head, a wry smile tugging at his lips. 'Brown, the priest, they all fell under her spell. I do not think she did it deliberately. It is just her nature. I'm looking forward to my life with Bala. I want a plain wife this time.' Venkat leaned towards Akal, looking him directly in the eyes. 'Sergeant, I want you to confirm that Kunti is gone from Fiji so I can get on with my life. Make it clear to Divya that her mother is not coming back so we can all move on. But do it without getting her hopes up too much. Can you do that?'

Akal frowned. Yet another person wanting him to investigate with their own agenda. So far, Divya seemed to be the only person who wanted the truth. Before he could respond to Venkat's pressure, Divya returned to them.

'Appa, what did you talk about? Did you talk about Amma?'

'Yes, *betee*, and your Sergeant Singh is going to find out what happened.' Venkat met Akal's eyes over the top of Divya's head. 'He will find out where she went. But you have to be prepared that he might not be able to bring her back.'

Cyclonic Storm

R.M.S. *Makura* Delayed

The R.M.S. *Makura*, which left
Auckland at 10 a.m. on Tuesday was
expected to reach Suva yesterday. It has
been delayed due to the cyclonic storm
which just missed Suva on its way to
Auckland. For those who are expecting
goods from New Zealand, they will have
a few more days to wait.

CHAPTER FOUR

The following morning, Akal commandeered the telephone at the main house, ignoring Parkins's scowls, and waited for the operator to connect his call back to the station.

'Suva Police Station.'

'Taviti,' Akal replied with some relief. He was guiltily grateful that Taviti was confined to the front desk as usual, despite his friend's desire to do some real police work.

'Akal. You made it to the plantation! My cousins didn't catch you and eat you?'

'They tried, but I'm too fast. I said hello to your uncle for you as I ran past him.'

'Ha! Now I know you are lying – you are so skinny my family would not even want to put you in the pot. Nothing but watery broth from you.'

'What is happening in Suva?'

'Man, you need to hurry up and figure this thing out. Your Mr Choudry came to the police station just now. The inspector-general looks like he is going to explode.'

'What did he want?'

'Don't know what he said to Thurstrom, but he recognised me on the way out. He asked me to remind you about the report you promised him and wrote down an address for you to send it to. Doesn't seem like he is going to let this go.'

Akal cursed down the phone.

'So, what have you found out?' Taviti asked, interrupting Akal's flow of invective.

'Nothing conclusive. She might have left with the overseer, Brown. Can you check into his movements for me? He left to go and join the war a few days ago. See if you can find him in Suva. If he has already left, see if there was an Indian woman on the ship.'

'You want me to actually investigate something? I'll get right on it.' Taviti's voice crackled down the wire, full of glee.

'Do it quietly. Do not let anyone know that the chief's nephew is doing any real work. That will be just one more thing for Thurstrom to blame me for.'

'Quiet as a mouse, bosso.'

After Akal hung up the phone and sat down at the table to eat, he watched on as Robert cornered Henry Parkins.

'Henry, there is a woman I need to speak with you about,' Robert said as he crunched down on his toast.

'Aha, looking for a little payment for services, are you? That isn't how I run my plantation, you know,' Parkins said, his laughter ringing about the kitchen.

'Anjali. She is pregnant. Shiri is her husband,' said Robert, sounding like he was talking through gritted teeth. 'She isn't getting enough food. Shiri says her pay has been docked because she can't work as hard. Do you know about this?'

'No, nothing. Brown took care of those things. But I am sure he followed the contract,' Parkins replied, growing increasingly firm through these sentences. He crossed his arms before finishing defensively: 'If she isn't working a full day, her pay is docked. It is in the contract.'

'Contract or no, the baby is at risk. And the woman. Do you want to lose a worker altogether?' Robert said pointedly. 'You already have an issue with a missing woman. Do you want new questions asked about a dead one?'

Akal winced. His job was already hard enough without the doctor stirring more resentment with Parkins.

Parkins nodded stiffly. 'Anjali, did you say her name is? I don't know all of them by name, that is what Brown and the *sirdars* are for. I'll find out who she is, and I'll see what I can do.'

Akal was sceptical. When they had first arrived, Parkins had given the doctor a detailed rundown of all the coolies who might need medical attention, belying the idea that he didn't know his workers well. He suspected that Parkins knew all about the pregnant woman and had done nothing for her thus far. In any case, Akal was glad that the conversation had ended with relatively little acrimony.

'Good man,' Robert said, reaching out to Parkins, who slowly uncrossed his arms and shook the proffered hand. 'I'm sure she will be grateful.'

After breakfast, Akal and Dr Holmes collected their horses from the stables and set out for the nearby township of Taveluka, for the doctor to continue his rounds and for Akal to ask some questions of the locals. After they passed the coolie lines and as the two houses on the hill receded behind them,

Akal felt the pressure in his head ease. It continued to lighten as they rode farther away.

Since his arrival to the plantation the day before, Akal had become aware of a growing sense of suffocation, as though the air was too thick to breathe and was getting stuck in his admittedly luxurious nostril hair. Could it be the investigation that was making him feel this way? Akal had not made any real progress, but he had been dealing with the Night Prowler investigation for some time, so he was used to treading water. It had to be the plantation itself.

Eating with the coolies last night had been an uncomfortable, warped reminder of home. In its domesticity, it had reminded him of both what he was missing and of his kinship with the indentured servants. As he sat cross-legged on the ground, Akal had felt his skin shifting over his bones, re-forming him from the accomplished favourite that he had been in Hong Kong – the version of himself that he was trying to hold onto – into the coolie officer that Mrs Parkins saw him as.

Akal gave his horse her head, and she was content to follow the doctor's horse. As indeed was Akal, hypnotically lulled by the rhythm of the brown cascade of the leading horse's swishing tail. Once more, the doctor was their guide. This was on his route of yearly inspections, undertaken so he could provide reports back to the British government on health conditions in the colony, reports the doctor had dismissed as futile. 'Selective reading, Akal. If it's any good, they'll bang on about it, and if it's bad, then they ignore it altogether. I don't know why I bother.' But bother he did, and would continue to. Akal had come to realise that the doctor felt deeply for all his fellow human beings. He felt vaguely fidgety when he thought that perhaps he, himself, didn't care enough.

They were on a well-travelled path, so there was nothing to do but watch the cane fields on the left of them and the river on the right. Eventually the cane fields ended, and the forest regained its dominion of the land, but it had been sufficiently beaten back so it did not impede their progress. It was certainly a more comfortable ride than the last one. Akal had fallen into a half-awake doze in the saddle when they arrived at the fledgling township, which was tenuously holding onto existence on the edge of the river.

Akal and Robert dismounted at the edge of the market, onto ground churned up from all the traffic. They tied the horses up to the hitching post, which looked as though it was never intended to last very long but was somehow holding on long past its expiry date. It was slanting to one side, and the wood was mottled and warped. The chances of it holding a horse that didn't want to be held were slim. In fact, the only structure in sight which looked as though it could survive the first thunderstorm was the pier, jutting out into the water with the assurance that it had the might of the British Empire behind it.

'Do you know where to find Mr Mahraj in all of this?' Akal asked, gesturing across the market, which sprawled along the riverbank by the pier and up into the lanes between the haphazardly placed wooden buildings. On the ride over, Dr Holmes had told Akal about Balaji Mahraj, one of the first indentured servants in this area to have completed his contract eight years ago, a *sirdar* during his contract. He had taken up one of the plots of land being offered to the free Indians and was now farming his own sugar cane to sell back to CSR. As Mr Mahraj was a leader in the community, Akal was hoping he had some knowledge of where Kunti might be or could provide some advice on who else they should speak with.

'Holding court somewhere with the other Indian men, no doubt,' Robert replied with a good-natured roll of his eyes.

They weaved their way through the market, redolent with the smells of earthy cassava, fresh tangy tomatoes, and sweet pineapple permeating throughout. Akal looked around eagerly, disproportionately excited by the meandering, sleepy market. He was determined to get some fruit and vegetables for the rest of his time on the plantation. They had a kitchen all to themselves, after all, a luxury he did not have in the barracks.

The market stalls they were weaving past barely qualified as stalls at all. They were composed of burlap sacks stretched out on the ground, with produce arrayed on top in precise piles: pyramids of tomatoes and okra, eggplants laid out in rows of four like soldiers in a parade. The stallholders were mostly Indian women of various ages, with faded saris and their wealth in gold on their necks and in their ears. The women sat on the ends of their sacks cross-legged, dark eyes watching them with muted curiosity as they passed. They would be the biggest topic of gossip for this market day, the Indian police officer and the European doctor striding through the market with purpose.

'There he is. I told you he'd be holding court.' The doctor pointed to a tree under which a group of Indian men were sitting on a woven mat, all dressed in cotton pants and buttoned-down shirts with leather sandals, the typical attire of the moderately well-off Indian man in Fiji. Akal recognised this as his father's dress code, the outfit of a respectable teacher. In their previous lives in India, these men, almost certainly all coolies who had completed their contracts, would never have had the opportunity to wear these clothes; they would have worn the *dhoti*, the simple loincloth of the labourer. He wondered how these men felt in their new clothes.

As Robert and Akal approached, one of the men rose and separated from the group. He greeted the doctor like an old friend, vigorously shaking hands with him. There was just a hint of a bow over the handshake. Subservience to the colonial masters was hard to shake.

'Doctor *sahib*, it is good to see you. What are you doing here? Surely it isn't time for your annual rounds yet?' After exchanging a few polite words with Dr Holmes, Mr Mahraj turned to examine Akal with narrowed eyes. 'And accompanied by a policeman?'

'I am Sergeant Akal Singh of the Fijian Constabulary, Suva Division. I am here to investigate the disappearance of a woman from the Parkins plantation. Her name is Kunti.'

Mr Mahraj's eyebrows shot up at this last statement and he responded in Hindi, leaving the doctor to take a step back and out of the conversation. 'What is this? The police investigating the disappearance of a coolie woman?' he scoffed. 'But of course, they sent the Indian police officer to investigate. Not important enough for one of the *gora* officers, eh?'

'I was given this investigation by Inspector-General Thurstrom himself. This is being taken very seriously,' Akal snapped. He had to bite his tongue when the Parkins said such things, but he wouldn't accept the same impertinence from an Indian. 'Do you have any information on Kunti's movements? Or perhaps you or your wife could identify some of her friends.'

Mr Mahraj slowly wobbled his head, lips pursed. 'No, no information like this. My wife does not know her.'

'No, neither of you knows her? Interesting.' Akal pretended

to jot something down in his notebook as the doctor looked on with curiosity. Robert couldn't understand the conversation, but he seemed to be picking up on Akal's machinations.

'Interesting? Why is that interesting? Nothing interesting about it,' Mr Mahraj blustered.

Akal kept the smile from his lips. He knew men like Mr Mahraj. They had some status in their own small communities and were not accustomed to having their pronouncements questioned. A direct challenge would see them walk away. Akal had found the best way to get information from this type of man was to appeal to their egos.

'Just interesting to an investigator when someone who should know something … does not know it. But I am sure you would not hide anything from me.'

'I tell you I do not know the woman. And nor does my wife.'

'No, of course not,' Akal responded soothingly. 'Did you know Brown, the overseer? He has gone off to fight in the war, I believe.' Akal kept his tone deliberately casual.

'Well, yes, him I knew. Of course, everybody knows him.' Mr Mahraj seemed relieved to be finally able to answer in the affirmative.

'What did you think of him? I have heard some stories about cruel overseers. Was he like that?'

After a brief pause, Mr Mahraj responded, words carefully chosen. 'He arrived after I finished my contract. But I dealt with overseers in my time as *sirdar*. He was no better or worse than any of the other overseers. So I have heard.'

'How did he treat the coolies? Did he do the right things? It seems the women are not being taken care of when they are pregnant.'

Mr Mahraj seemed puzzled by the questions. 'Yes. Yes, I heard he did. What sort of questions are these? I thought you were looking for a missing woman.'

'I am trying to see if there was a reason for her to run away. Perhaps her work was too hard?'

'Everybody's work is too hard. That is no reason to run away. Wherever she is, I guarantee her life has not gotten any easier. Stupid woman.'

Akal tilted his head to the side. 'Maybe she did not run away. Maybe she was kidnapped as they said in the newspaper. What do you think of that?'

'Hmph. Who would kidnap a coolie woman? What for? I know she is very pretty, but hardly worth all this trouble.'

'So ... you do not know her, but you know she is pretty?' Akal asked sharply, seizing on this crack in Mr Mahraj's story.

Mr Mahraj shifted from one foot to the other. 'Yes.'

'Very pretty?'

'Yes ... no ... just pretty. What are you asking me this for anyway? I cannot help you. Go ask somebody else your questions.'

Mr Mahraj abruptly turned away from Akal and towards his entourage, pointedly presenting his back to Akal. Before Mr Mahraj even sat down, the questioning started, all the men leaning in and talking over each other until a sharp *'Arre yaar, chup'* from their leader stopped them short. The rapid-fire conversation restarted more civilly, conducted in low tones, with frequent unsmiling glances over at Akal and the doctor, gliding over them without ever making eye contact.

Akal quickly filled Robert in on the details of his exchange with Mr Mahraj.

'They all rely on Parkins and Brown. He's the only one with a mill around here,' the doctor mused, after Akal finished describing Mr Mahraj's evasiveness.

'Sugar.' Akal snorted. 'I don't even like sugar.'

Disbelief was writ large on the doctor's face, one bushy eyebrow shooting all the way up to his hairline. 'I saw you inhaling those little brown dumplings after the last match. What *are* those things? I can't eat more than two bites.' He shuddered.

'*Gulab jamun.*' Akal grinned. 'They have to be sweet, to please the gods! My mother's *gulab jamun* are the best.'

'Of course they are,' the doctor replied with just a hint of a smile.

'Well, we aren't going to get much more out of this lot,' Akal said, looking around at the curious crowd. 'Now, where are we going to set up this clinic of yours? It would be good to do something useful.'

'*Beta.* Mr Police Officer.'

The whisper was coming from down low. Akal turned around looking for the source of the conspiratorial whisper, until he realised that it came from around the corner, just inside one of the lanes. A tiny old lady was sitting behind her impromptu market stall, leaning against the splintery wall of a nondescript building, with her legs drawn up under her plain, faded cotton sari. Like so many others, she had small piles of vegetables, neat but sparse, the scant extra produce from a small home garden. Akal wondered if this was her sole support in life. Surely not.

'*Namaskaram*, Aunty.' Akal squatted down and smiled reassuringly to her. 'Have you sold much?'

'A little bit. No matter. What I don't sell, I'll eat. Nothing will go to waste.' Her rheumy eyes considered him, creases at their sides deepening. Akal felt pinned by her gaze, by a force of will that seemed out of place in the diminutive woman with her humble stall and threadbare clothes. Her strength did not come from any of those things. It seemed rather that she had let go, was unconcerned about what happened around her and was focused purely on this moment. She crossed her legs and leaned forward, gesturing him closer.

'Where is your doctor *sahib*?'

'He found a room to set up as a clinic. Did you need to see a doctor? I can take you to him.'

'You are asking about Kunti?' she asked, ignoring his question.

'Well ... yes. How did you know?'

She laughed, her hunched shoulders moving in rhythm with a laugh that sounded more like a series of cracking, wheezing coughs.

'A goat can't fart around here without every man in town giving his opinion on it.' She nodded over to Mr Mahraj's cohort of cronies, still deep in discussion. 'They were all picking up cow shit for fire to cook their dinner in India, but here in Fiji they think they are big men. But for the women? Nothing changes for the women. Or only for the worse. Kunti thought it was going to be better. Now what does she think?'

The old lady paused and looked away to the bustling market. When she looked back, she had eased the bitterness from her expression, now neutral and inscrutable.

'Aunty?' Akal prompted, curious to see where this would

go. The older women in his village in the Punjab had always had a very efficient information pipeline, exchanging gossip as they went about their daily chores. He wondered if that same system had evolved here in Fiji.

'I knew Kunti. She was a beautiful girl, but everyone will tell you that. There are other beautiful girls on the plantation, of course. But Kunti was the one everyone noticed. They just think it is because of how she looks. They don't realise it's because of how she looks at them.' She paused, pinning Akal with her gaze again. 'You see? It was the same for me when I was younger.'

Akal could believe it. He couldn't quite imagine how she would have looked in her youth through the wrinkles and the wiry grey hair and the sun-spotted skin. But the strength of her gaze was compelling even now, and a scant quarter of that strength coupled with the glow of youth would have drawn any man.

'Watch out, Aunty. I am only a weak young man.' He clutched his chest and shot her a grin. 'I'm not sure I can resist you when you look at me like that.'

She cackled her painful laugh.

'*Haramin*, cheeky boy. Listen now. Kunti should have known better. She should have known that around the *gora* she needed to look down at her feet. Not straight in his eyes. I told her to be careful. I don't know if she even knew what she was doing.'

As Akal bit at his lower lip and considered how to ask the old dear to stop being mysterious, she finally got to the point: '*Acha ha bahya*,' she chortled, wobbling her head side to side as she laughed. 'I'll start from the beginning.'

Akal gave a silent sigh of relief.

'Kunti arrived, let's see, three years ago now, yes, I think that's right. With her husband and Divya. Oh, such a lovely family, it almost hurt my heart to see how gentle they were with each other. The first time I saw them, they were coming into the coolie lines from the depot with all their *jahajibhai*, their ship brothers. They were walking together, the parents carrying all their possessions and the little girl running around them, talking, talking, talking about everything she could see and everything she was going to do and would there be other children here. Kunti and Venkat answered her questions and pointed out other things for her to look at. I thought to myself – that is not going to last. The coolie lines will take the chatter from that little girl's mouth and the light from her mother's eyes and the smile from her father's lips. I had seen it before.

'But it did not happen, not at first. They did not let the coolie lines break them apart. Maybe it would have been better if they had broken a little bit, if Kunti had become a little less, if the light had faded. Then maybe she would have looked at her feet and not in the *gora*'s eyes and he might not have seen her.'

'You said you told her to be careful?' Akal prompted after a long pause. The old lady seemed lost in her memories, staring into the dim laneway as though she had a direct line of sight into the past and could see the family there, with the little girl chattering away as she had the first day they arrived. She turned and looked at him, eyes gradually coming into focus.

'Yes. He has done it before, you know. Another woman, Magamma. Like Kunti, but with just a ship marriage and no children, so it did not matter so much.'

'A ship marriage?' Akal asked.

'She wanted to come to Fiji, and she couldn't go on the

ship unmarried. So, the *arkathi*, the one who recruited her, arranged for her to "marry" one of the men who was going to be on the ship. Most of the marriages here are like that, no ceremony, nothing registered anywhere. You just agree that you are married. Then later, if you're not happy, you agree that you aren't married anymore,' she explained, shrugging philosophically. Akal was shocked. This was not marriage as he knew it.

Aunty resumed her story. 'As I was saying, Magamma's husband was glad the *sahib* had taken a liking to her. They got better food, lighter work. When she finished her contract ... well, I think the *gora* was bored of her by then, so she went. She left the ship marriage and found another husband. They have a little cane farm. Sometimes I see them here at the market. She seems happy now.

'When Kunti came, I knew he would treat her the same way. But she wasn't the same. She was happy before. I do not know too much about how and when he started using her, I just know that I saw the family here at the market a year later, and what a difference. Venkat was quiet, the little girl just walked, holding both her parents' hands and not saying a word. Kunti looked down at her feet now. The women talk, I know what happens on the plantation. I'd heard the stories already, but I still thought maybe they'd be like the family I saw the first day. Now I knew that wasn't to be.'

'This other woman, Magamma? Where can I find her?' Akal didn't know what Magamma would be able to tell him, but he sensed that her story would help him uncover the truth of what happened to Kunti.

The old lady proceeded to give him lengthy directions, replete with colourfully described landmarks and commentary on the character of any of the people she mentioned and a complete history of the building of any of the homes along the way. Still, at the end of it all, he had a mental map of the township and he thought he'd be able to find the place.

'*Shukria*, Aunty,' Akal said. 'Thank you very much. I don't think anybody else has told me the full truth about anything in this investigation. Thank you for your bravery in calling me over.'

The old lady beamed at him, showing him more gum than teeth. 'Kunti was a nice girl. I hope you find out what happened to her.'

'Now, could you help me with one more thing?' Akal asked. 'Could you pack me some of these tomatoes and beans? I'm going to cook some dinner tonight.'

Akal walked away with some vegetables stowed carefully in his pack so they wouldn't get crushed, his lighter wallet matching his lighter heart at the old lady's joy as he handed her the coins.

Akal and the doctor scarpered from the marketplace when they realised that a storm was coming. Pushing the horses into a faster trot as the clouds grumbled above them, they were still dry when they made it back to the plantation. They hastily stabled the horses and were scrambling back up the hill to Brown's old house when the heavens opened. Warm blobs of rain, too fat to be called drops, exploded on contact to form a spray of smaller drops, blinding them. It was already hard to see as the clouds had closed ranks abruptly, thrusting them into an early twilight.

The two men eventually dragged themselves up the steps of the small house and collapsed onto the wooden chairs to drip dry. They shed their boots, thumping in a shower of mud to create arcs on the rough wooden planks. Sodden socks joined the boots in untidy piles. Without looking at Akal, the doctor stripped down to his skivvies and disappeared inside with his bag. Akal, his wet clothes clammy against his skin, prayed for the doctor to hurry.

Dr Holmes returned a while later in dry clothes, rubbing his hair with a towel. He held another towel, which he threw to Akal. Akal caught it instinctively and immediately started drying his face. This was a futile exercise thanks to the water dripping down from his sodden turban and he quickly stopped before the towel got soaked.

As he lowered himself into one of the chairs on the verandah, Holmes told Akal, 'Lucky for us, Parkins's overseer must have packed lightly for the war. He even left his clothes behind. I grabbed a few things out for you. Go on, get in there and get changed.'

Akal gratefully squelched inside and quickly divested himself of his wet clothes, leaving a dripping pile on the floor. Perhaps he should have followed the doctor's lead and stripped off outside, but something about that had seemed disrespectful towards the doctor, no matter that the doctor had stripped off in front of him. It was even darker inside and he opened his bag blindly, feeling around for his spare underwear and singlet. Fortunately, his waterproof bag had done a reasonable job of keeping everything dry. The clothes that Dr Holmes had found had fit his own frame well, which meant they were both loose and short on Akal, leaving ankles and wrists exposed. His final job was to unwind his turban and hang it up to dry. With his hair sticking to his face, he looked like a hastily constructed scarecrow. When he reemerged outside, the doctor openly grinned.

'Well, it'll keep you warm, at least. They do grow you tall in the Punjab, don't they?'

Akal shrugged and the sleeves lifted to almost his elbows, causing both men to chuckle.

The doctor had scouted out the kitchen and had a tin mug in hand and an open packet of the dangerously solid crackers in the other. There was a second mug perched on the arm of the other chair. Akal sat down and grabbed the mug before it could fall.

'Gin?' asked the doctor, gesturing with a flask. 'I know you Sikh fellows aren't supposed to drink, but I've seen a fair few sore heads under those turbans in my time.'

'Yes, please, Doctor. Might warm me up.' Akal rubbed at his arms, prickly with goose bumps.

They both settled in and lapsed into moody contemplation of the rain lashing down furiously, as they sat in the haven of the balcony. Akal felt his bones loosen as the gin warmed him from the inside.

'This reminds me of the monsoon rains at home,' Akal said, breaking the silence.

'Ah, so you have some experience of this. This is nothing like the rain in England. It is always raining, but it's never like this,' Robert said, gesturing out to the deluge. 'Often it is more mist than rain. You don't get rained *on* so much as you catch the mist in your hair. Certainly nothing to prepare me for this sort of onslaught. The first time I saw a proper storm in Suva I was at the bar at the Grand Pacific. You know you can sit out the back and look out to the ocean? I watched the storm come in. The rain and wind bent the coconut palms almost in half, leaves whipping the ground, while the ocean tossed and turned like a restless giant behind them. It was magnificent.'

'As long as you don't get caught in it,' Akal said, ruefully inspecting his exposed wrists in his borrowed clothing and prompting a quiet laugh from the doctor. 'Where else have you worked, Doctor? India perhaps?' Akal asked, thinking of how vocal the doctor had been about the treatment of the Indians on the plantation.

'Who, me? No, this is my first time working in one of the colonies. I was always happy enough in my practice back home. It was my relatives who drove me out of England,' Robert said, laughing at Akal's aghast look. 'Not literally! It was just that, six months after Samantha passed away, they started badgering me to remarry, introducing me to women half my age, for God's sake. They didn't seem to recognise that I did not want to move on. I kept telling them that I wasn't going to find my heart hiding in the skirts of another woman. They just wouldn't listen. When they found a young woman who looked uncannily like Samantha, well – that was the last straw. One of my friends told me about this post and I signed up straightaway. No interfering relatives out here.'

Akal shook his head slowly. This did not make sense to him. The doctor's family seemed to know what was best for him. Why had he fled halfway around the world to this tiny, inconsequential colony to avoid marrying? Akal noted with horror that he sounded like his own mother.

'More?' The doctor topped his own mug up and offered the flask to Akal.

'Yes, please.'

'Gin will make it all better.'

'Can't make it worse.'

'Not getting very far with the investigation?'

'What investigation?' Akal snorted. 'All I've got is some people saying she must have run away and a few saying she never would. It is all just speculation. But something about this whole situation makes me uneasy. Do you feel it as well, Doctor?'

'I'm English,' Robert replied with a wry grin. 'We don't *feel* anything. You Indians are much more in tune with sensing things in your environment. I think it's because you are so much closer to your many gods than we are to our one.'

'I always felt your God wasn't very interested in his people. Why is that?' Akal asked, feeling quite daring. The gin was loosening his tongue along with his other muscles.

'I don't know. We like to maintain a bit of distance. I guess He respects that and leaves us to it.'

'We don't do distance in India.'

'I noticed.'

They both grinned.

'How old are you, Akal?' Robert asked casually.

'Twenty-five,' Akal responded, wary of where this was going.

'About time you got married, isn't it?'

'Have you been speaking with my mother?' Akal asked with mock dismay.

Robert chuckled. 'She's on your back about it, is she?'

This saying Akal had heard before, mostly with men complaining about their wives. 'She has just finished marrying off my sisters. It seems it is now my turn,' he said with a rueful smile.

'Will she pick a nice girl out for you in India?'

'Yes, but I don't know when I can go. I had arranged to go home for a long visit when I was in Hong Kong, but then ...' Akal hesitated. 'I was sent here instead.'

'Yes, I had heard there was a problem in Hong Kong.'

Akal frowned into his glass. 'Everyone has heard about the problem in Hong Kong.'

'I don't pay much attention to gossip. I would rather get it from the horse's mouth.'

Akal looked at him blankly.

'I would rather hear it from you,' Robert clarified.

Akal was quiet for a few minutes, knuckles white as his internal battle raged, fear against the desire to bare his soul. On this trip, the doctor had shown himself to be unfailingly kind, patient with the foibles of those in his care. The only people he seemed to be roused to anger with were the administration in Suva and the Parkinses when they behaved poorly towards Akal or their workers. He felt safer with the doctor than he had with anybody else since he arrived in Fiji.

They both stared out at the rain, though Akal could feel the doctor glance over at him a few times. Finally, Akal cleared his throat and shifted in his seat, suddenly feeling every millimetre of bone connecting directly to the wood below.

'You will think I'm a fool.'

'I regularly see people at their worst, Akal. I can tell the difference between an idiot and somebody who did one stupid thing.'

Akal nodded and was quiet again, this time to gather his thoughts and wrestle with how to best tell the story. Eventually, he gave up and just began at the beginning.

'The thing is, Doctor, it all started when I met a girl ...'

Akal was admiring the tangle of vibrant orchid blooms at the Hong Kong botanical gardens, as he often did when he needed a moment of quiet, when Emily Strahan 'accidentally' bumped into him.

'Oh, I'm ever so sorry,' said the young woman after they had both recovered from the collision, holding her hat as she craned her head back to talk to him. She was tiny, and with his height, the top of her head was just above his elbow. '*Namaskaram, mujhe maaph kar do*,' she continued, repeating her apology in flawless Hindi.

'No, please,' he stammered, automatically replying to her in English. 'I'm sure it was my fault.'

The young lady's eyes widened in surprise at his inanity for a moment, before she started giggling behind her hand. He joined in, laughing helplessly.

'I am sorry I was in your way, Miss,' Akal said, when they had both stopped laughing. 'I will leave you to enjoy the orchids.'

'Oh, no, won't you stay?' she responded, cornflower-blue eyes pleading. She swept a graceful arm towards the purple blooms. 'I didn't mean to chase you away from this beauty. Surely we can admire the orchids together.'

Akal hesitated, aware that he had already broken the social boundaries by laughing with this pretty, blonde-haired English rose. But she sounded so plaintive. There couldn't be much harm in just standing together for a few minutes.

'*Mera naam* Emily *hai*,' she said without looking at him. They were standing a few feet apart, not so close that anybody might think they were there together.

'*Namaskaram*, Miss Emily. *Mera naam* Sergeant Singh *hai*,' Akal answered, feeling very daring. He dared a quick glance over at Emily, who was carefully considering the orchids, and equally carefully not looking at him. He jerked his eyes back forward. 'You speak Hindi very well. Where did you learn?'

'Very well for a *gouree*, you mean?' she asked tartly.

'Oh no ... I ... oh ...' Akal stuttered, searching for the right thing to say, until Emily's peal of laughter told him that it wasn't necessary. He glanced around nervously, but there didn't seem to be anybody nearby.

'I was born in India. I have never even been to England,' Emily said, her voice light with suppressed mirth from her previous teasing. 'I think I might have learned to speak Hindi and Nepali before I learned to speak English.'

'And what brings you to Hong Kong?' Akal asked.

'My father has decided it is time I get married. He is taking me to London to launch me. Launch me where, I don't know,' she said. The mirth had disappeared, and she sounded grim by the end. 'I don't want to go. I just want to go home to India.'

They were silent for a moment and then both turned to face each other in the same moment. Emily smiled at him wistfully.

'I miss my *ayah*,' she said, her voice so low he had to take a step closer. 'I miss *momos* and *chai* and the smell of the spices as my *ayah* ground her own *masala*. I miss the peace of the hills in the morning. I miss ...' she hesitated before continuing, 'my friends on the plantation.'

Akal wondered what the story was behind the hesitation.

'What are *momos*?' he asked instead, not wanting to be impertinent.

She brightened and began a long and rapturous description of the dumplings which were a local speciality all over the

Himalayas, concluding with, 'I tried the Chinese dumplings. They just aren't the same. I miss the spices of India.'

'I don't think there is anywhere in Hong Kong one can find *momos*,' Akal said, musing on the problem. 'But if it is spice you are missing, there are plenty of stores with Indian snacks. *Samosas* and *bhuja* and all the *ladoo* you could possibly want. There are even some south Indian snacks you may not have tried before. Have you ever had *idli*?'

'No,' she said, her face quick with interest. 'I would love to try them, but my father doesn't allow me to leave the hotel. I'm not even supposed to be at the botanical gardens, but it's so close that I can walk over and back without anyone noticing.'

'I'm sorry for that,' Akal said. 'Perhaps your hotel could arrange something?'

'Oh, I don't think so. It's very stuffy. They don't even like to prepare Chinese food. It is mostly *very European*,' Emily said, rolling her eyes. She tilted her head and smiled pleadingly. 'Could *you* bring me something? Could we meet here again? Please say yes. This is the closest I've had to real company since I arrived.'

She sounded so wistful, Akal couldn't say no.

'I walk in the park most days at this time. I could bring something tomorrow?'

The brilliance of her smile had Akal pushing aside any niggling doubts about the advisability of meeting a wealthy young European woman in the park. He knew nothing could come of it, but what harm could there be in spending a little time with her, bringing her a little joy from home? They arranged to meet again, and Akal walked away with stars in his eyes.

The next day, Akal left the station for his walk a little early, detouring via his favourite *samosa* vendor. He entered the botanical gardens and headed towards the orchids. Akal followed the path farther into the park, past the carefully sculpted gardens and the more untamed lush greenery, with a sense of mounting excitement. He had a wonderful life in Hong Kong. Excellent work for which he was well-regarded, good friends among the other Punjabi police officers, and the excitement of living in this vibrant hub of the Raj. But it was a life full of men. The chance to spend some time in conversation with a woman, a *lady*, was unheard of. It felt like an adventure. Or perhaps a dream, not quite real.

Akal turned the corner and arrived at his destination, his heart in this throat. And there she was, her slender figure encased from wrist to ankle in a pale blue dress of the finest cotton, her parasol twirling as she turned towards him.

'Oh, I'm so glad you came,' she trilled, gesturing him over to her.

Akal lifted the paper bag, slightly stained with oil, and gave it a little shake. 'Of course. You sounded so sad yesterday, I had to bring you some *samosas*.'

'Oh, how wonderful, thank you so much!' she exclaimed, clapping her free hand against the one holding her parasol and tilting her head up so she could meet his gaze.

Akal drank in her luminescent face, her peach skin glowing with the heat of midday Hong Kong. He felt a blush climbing up his face, which was mortifying, which naturally just made him blush more. 'You are welcome, of course. Though you should try them first. Maybe you won't like them,' he said, trying to distract from his awkwardness.

'I know I'm going to like them. Anything after the bland food at that hotel,' she stated firmly.

'I know a spot with a couple of benches,' Akal offered tentatively. 'They aren't too close to each other, so even if somebody passes us, they won't necessarily think we are sitting together. But we could still talk when nobody is around.'

'That sounds brilliant!' she exclaimed. Akal was starting to recognise that Emily rarely said anything prosaically. She exclaimed and proclaimed, purred and pouted, but never said anything simply.

Emily trailed him to the benches in the shade of two large trees a few hundred metres away, set back such that anyone on the path would not see them. Akal handed her the bag with two *samosas* and kept one *samosa* for himself. With her first bite, she closed her eyes and sighed. When Emily opened her eyes again, she smiled at him with such gratitude, he thought he could see tears. He bit into his own *samosa*, and the experience was so much more vivid than usual. The crunch of the flaky pastry, the cumin-scented steam wafting from the inside of the samosa, the melting softness of the spiced potato-and-pea filling. It was the best *samosa* he had had in an age.

They were quiet as they ate, sitting on their respective sun-dappled park benches. Akal finished his and snuck a glance at Emily as she daintily worked her way through her second, visibly savouring every bite. Her joy at the snacks made Akal feel like a hero.

When she had finished her *samosas*, Emily favoured him with another of her brilliant smiles, and said, '*Bahut dhanyavaad*. You don't know what this means to me. Not just the *samosas*, but your kindness.'

Akal smiled, more comfortable with her gratitude now that they had eaten together. 'You are most welcome.' Then, he frowned and asked, 'Does your father know how very unhappy you are?'

Emily sighed, her posture remaining stiffly upright and her chin high as she said, 'He simply does not care.'

She proceeded to tell Akal more of her history. Her father had gone to India as a poor man, bringing his wife, Emily's mother, with him, and made his fortune on a tea plantation in Darjeeling. Her mother died when Emily was quite young, so Emily had been raised by her Indian *ayah*, the nanny she had had since she was born. She had never set foot in England in her life. Her father had left her at his plantation with no Europeans in sight, only the Indian servants to care for her. She mentioned a young man, Koushik, enough times that Akal wondered if this was the 'friend' she missed so much.

Her father was now going back to London in triumph, to establish himself in English society with the wealth he had wrung from India. Emily was part of his plan. He had bestowed on her an enormous dowry so she could snare an impoverished member of the aristocracy for a husband. Nothing less than an earl would do. This, her father reasoned, would open the drawing room doors of the establishment for himself. And he had good reason to expect it to be so; it was a well-established pattern for the nabobs returning to England. Her father was little concerned whether she wanted a life in England or not.

They were stopping in Hong Kong for her father to conduct some business. He had forbidden her to do anything or meet anyone while they were there. She wasn't to leave the hotel. On her behalf, he had declined invitations to all of the soirees that were a regular feature of colonial Hong Kong life. After all, she concluded bitterly, how could she take London by storm if stories of her heathen ways had already travelled over from Hong Kong?

'But enough about my tale of woe, I want to hear more of your life,' Emily declared. 'How did you come to be in Hong Kong?'

Akal told her his story. After his father had fallen ill when Akal was eighteen, he had had to find a way to support his family. Akal had gone to his childhood friend Heminder to see if he could get a position in Heminder's father's company. Heminder's father, having known Akal from childhood and being well aware of Akal's abilities, was eager to take him on. The problem was, he had insisted that his son work his way up, so Heminder was currently a clerk on relatively low wages. He could hardly bring Akal in at a higher position than his own son. Instead, he had offered to introduce Akal to a friend of his who was looking for Sikh men to take to Hong Kong to join the police force there. The recruits were mostly ex-*sepoys*, the Indian Army's infantrymen. As a green boy of eighteen, with no military background and a pacifist teacher for a father, Akal would not normally have made it through the front door. But with Heminder's father's recommendation, Akal secured his position as a new recruit for the Hong Kong police force.

'And since I arrived six years ago, I have performed my duties quite well,' Akal concluded, attempting to be modest. 'I was the youngest Indian officer in the history of the Hong Kong police force to be promoted to sergeant,' he added, ruining any pretence of modesty.

'That's a wonderful achievement, Akal,' she said, gazing over at him in admiration. 'You know, I've been reading the newspaper from cover to cover, and the back issues, given I have little else to do at the hotel. I read an article that mentioned a Sergeant Akal Singh. Could that possibly have been you?'

Akal flushed again and nodded shyly.

'How exciting that you are in the newspaper! You must be so proud. How did it come about?'

Akal told her that he was working on a project with the wealthy families of Hong Kong, to help them secure their houses against burglary. The owner and editor of the *China Mail*, an English-language newspaper in Hong Kong, was one of the wealthy Europeans he was helping. The man suggested running an article about the project to promote the good work the police force was doing, which the inspector-general was very happy with. Even though Akal had done almost all of the work, of course the article largely credited the success of the program to the inspector-general, with Akal only mentioned once as having assisted his superior officer. Akal was happy that he had been acknowledged at all.

'Well, it sounds fascinating! Though of course I only understood some of the details in the article. Perhaps you could explain it to me the next time we meet? Over some more snacks?' Emily asked with a winning smile.

They parted on the promise to meet the next day at the benches, with whatever snacks Akal could procure.

The next time they met, Akal's downfall commenced in earnest.

As promised, over another round of *samosas*, Akal told Emily all about his project. He told her about the houses that he helped to secure, and found in Emily a fast-moving and incisive mind. Curious about the Hong Kong society she was being kept hidden from, Emily asked Akal all about the wealthy families he encountered in his work. How did they come by their wealth? Where did they live? Why were they in Hong Kong? What sort of items were they trying to secure? How had they treated him? Did they take his advice?

These questions about his work were interspersed with questions about Hong Kong landmarks that she was not allowed to experience. They heard the gun salute ringing at noon as they sat on the benches one lunchtime, which led to Akal providing the colourful history of the Noonday Gun. He described the trip to Kowloon on the Star Ferry and the view back to Victoria Harbour as the ferry chugged away from Hong Kong Island.

Her interests were so wide-ranging, often connecting back to her fears of failure in London, that Akal didn't even notice that he was telling her things he ought to have kept to himself. Or perhaps he did notice, but he pushed that nagging voice away, and drowned it out with the sound of Emily's praise and laughter.

They kept meeting thusly, Akal providing a variety of snacks including the *idli* that Emily hadn't tried before and ended up enraptured by. It wasn't until their fourth meeting that Emily asked some questions that made Akal a little wary. She manoeuvred the conversation to asking about the safe that Akal had been recommending, a new design on which Akal had done extensive research and which had been procured for the wealthy Hong Kong families at some effort on his and the inspector-general's part.

'So, it definitely can't be broken into?' Emily asked, with an urgency that Akal didn't understand.

'No,' Akal replied shortly. His abruptness seemed to jolt her back to herself.

'Oh, well, that's excellent, Akal. You are so clever. Your

inspector-general must be so glad to have you with him,' she cooed.

But the spell was broken, and Akal was suddenly, uneasily aware of the impropriety of their position, still on different benches but inching closer to each other on each subsequent meeting. He excused himself earlier than usual, claiming work commitments. Emily looked so crestfallen at his early defection that he couldn't find the willpower to say no to one more meeting, and one more round of snacks, the next day.

That afternoon, Akal met with the inspector-general, as he did regularly, to update him on the progress of the project, which was wrapping up.

'Well, Singh, it seems that your efforts have been put to the test. We've had two burglaries the last couple of nights. The Cummings and the Hamptons. Both times, the thieves got all the valuables which were left out, but didn't get anything that was in the safe. They knew where the safe was, which is unusual in itself, given how well you had them hidden. And they gave it a good try to break in, chisel marks all over the place. But they couldn't break it.'

As the inspector-general continued giving details of the break-ins, Akal felt his world shatter. They were both houses that Akal had described in detail to Emily, including the locations of the safes. Akal couldn't manage to keep the horror off his face, and eventually the inspector-general trailed off and looked at Akal quizzically. He forced the words past the constriction in his throat.

'Sir, I believe I might know something about these burglaries.'

The next day, Akal had to force a smile as he approached Emily on the benches. He forced himself to sit where he had the day before, just a touch too close to be appropriate. He forced himself to describe the *masala vada* in glowing detail to Emily, another new south Indian snack for her. And he forced a friendly tone as he said, 'You were asking about the new safe I've been recommending. I wish all my clients were as interested in modern advances. The family I was working with yesterday are clinging to their old safe, even though I told them that thieves were beginning to understand their mechanism.'

He wondered whether she could possibly be fooled by what sounded like complete artifice to his own ears. But she didn't seem to notice. She blinked at him a few times, and then looked down at the paper bag on her lap, picking at the crumbs of deep-fried *chana dal* as she asked with an air of studied casualness, 'Oh, interesting. Which family is that?'

His suspicions thus further confirmed, Akal struggled for a moment to contain the sick, angry, frightened feeling which made him want to do something – curse loudly, run, hit one of the trees, anything other than sit here and return Emily's lies with his own. He stuffed the rest of his *vada* into his mouth to give himself a moment to push down the melange of emotion, and coughed as he forced the bite of food, like dust in his suddenly desert-like mouth, down. A few more indiscreet details on the family, the house, and the safe, all rendered in the same false tone, and the trap was set.

That night, Akal and five trusted constables were hidden in locations surrounding the house in question. The owner of the home was a childhood friend of the inspector-general's and had agreed to the venture against his wife's outraged refusals. She had only acquiesced after they reassured her that she could remove her real jewels from the house; they replaced these with some paste costume jewellery that the police department hastily found. The family had ostentatiously vacated the home for the evening to go to a ball.

Akal, along with one of his constables, had a vantage point in a sheltered nook at the back corner of the gardens of the house. From there, they could see both the back entrance to the house, and into the library, the room containing the safe. They had secreted themselves away in their little niche just after sunset, well before the family departed. At eleven o'clock that evening, after the household servants had sought their beds, the thieves came.

Akal watched as two figures slipped from the shadowy gardens at the side of the house and stealthily slunk up to the back door. In the dim moonlight, Akal caught a flash of one of the men's faces, the one who was standing watch as the other broke the lock to the back door. He recognised him immediately.

Charles Coventry was well-known to Akal. He was the youngest son of the Earl of Blackwood, and had been sent to Hong Kong in disgrace to oversee the family's business dealings and learn some responsibility. Instead, he had found a similarly rowdy set in Hong Kong and continued his scapegrace ways, only setting foot in the family offices to help himself to any ready cash. Akal had arrested him a number of times, incidents which had always been hushed up by his family. After the last one, his father had finally washed his hands of Charles.

Charles's accomplice made short work of the door and they were inside the house quickly. Akal kept his binoculars trained on the library window. The thieves would find few loose valuables in the house, the family having secured everything they could against the slim possibility that the thieves might get away. Sure enough, within minutes, the library door opened, and the two thieves slipped inside.

The two shadowy figures made their way unerringly to the safe, exactly where Akal had described it to Emily. Akal pushed away the recriminations that kept bubbling up in his mind. Dwelling on his foolishness was an activity for later, after the situation had been rectified. Once again, Charles stood lookout as his accomplice cracked the safe. They unceremoniously scooped the contents of the safe into a black sack and silently slipped back out of the library, to exit the house the way they came.

Akal and his constable slipped through the hushed streets of Hong Kong like wraiths, following the pair down towards Victoria Harbour. They maintained as much distance as they could while still keeping the thieves in sight. Though he couldn't see them, Akal knew that the other four constables were somewhere behind them. Charles and his accomplice arrived at their destination, a small, nondescript office in a rundown part of the harbour. The only distinguishing feature of the office was the fact that the single window at the front of the office glowed with the light of a lantern in an otherwise dark and deserted street.

The two criminals stepped inside, and moments later, Akal saw the silhouette of three people in the window. He waited anxiously for the other constables to arrive. When they did, they moved quietly and efficiently to the door that Charles and his accomplice had just entered, skirting around to ensure that they couldn't be seen through the window. At Akal's nod, one of the constables flung open the door and they rushed in, catching the three conspirators by surprise.

Charles Coventry and the safe-breaker, a man Akal hadn't seen before tonight, were standing around a table sorting out the night's haul with Emily, who had presumably been waiting for their return – until the six police officers burst in with their firearms drawn. All three of them froze in place, faces white and stark with shock. The necklace Emily had been holding slipped from her nerveless fingers to clatter on the table, the only sound in the room.

'You are all under arrest,' Akal said, breaking the silence and prompting three of the constables to come forward with handcuffs. It was at this point that Charles found his voice and started protesting loudly.

'How dare you, get your hands off me,' he said, struggling against the constable who was trying to restrain him. He looked at Akal. 'You again. You should know better. My father is the Earl of – '

'I know who your father is.' Akal cut him off, indifferent to whatever threat Charles had been about to utter. He kept his eyes trained on Charles, ignoring Emily's frightened face. 'And I know that after the last time I arrested you, he disowned you.'

'We'll see about that, won't we,' Charles said, a smirk playing about his lips. 'Pater is big on respectability and the family name. I don't think he'll allow this to be bandied about once he hears what has happened.'

'The Earl has told the highest levels of the administration here, including my inspector-general, that he has wiped his hands of you and that we are not to contact him about any matters pertaining to yourself. He was quite clear that we were to treat you as plain Charles Coventry, whatever the consequences. It seems he thinks that the family name will suffer less from a sharp excision than to be continuously dragged down by the likes of you,' Akal said dispassionately.

Charles stilled, breathing heavily from his exertions.

'Well, look at you,' he sneered. 'You think you've caught me this time, don't you? I'm not so easily done for. After all, I led you astray with pretty little Emily here, didn't I?'

Akal's eyes flickered over to Emily, who was standing quietly in the midst of the confusion. The constable was standing behind her but hadn't put the handcuffs on her. She caught Akal's gaze for a moment and looked stricken, but quickly looked down to the floor. The other police officers in the room looked puzzled.

'Oh, you don't know, do you?' Charles said conversationally to one of the constables standing near him. 'You haven't heard about how your much-vaunted Sergeant Singh gave me all the information I needed for our last couple of burglaries, because a pretty girl asked him nicely.'

Now the constables' eyes grew large as they looked at Akal with disbelief tinged with doubt.

'Never mind all of that,' Akal said briskly, trying to close the encounter before any more sordid details could escape. Though he knew it was probably too late to hope it would all quietly go away. 'Let's get you all down to the station.'

Akal spent the next two days with a growing sense of unease. The morning after the arrest, he had arrived at the Central Police Station expecting to debrief with the inspector-general about the case. Instead, he had been assigned a menial filing task, keeping him sequestered away in an airless room in one of the newer blocks of the station by himself. When he tracked down a fellow Sikh police officer he was friendly with and asked him what was going on, the officer wouldn't meet his eyes and quickly walked away, muttering that he didn't know anything. After that, Akal realised that nobody would meet his gaze.

The afternoon of his second day of filing, Akal was called to the inspector-general's office. He left his filing purgatory with both relief and reluctance. It seemed like nothing good could come of this interview. Akal walked back into the bustling main block of the station, and up to the inspector-general's offices. As he waited in the corridor, he appreciated anew the high ceilings and the elegant windows, facing down the hill to the harbour below them.

Akal heard his name being called and turned to see Inspector-General Rutledge standing at his office door. The stout, red-haired man gestured for him to enter. They automatically assumed their regular positions in the armchairs in the centre of the room, and the inspector-general met his gaze steadily. At least this hadn't changed.

Akal had first met Rutledge in Punjab, when Rutledge was recruiting Sikh police officers for his upcoming role as inspector-general of the Hong Kong police force. They had been introduced by Heminder's father, who had recommended Akal. Rutledge had seen past Akal's lack of military experience and not only recruited him but taken him under his wing. He valued Akal's excellent written and spoken English, as well as his keen analytical abilities, and had put Akal to work on some of the trickier cases that came his way. Akal's career had seen a meteoric rise under the inspector-general's watchful eye.

'The governor is calling for your dismissal.'

Akal couldn't hear for the roaring in his head. He didn't respond, but the inspector-general proceeded regardless.

'It seems that one of your constables was loose-lipped and word has spread of your indiscretion with the Strahan girl. I've asked this before, and I'll ask it again – how could you have been so foolish?' he said, shaking his head in bewilderment. 'To lose your head over a girl. An *English* girl, no less. What did you think would come of it?'

Akal shook his head, lost for words, mouth dry. 'I didn't expect anything,' he finally said weakly. 'She was lonely and missing home. I just wanted to be her friend.'

'Her friend? Surely you must have known that that was impossible,' Rutledge said, incredulous.

'Yes, sir,' Akal replied woodenly. 'In any case, I do now.'

'They targeted you, did you know that?'

Akal shook his head.

'Apparently the girl met that Coventry scoundrel at her hotel. He managed to convince her that he could get them both away from their families; he just needed some capital. Didn't bother to tell her that his family had already wiped their hands of him. He is the one who told her how to find you and what to ask.'

'What has happened to Miss Strahan?' Akal asked.

'Her father is painting her as an innocent, caught up in a vendetta between you and the Earl's son. I know it is a piece of nonsense, but the die is cast. The governor would rather punish you than offend a man as wealthy as Strahan.'

They sat in silence, Akal struggling to find a solution. He glanced at Rutledge and saw he was frowning and staring into the distance, a sure sign that he was also wrestling with the situation. Akal considered his commanding officer and felt the shame of his failures anew. Akal knew that he owed his early elevation to sergeant to the inspector-general's faith in him, a faith which it seemed had been misplaced.

When the inspector-general broke out of his reverie and caught Akal's gaze, Akal felt compelled to say, with quiet dignity, 'I am very sorry to have disappointed you, sir.'

Rutledge shook his head slowly.

'I am disappointed, Singh, I can't say I'm not. You are too smart for this. I'm disappointed to lose my best man, but I can't save you from this.'

These words hung in the air. Akal sat numbly in the seat, unable to move, unable to think, barely able to breathe. He felt like he had split into two, one version that understood that his world had just ended, and the other that was still running through what he needed to do for the next house in the security project. He almost didn't hear the inspector-general's next sentence.

'There is one remaining option. It might leave you with a very slim chance to redeem yourself.'

These words pierced through the mental fog Akal had been mired in and created a spark of hope. He leaned forward eagerly. 'Yes, sir, anything. What can I do?'

'I could send you to Fiji. They are crying out for qualified officers. Perhaps there you can get a fresh start, rebuild your reputation.'

The small spark of hope immediately withered, and Akal considered Rutledge with dismay. 'Fiji? But it's a tiny colony, isn't it? In the middle of nowhere. Surely there is something else I could do?'

'It's that, or outright dismissal and be sent back to India with no reference and a black mark on your record,' Rutledge shot back. 'You dallied with an English girl and gave her information that was used in a string of burglaries involving some of the wealthiest families in Hong Kong. Did you think there wouldn't be consequences?'

'No, sir, you are correct, of course,' Akal said faintly.

'Well, you had better pack your bags. No matter which way you decide, you have a long journey ahead of you.'

'Hmmm ... that is quite the fall from grace, Akal,' Robert said with a sigh. 'But not an unusual story a young man tripped up by a beautiful woman. It happens all the time, but your story has a more spectacular outcome than most.'

Akal had kept the emotions at bay during the storytelling, focused on getting the details right. But now a flush of shame crawled up his face. He surged to his feet, suddenly restless. 'I have to fix this, Doctor. I have to. I can't face my family until this is fixed. I need something to make Inspector-General Thurstrom see past my mistakes and see what a good investigator I am.'

'Surely Thurstrom sees some redeeming qualities in you?'

'Yes. I'm his best bowler,' said Akal wryly, stopping his pacing to lean on the verandah railing, and stare fixedly out into the rain.

The doctor stood and joined him at the railing, putting his hand on Akal's shoulder. '*I* can see your value. And I know John Thurstrom. He knows what's important. He'll come around.'

They were both quiet, unsure what to say after Akal's deeply personal revelations. Akal moved to the door to break the moment. 'I'm going to get the lantern. I don't think we are getting the light back today.'

'Good idea. See if you can find some other food, eh? These crackers are like punishment. I'm not sure what crime I committed to deserve them.'

Akal's mood brightened. 'Of course, Doctor. I completely forgot I bought vegetables this afternoon! Let me go prepare them.'

Akal returned with not only sliced tomatoes and quickly boiled beans for their dinner, but also a bottle of Dewar's whisky, found as he was rooting around for a pot. They drank late into the night, swapping increasingly improbable stories of feats of cricket prowess as the storm raged unabated.

Chop Chop

We have previously ventured our shy opinion on the Night Prowler question and will not repeat it here.

The speakers at last night's meeting put all sides of the question very plainly and lucidly. We confess by the way, that we are rather glad the 9 o'clock curfew for the natives and the Indians was unpopular, being regarded by most of the speakers as both unfair and likely to prove profitless.

One does not need here, in spite of occasional scares such as this, to emulate the harshness which may be necessary in parts of South Africa, in dealing with the native population.

CHAPTER FIVE

Akal spent his second night on the floor in the small sitting room of the overseer's house, while the doctor took the narrow bed in the equally small bedroom. On the first night, Akal had rummaged by lantern light in the chest of drawers in the bedroom, looking for something with which to improvise a bed. In the bottom drawer, he had unearthed some scrunched-up sheets of dubious colour and cleanliness. This was as good as he was going to get while on the plantation. Robert had tried to swap with him on the second night in the interests of fairness. Slurring, Akal had assured the doctor that he was very used to sleeping on the floor, where he had passed many a night as a child in India whenever the family had guests.

In the early hours of the morning, Akal awoke out of his restless doze, fully clothed in his borrowed outfit. He shifted around atop the sheet, trying to get comfortable, and trying not to think about exactly why it felt a bit crunchy. Akal realised at that point, that while he may have slept on the floor in his youth, he had always had some form of mattress, no matter how threadbare – and that his child's bones might have been more forgiving.

The assault of rain against the tin roof was too ferocious to be soothing. Akal kept his eyes closed but could not still his mind. His thoughts kept returning to Hong Kong, to the orchid house. It was as though he was a spectator watching his own ruination, helpless to change anything, as Emily wrapped him around her little finger. At some point, sheer exhaustion must have overcome all the discomforts to drag him back into a restless unsatisfying sleep.

Akal awoke to warmth on his face. Blinking his eyes open gradually, he realised the warmth was from the first rays of sunlight, which were peeping between the slats of the wooden window covering and crawling across the dusty floor to where he was lying. With a groan, he dragged himself up to sit. The nights on the floor had left his back aching, and the long rides of the past couple of days had left his thighs on fire.

Akal stretched half-heartedly to loosen up his aching muscles, then limped out to the verandah and collapsed into the rickety chair that by unspoken agreement was his chair now. The day had dawned clear, clouds spent after a night of furiously pouring themselves out onto the swelling earth. The kitchen had been bare the night before, and he had used the last of the fresh water in the urn for the beans. No doubt the tank at the side of the house would be full after the rain last night, but that seemed like such a long distance to travel. Akal resigned himself to living with the foul taste in his mouth, his parched throat, and his grumbling stomach. All in all, the day was not starting well. After what felt like hours, just as Akal was preparing to rouse himself to go fetch some water, Robert wandered out onto the verandah, yawning and scratching his stomach.

'Bloody hell, Singh. Maybe we shouldn't have drunk that Dewar's.'

Akal just looked at him balefully. At least the doctor had slept in a bed.

'Let's get up to the house and see if we can get some breakfast,' Dr Holmes said around another yawn, and looked at Akal with a hint of a smile. 'Hope your clothes have dried. Not sure how credible you are as a police officer with your ankles hanging out.'

They had not dried, but Akal dragged them on anyway, cringing away from the clammy cloth until it warmed from the sun and his body. Despite the dampness, he was much more comfortable once he got into his own clothing and rewound his turban around his head. The soaked boots were the least comfortable part about it all. Luckily, his waterproof pack had kept Akal's spare socks dry, but that luxury did not last long inside the wet boots. The doctor elected to keep his borrowed outfit on, given it actually fit him.

They squelched their way up to the big house, each step squeezing little rivulets of water out of the sodden earth to run a few centimetres down the hill before being reluctantly absorbed back into the ground. By the time they arrived, Akal was nauseated and light-headed. A whistling sound reignited the sharp pain in his skull.

'Sounds like Henry has the kettle on. The kitchen is around the back, let's go directly there,' Robert said.

As they came around the corner of the house, the vista opened out to the other side of the hill, a part of the plantation Akal hadn't seen before. Miles of cane fields spread out below them, tame and orderly, bordered in the distance by a brown winding river. Beyond the river, untouched forest claimed dominion over the land, lush, dark, and implacable.

The sound of a man and woman arguing distracted Akal from the view.

'Is that Mrs Parkins?' Akal asked, headache temporarily

pushed to the background. Everything he had heard about Susan Parkins, and his own experience of her, made a trip out to the plantation seem unlikely.

'Sounds like it. I wonder when she arrived,' the doctor mused.

Akal put his hand on Robert's arm to get his attention, and then silently gestured that they wait for a moment. If the Parkinses were arguing, Akal wanted to get some inside information on what they were disagreeing about. He flattened himself to the side of the house and moved to stand under the open window, where he could hear the argument unfolding. It was indeed Mrs Parkins, and she didn't sound happy.

'I just can't believe you let him stay in John's house,' Susan hissed.

'What else could I do? Robert insisted that they stay together. I couldn't exactly let the doctor stay with the coolies. Do you think that would have been better? God knows what they would have told him,' her husband retorted.

'You should have convinced the doctor to stay in the house without his coolie detective.'

'I'm not the politician. You are. And you weren't here, were you?'

They were both silent for a moment and Akal heard footsteps briskly walking out of the room. He was about to signal to Robert that they should resume when he heard Henry Parkins mutter to himself.

'What does it matter, anyway? Why do you have such a bee in your bonnet about where the bloody Indian stays . . .?'

Why indeed, Akal wondered. He resolved to have a better look around the overseer's house.

They climbed up the back stairs to the kitchen and found

Mrs Parkins walking back into the kitchen. She looked past her husband and stiffened when she saw Akal and Robert. 'Oh. You,' she said.

'Yes, you have met both Dr Holmes and the constable, haven't you?' said Henry, with a sly look that suggested he was eager for Akal's reaction to his demotion.

'Sergeant,' Akal said automatically, gritting his teeth as he watched both Parkinses smirk.

'Could you see to some breakfast for them?' Henry asked his wife.

Susan Parkins pursed her lips in disapproval and her husband shot her a warning glance.

'Do you know where the roti and eggs are?' he asked pointedly.

'Of course I do,' she snapped. 'And why is there no proper bread?'

Henry looked at her incredulously. 'Where would I get proper bread from? It isn't as though you are here to bake it for me. I had to get a coolie woman to cook for me and I can't afford to have her away from the fields every day.'

On that note, Parkins turned back to Akal and the doctor. 'I've got to go. Busy day. I've got my own job to do, as well as the job my overseer should be doing. This bloody war.' On that pronouncement, he jammed his hat on his head and stomped down the back stairs.

Susan Parkins seethed as she looked around the kitchen for the breakfast accoutrements with no success. She opened the lopsided sideboard cupboard doors and slammed them shut again once she found only a hodgepodge of chipped crockery. Robert and Akal gave each other wry looks, eyebrows raised. Robert cleared his throat and said cautiously, 'Susan, we can probably take care of ourselves. We had breakfast here yesterday.'

'Oh, you have been making yourself at home, have you?' She glared at Akal. 'That is why I came out here. God knows I did not want to. That track is a disgrace. I had to have an escort, and even then, I didn't feel at all safe coming out here.' She looked around the rudimentary kitchen with its rough-hewn planks and mismatched crockery, sneering. 'But I knew Robert would be too soft with you. *I* will make sure you do what you need to, and then get out of here. I don't need this nonsense about some coolie woman distracting Henry from the election.'

Before Akal could respond in no uncertain terms that he would do what he needed, election or no, Robert put a restraining hand on his arm and said, 'Susan, we do not want to be here any longer than we need to. I'm sure we will be out of your hair very soon.'

The doctor's soothing tones seemed to mollify her somewhat. Akal could see her jaw unclench but her eyes hardened again every time they passed over him. Her anger, which had puzzled him the first time they had met, was now prompting Akal to be angry in turn.

'See that you do.' She flipped her hand dismissively towards the stove. 'You may take care of your own breakfast. I am going to rest. The journey yesterday was very fatiguing. And be quiet. I don't want to be disturbed.'

Akal joined his hands and bowed to her departing figure, mockingly. 'Certainly, *mehamsahib maharani*,' he muttered.

Robert huffed an amused sound at Akal's performance, then began the breakfast preparations, while Akal sank into a chair at the table and cradled his head in his hands.

The creaking of floorboards roused Akal out of his stupor a few minutes later. Somebody was moving around the house. It was somebody heavier than Susan Parkins; she hadn't made a sound as she had left the kitchen. Had Henry Parkins returned to the house to talk to his wife? Akal's senses went on alert. He waved at Robert to catch his attention and then put a finger to his lips, indicating the doctor should be quiet. Robert looked puzzled, but nodded.

Akal slipped his boots off and eased himself into the corridor and quietly inched his way towards the living room. He realised, as he got close enough to distinguish the voices, that it wasn't Henry Parkins he could hear. There was another man in the house.

'Of course, I'd rather be in Suva with you. But I have to take care of a few things here.' Susan's voice floated out to the corridor, lighter, happier than he had heard her before.

'What things? I thought your work was in the ballroom, not the plantation.' The man sounded European, based on his accent. There was a teasing lilt to his voice, but also some genuine curiosity threaded through the words.

'I just need to make sure Henry keeps his house in order. I'm taking care of everything in Suva for the election, but he could mess everything up, like he did in Sydney.'

'Is it so important, Susan? It's just the Planters' Association.'

'Yes, it is. It's incredibly important. I can't believe you are asking me that,' she said, sounding to Akal like she was both surprised and hurt. It seemed somebody *could* affect the otherwise cold woman, just not her husband. 'I've got a second chance here. To be somebody, to make some changes, to do something good for the planters of Fiji. Women don't often get these chances. Even in Sydney, I would have had to make suggestions to Henry from the background. He would have done what I told him to, but nevertheless, I would have had to go through him. Here I can make changes myself. Without asking first. In Henry's name, of course, but still, on my own.' Her voice had grown louder and more impassioned throughout the speech, and the man replied with equal fervour.

'Have you thought about what it means for us? If he gets this Planters' Association presidency, then he might have to live in Suva. How is that going to work? I'll never see you.'

When Susan Parkins spoke again, the tender voice was back.

'Don't worry, Lewis, Henry and I understand each other. He won't be coming to Suva. Nothing has to change between us.'

They didn't speak again for a while. Akal didn't recognise the name Lewis. The man must be on the fringes of Suva society, as Akal thought he knew most of the Europeans by name.

'I'd better get back to Suva,' Lewis said, his tone questioning, as though inviting Susan to contradict him.

'Yes, of course,' she replied.

Akal needed to see who this Lewis was. He walked into the living room and stopped short when he saw Susan Parkins standing close to a tall, red-haired European man Akal had never seen before, her hand on his upper arm. They sprang apart when they saw Akal.

'My apologies,' Akal said in bland tones. 'Dr Holmes sent me to look for a tea strainer.'

Mrs Parkins scowled at him and said, 'So you think you can just wander around my house at your own leisure? Why would there be a tea strainer in the living room? Get back into the kitchen.'

Akal continued as though he had not heard her, with a

malicious sense of satisfaction over how much this would infuriate her. He looked at the man and said, 'I am Sergeant Akal Singh of the Fijian Constabulary, Suva Division.'

The man cleared his throat, a flush blooming across his freckled, tanned cheeks. 'Hello there. I am Lewis Robinson. Nice to meet you.' He nodded uncomfortably at Akal.

'And what do you do here at the plantation?' Akal asked, careful to keep his voice curious but gentle.

'Oh, no, I don't work here,' Lewis replied. 'I just escorted Susan ... Mrs Parkins ... from Suva.' After a glare from the lady in question he hastened to add, 'I'm headed back now.'

'He has nothing to do with the missing coolie,' Susan Parkins snapped. 'Stop asking him questions and get *out*.'

Akal inclined his head at her, seething inwardly but giving her no indication of it. 'It was nice to meet you, Mr Robinson. Enjoy your rest, Mrs Parkins.' And with all the grace he could muster, he turned and left the room. He really needed that cup of tea.

Hot roti and tea restored Akal's spirits and he left the house with more of a spring in his step.

'Did Susan tell you where her husband will be working today?' the doctor asked Akal as they walked down the hill to the overseer's house to get their packs, and then on to their horses.

Akal snorted. 'I'm not sure if she remembers she has a husband. She seemed a little wrapped up in the man who 'escorted' her from Suva.'

'Yes, I thought I heard you talking to somebody. Who is he?'

Akal filled him in what little he had learned about Lewis Robinson.

'Henry can't be too happy about this,' the doctor mused.

'They seem to live very separate lives,' Akal said.

'That's true. Maybe Henry doesn't mind,' the doctor said, sounding very doubtful.

'I just wish I had been more alert this morning so I could have spoken with Mr Parkins then. Now we have to go find him,' Akal said with a sigh.

'Henry didn't really give you much opportunity. He just stomped off. I haven't seen him this agitated before. I don't know if it is because of his wife, because his overseer took off, or because of this missing woman. He has a lot going on.'

As they approached the stables, they saw a native Fijian man leaning bonelessly against the wall of the wooden structure.

'*Bula*,' he called out to them.

'*Bula*,' they chorused back at him. Neither said any more, as neither of them could speak much more of the native language. The Fijian man peeled himself off the side of the building and sauntered towards them, sun gleaming off of the glossy, near-black skin on his outstretched arm.

'I'm Timi. Who are you?' the man said, luckily in English. He beamed a gap-filled smile at them while vigorously shaking their hands.

'I am Sergeant Akal Singh of the Fijian Constabulary, Suva Division,' Akal said, surreptitiously rubbing circulation back into his hand after Timi finally released it. 'This is Dr Robert Holmes.'

'Ah, you here about that woman who ran away, huh? Beautiful woman, I heard. You Indian men, you need to take better care of your women. We don't have our women working for the *kaivalagi*. Our women are not running away.'

Akal ground his teeth. Could nobody in this country see the difference between him and the coolies? Women in his family were protected. He ignored the comments with some effort, and the doctor jumped in while Akal struggled with his temper.

'Where is your village?' asked the doctor.

'You know the Navua River?' Timi asked, gesturing in the direction of the river Akal had seen from the top of the hill. 'We close to here, at the river. Good fish in that river, best in Fiji. You come by, we give you a good feed. The Lavuwala village,' he concluded with a self-satisfied nod.

'Right, we might just do that,' responded the doctor blandly. Akal did not think they would be getting that 'good feed'. Robert's preferences for simple food had become quite clear on this trip. Unlike Robert, Akal was interested, but he didn't imagine the inspector-general would be happy to hear about a side trip to a village to eat fish.

'I come to see Mr Parkins, tell him we seen some things in the river. Could be his or his Indians'? Maybe he wants us to dive for him, get them back?' Timi volunteered the information cheerfully.

'What sort of things?' Akal asked sharply.

'Looks like a dress. Don't know how it got there but it's stuck on a tree in the middle of the river. The river is strong after all the rain, need a good swimmer to get it. Only my boys can do it.'

Akal and the doctor exchanged a glance. It was a long shot, but as it was, they were going to go back to Suva empty-handed.

'Why don't we come and take a look?' the doctor suggested.

'I can let Henry know what it is and make sure he uses your boys.'

'Sure thing, bosso.'

They rode through the cane field to the river. On horseback, Akal's head was above the sugar cane, and in any direction he looked, there was a calm sea of green. As they moved, the long leaves slid along their shoulders, sending sinuous ripples through the nearby stalks, which settled back to stillness as they moved away.

Under any other circumstances, Akal would have found this soothing, but unfortunately, he had a passenger: Timi was riding double with Akal. The Fijian man had eyed the horse doubtfully, but once he was settled in the saddle, Timi had picked up the rhythm and relaxed into a slouch. Then he commenced regaling Akal with improbable stories about the swimming and fishing prowess of the boys in the village.

'Can you swim, Mr Police?' Timi asked him when he had finally run out of tall tales.

'No. Sikhs don't swim.'

This was not true. Punjab was the 'land of five rivers', but Akal had not grown up near any of them. He had never felt the lack of this skill until he came to Fiji, where the locals were as comfortable in the water as out. Even the Britishers would venture in, albeit much more timidly and with swimming costumes that were comically voluminous compared to the near nakedness of the Fijian men.

When Taviti had realised how uncomfortable Akal was in the water, he had been embarrassed for Akal, as though he had exposed a major character flaw. Since then, Akal had behaved as though swimming was beneath his status as a Sikh warrior, while privately trying to figure out how he could learn on the sly. He had a vague notion of one day jumping into the water and swimming with strength and grace, demonstrating to Taviti and anybody else who was around that while he didn't know how to swim, he needed no lessons and could just pick it up by sheer dint of his exceptional physicality. Akal knew how absurd this was, but he still hoped to make it happen one day.

'What's a Sikh? You are different from the other coolies?' asked Timi conversationally.

Akal sighed. 'Sikhs are warriors. We are renowned for our strength and agility. For our bravery and ruthlessness in the battlefield. We are not coolies.'

He enunciated the last sentence carefully, emphasising each word.

He could feel Timi shrug behind him. 'If you say so. You are Indian. You work for the Britishers. Seem like a coolie to me.'

'Well, I'm not,' Akal replied.

He didn't realise he'd raised his voice until the horse skittered underneath him. This didn't go unnoticed by Dr Holmes, who turned around in his saddle to see what the commotion was about. Akal shook his head sheepishly and the doctor turned back to the front. 'I am not a coolie,' he continued at a moderate volume, embarrassed that this foolish man was having such an impact on him. 'I am a police officer. Not a labourer in the field. I am free.'

'Oh, I see,' said Timi in a tone that made it clear that he did not understand in the slightest. 'So ... you can live where you want to, then?'

'No. I live in the barracks.'

'Go fishing when you want to?'

'No. Sikhs don't fish.'

'Drink what you want to?'

'No. Sikhs don't drink.'

He hoped Timi couldn't smell the alcohol still in his system from the night before.

'Sounds like a coolie to me.'

Timi sounded satisfied that he had reasoned the situation through and come to the same conclusion he had in the first place.

'Constable Coolie.'

'I'm a sergeant!' Akal protested.

'*Sergeant* Coolie, then.'

Akal fought the urge to have the horse rear back suddenly and buck the annoying man off. He had realised sometime in the middle of this exchange that Timi was enjoying needling him, but even this knowledge could not take the sting out of the words.

The cane field ended abruptly, and they emerged into the brightness of the morning with the Navua River stretching out ahead of them. It looked like a river of *yaqonya*, the sedative drink that the native population drank by the bowlful. Swirls of silt in eddies of brown water were the only real clue to how fast the river was flowing.

There was a coconut tree growing out of the opposite bank of the river, its trunk almost horizontal above the water. One of its older branches had started to come away and was hanging off the trunk, the tip of the branch and crumpled dead leaves trailing in the river. Tangled among the leaves and snagged on the branch was a piece of cloth, some of its mud-stained length flowing with the water. The current was tugging at the branch, causing the occasional ominous creak as it pulled farther away from the trunk.

They dismounted and got as close to the river's edge as they dared, straining to see. 'It looks like a sari,' Akal said quietly to the doctor.

'Do you think it could be Kunti's?'

'It might be. But how could a sari have come all this way? That was a half-hour horse ride to get here.'

Timi had been watching them curiously. 'What do you think, boss?' he asked. 'You want I get the boys to swim out and get it?'

'Yes, quickly,' replied Akal. 'I don't know how long that branch is going to hold.'

'Sure, we'll be quick. What have you got?'

Akal reminded himself to thank Taviti when he got back. At Taviti's prompting, Akal had brought some tobacco along to bargain for some *otha*, an edible native fern found inland, which Taviti thought Akal might enjoy. Akal had unwrapped the parcel last night and seen that the tobacco had remained dry inside his waterproof pack. The musky, earthy aroma had permeated from his nose to his chest, warming him from the inside.

He'd tried smoking it once, early in his time in Hong Kong, crumbling the end of the rope of tobacco into a paper and carefully wrapping it, as he'd been shown. He'd enjoyed the ritual; he found the smell of tobacco hypnotic. When lit, the sweet notes turned into burnt toffee, like when his mother had been making desserts for temple offerings and taken the sugar syrup too far. With mounting excitement, he had taken his first inhalation ... which immediately dispelled any romantic notions he'd had of becoming a smoker and bonding with white and black men alike in hazy rooms. With eyes and lungs searing, he had concluded between coughing fits that he had best stick to the vice with which he was already comfortable. Gin may have occasionally caused his head to pound, but it had never made him cough so much he couldn't breathe.

The deal was struck with little negotiation. Timi seemed to be satisfied with the small coil of tobacco that Akal gingerly unwrapped to show him. The doctor looked on, providing helpful commentary on the exceptional quality of the tobacco. After a handshake, Timi shouted across the river until a teenage boy emerged from the trees.

The boy came right to the river's edge and leaned out over the water, straining to hear what Timi was shouting over to him, leaning on the same bowed palm tree for support. Akal could see the tree visibly swaying, and the length of cotton, which had been flowing smoothly, started to roil more chaotically.

Timi shouted louder and started gesticulating wildly, trying to push the boy away from the tree by sheer strength of will, his rapid-fire Fijian interspersed with English. '*E muri*, shit, get back,' he raged, no doubt fearing that his tobacco would disappear if the sari was dislodged.

The youngster seemed to understand, and, grinning, jumped back and held his hands up in mock horror. He then proceeded to parody Timi, waving his arms about while shouting '*E muri*' and adding some hops and jumps for good measure, until finally he collapsed against a tree on the fringe of the forest, roaring with laughter. Timi stood muttering on his side of the river, visibly annoyed.

'Can you hurry him up? This is a serious business,' Akal asked, frowning at Timi. He wanted to savour Timi's discomfiture, but unfortunately the urgency of the situation precluded gloating.

'He's a stupid boy. My cousin-sister's son. Idiot,' Timi replied before turning back and yelling across the river again. Something he said must have sunk in because the boy stopped laughing, nodded, and straightened up to merge seamlessly back into the forest, going from leaning against the tree to a lazy ground-eating lope instantly. Akal was reminded of a young British officer he had served under in Hong Kong, an incredible bowler with a run-up that displayed such casual elegance Akal couldn't help but be inspired.

'He's gone to get my sons. They'll get the clothing and bring it this side. Then we all have a smoke together.'

Akal had a sinking feeling there would not be an opportunity for relaxing with the locals anytime soon.

The retrieval of the cotton sari was a precarious and nerve-racking thing, at least for the doctor and Akal. The boys returned after what seemed like an interminable wait, during which Akal stared tensely at the tree branch, willing it to stay in place, flinching every time it gave a particularly loud creak. The three boys who were to perform the operation seemed unperturbed by the fast-flowing water. There was some horsing around while they unlooped a length of rope and conferred with each other, presumably on the best way to proceed. All three of the grown men on the other side of the river became increasingly nervous, and when one of the boys grabbed the rope and started running away, laughing, Timi snapped. This time the shouting and gesticulating was accompanied by foot stamping and the boys stopped their hijinks almost immediately.

'They are just showing off,' Timi said, shaking his head in annoyance. 'They want to prove who is the best swimmer. Don't worry, it'll be quick now.'

It was indeed quick. Batu, Timi's eldest son, tied a rope around his waist while the other two arranged themselves on the edge of the river, a little way back so they were safely out of the slipperiest part. Batu then sat on the edge of the river, close to the tree where the sari was caught, the bank falling away steeply below him. He reached down to grab some protruding tree roots and, flipping himself around to face the riverbank, wriggled and slid himself into the water.

He clung to the tree roots for a minute while he adjusted to the fast-moving water, then used the current to propel him down until he was under the tree, all the while keeping a grip on whatever he could find on the riverbank. The doctor let a breath out explosively when the boy reached the tree.

'Bloody hell, Timi. Is he going to be alright? Getting that dress is not worth your son's life.'

Timi grinned at him, relaxed now that the boys were doing what they were supposed to be doing.

'All fine, Doctor. We swim in this river all the time. This is a bit faster than usual, but nothing to worry about. My Batu is the best swimmer in the village.'

They continued to watch, Timi calm and Robert and Akal still tense despite his reassurances. The young boy reached up to give the tree trunk a push, testing how firmly it remained rooted into the earth at the edge of the river. Evidently satisfied that the tree was stable, Batu shouted something to his brother and cousin, who came to more alert positions. With a powerful push of his legs, Batu propelled himself away from the relative safety of the riverbank, half coming out of the water, before landing back into the river. He immediately reached up and grabbed one of the tree branches firmly in his hands. Batu shook his head, water flicking from his face and hair. He flashed a quick distracted smile at his father while he got his bearings. Timi called something that sounded like it was intended to be encouraging.

Batu then worked his way up the tree, selecting the branches that looked more securely attached to the tree trunk, all the while struggling to maintain his position against the water. Occasionally it would splash up into his face and he'd have to stop and shake his head again to clear his eyes. As he got close to the branch where the sari was caught, the creaking started to get louder as the tree bowed closer to the water, pulled down by his weight, despite how slight he appeared to be.

Finally, he got near enough to reach out and grasp the cotton sari. One tug and the branch it was caught on gave up its tenuous connection back to the tree and joined the water rushing downriver, knocking a startled Batu loose. As he disappeared under the rushing water, the two boys on the bank came to life with a shout and started hauling back on the rope, which until now they'd kept fairly slack to give Batu room to move. Timi was yelling at them, tendons in his neck taut as he pumped his arms as though he was on the other side, pulling the rope in with them. Akal now saw the real man, the father, emerge from behind the boasting and the needling and the nonchalance.

The rope came out from the murky river in jerks, showers of water shuddering off each time the rope tightened as the boys furiously hauled it in. It had passed under the bowed tree and seemed to be moving closer to the same side of the river that the boys were on. Akal found himself standing next to Timi at the river's edge, slightly downstream from where he had been, although he had no recollection how he got there, straining to peer into the murky water at the point from which the rope was coming.

After what seemed like an hour, though it was probably just a matter of seconds, the rope came to a halt at the edge of the river. Batu's hand emerged from the water, scrambling for a handhold among the roots and clumps of dirt of the steep riverbank. His other hand followed, sari tangled around his forearm. Finally, after another agonising pause, Batu's head appeared above the water. Timi exhaled gutturally. The boy hung for a minute, resting against the riverbank, before he squared his shoulders and dragged himself up, hands grabbing for roots and feet slipping against the mud with the other two boys keeping the rope taut and bellowing encouragement. Finally, with a last heave he was up and over, lying face-first into the grass until his comrades came bounding over and pulled him to stand, laughing and thumping him on the shoulder. Batu was not laughing. When he saw his father, he held the sari aloft and gestured for them to come over.

'That's my son! He got it!' crowed Timi, all fear banished and back to his braggart ways.

'You are all mad,' barked the doctor. 'He's just taken ten years off my life. If I wasn't already grey ...'

Akal realised that the doctor was unsuccessfully trying to suppress a relieved grin.

'What was your plan now, Timi? I'll tell you, after seeing that, I'm not swimming over there,' Akal said, nodding at the tumultuous river.

'We'll have to go upriver. There is a section a little way up where we can cross. Don't worry, Constable Coolie, I'll get you there and you'll hardly even get wet.'

The doctor, Timi, and Akal forded the river upstream in a shallower and slower moving spot where they could cross on mostly dry rocks. It was still an anxious crossing, and Akal had to temper his urge to hurry in order to concentrate on his footing. He was conscious of every minute that ticked away as they hurried to where the boys were waiting, flopped onto their backs, having a nap as far as Akal could tell. All except for Batu, who was sitting cross-legged and staring at the sari. He stood in one sinuous motion, sari in hand, as they approached. He handed the sari to his father, who grabbed him in a hug, crowing his praises. Batu was still in his father's exuberant embrace when Timi finally noticed that his son was ashen and silent.

Timi handed the sari back to Akal without turning and continued talking to his son. The thin cotton had partially dried, so it was no longer dripping. Akal examined it portion by portion, careful to keep it from dragging on the ground. A few thinner patches had completely dried and were stiff and crunchy, shedding a fine layer of dirt when handled. This was the simplest of saris, plain cotton with faded remnants of a print along the border, smudges which might have been dark blue. It was impossible to tell what the original colour of the fabric had been, as it had been stained a patchwork of tan by the muddy water of the river. But standing out in stark relief along one end of the sari was a large, rust-coloured stain.

'What do you think it is?' Akal asked Robert, dreading – but knowing – the answer.

'Blood,' declared the doctor. 'A lot. And to have stained like this, it had to have dried before the cloth went into the river.'

Timi approached them as they stood contemplating the stained cloth. He looked shaken and grave.

'You looking for a woman, right? Indian woman?'

Akal nodded as the doctor continued to examine the sari.

'You think that's her dress?'

Akal nodded again, wondering where Timi was going with this. For his part, Timi paused, lost for words for the first time in Akal's short acquaintance with him.

'Maybe we found her.'

Timi told them Batu's account in a garbled fashion, his grasp of English losing cohesion with the stress of telling tales of the dead. With some difficulty, Akal pieced together the story.

When Batu had grabbed the sari, it seemed like it was caught on something under the water, not just the tree. He yanked it and a face started to come up through the water towards him. He had been startled not only by the branch giving way, but by the watery face appearing from the murky depths. When he had been knocked into the water, he had managed to hold on to the sari, effectively dragging the body downriver with him. Batu was not completely sure where the body had ended up. At some point, it had unravelled from the sari and gone its own way, but he thought it might be near the riverbank as well, given that was where the current had taken him.

'We need to get back in there and find her,' said the doctor.

'Can your boys do it?' Akal asked Timi.

'Gonna take a whole lot more tobacco.'

She did not come out of the water easily. First the boys fought each other over who would do the diving and show off to their guests. Then they fought the current, the tangled ropes, the silt swirling through the water making it impossible to see. The search was completed entirely by touch. There was a heart-stopping moment when part of the riverbank unexpectedly gave way. But eventually, groping their way along the shallows and feeling with hands and feet, they found her.

Her journey to dry land went in fits and starts. The boys in the water lifted her as best they could, and the men at the top of the riverbank grabbed her and hauled her up. She came out of the river with her back sliding along the mud, slumped forward with her hair covering her face, water streaming from every inch of her limp body.

And as she came up, they discovered she was not alone.

The second body bobbed up to the surface after the first had been retrieved, emerging next to an unsuspecting young man, one of Batu's helpers named Peni, who was already a little shaken at having handled a dead woman. Peni turned to chastise whoever had bumped into him in the water, only to be confronted with a floating linen-covered back, the body's head, arms, and legs disappearing into the brown of the river. He had screamed and started clambering up the embankment himself before his friends could start pulling him out. During the whole procedure of retrieving the second body, Peni had sat shivering in the sun, staring into the distance, not able to respond when anyone talked to him.

When he caught wind of the second body, Akal joined one of the boys who was noisily vomiting by the trees, as far from the bodies as he could make it before the nausea took over. He had seen dead bodies before in the line of duty, but they had always been recently deceased; he had never seen one that had been in the water for God knows how long. The other boys, including Batu, had managed to hold onto their stomachs, but they were all standing as far away as they could and shifted from foot to foot, seeming as though they were ready to take off at any moment. The only person relatively unaffected was the doctor, though even he had flinched when the second body came out of the water.

When there was nothing left in his stomach, Akal went back to where the doctor was kneeling over Kunti's body. Even the lingering smell of vomit could not overpower the stench from the second body. Akal could feel his gorge rising again and struggled to control it.

'Breathe through your mouth,' the doctor said, without looking up from his examination. 'If you are going to throw up again, get back with the others.'

Akal followed this advice and got his nausea under control, all the while focused on Kunti's face to avoid looking at the bloated male corpse beside her. She had clearly not been in the water as long as he had. Her skin looked wrinkled in places, to the extent Akal's fingers did if he had them in water for too long, but her features were not distorted. She was easily recognisable as the woman in the photograph that Father Hughes had shown him a few days ago.

Even grey with death and weary from the difficult life which had preceded it, Kunti's beauty shone through. Her eyes, thankfully closed, slanted upwards away from prominent cheekbones and a mouth too wide for prettiness, but compelling nonetheless. Hollowed cheeks and emaciated arms were indicators of an existence where meals were hard fought for. She was clad in the *choli* and petticoat she had been wearing under the sari they had retrieved earlier, the thin wet cotton transparent and plastered to her skin. There was a puckered hole in the middle of her chest, the edges of her *choli* charred around the hole. She was extremely slender all over, which made the gentle slope of her midsection all the more apparent.

'Doctor?'

The doctor looked up and followed Akal's line of vision.

'Yes. I would say about four months along, though it is often difficult to tell with coolie women.'

Akal was puzzled. Why hadn't anybody mentioned it?

'As for this fellow, he's been shot as well, but at least she had the dignity of knowing who killed her,' the doctor said, nodding at the other body. Akal instinctively looked over, much to his regret. The doctor moved to kneel next to the male corpse. He lifted the head and gestured for Akal to stand behind the dead man.

Akal steeled himself to look closer and saw what the doctor meant. The back of the man's head was caved in and lodged in the mangle of bone and flesh was a bullet. The doctor gently lowered his head back down and stood up.

'Who on earth is he, Doctor? Do you recognise him? I do not think I've seen him in Suva.'

'Who can tell with his face like that? But no, nothing looks familiar.'

They were both reluctantly scrutinising the body, searching for anything to identify him by when Timi approached them. He was walking with an older, portly Fijian man, and instead of his usual lazy gait where his feet barely cleared the ground, he was striding crisply.

'Chief, these are the men I told you about. Dr Holmes and Sergeant Singh,' Timi said to the older man.

'Doctor, Sergeant. I am Sukuna,' the chief said with a civil nod to each of them. Each word was uttered in a slow and solemn tone, perhaps an indication that he generally only spoke English at formal occasions. He was dignity personified.

'Chief. Thank you for your assistance. The Fijian Constabulary is in your debt.'

Akal sincerely hoped Chief Sukuna would not call in the debt at that moment, as he had no more tobacco with him.

'Is this the woman you were looking for?'

'Yes, we believe so. No other Indian women have been reported missing in this area.'

'And how did Mr Brown end up in our river?'

'Brown? Parkins's overseer? Are you sure?' Akal asked sharply. He could not quite believe that the misshapen body was going to be identified that easily in this investigation where nothing had come easily, not even breakfast.

'I believe so. His face is ... I think that is his face. Let me see his right hand.'

The doctor carefully lifted the right hand. Despite the loose flesh sagging towards the ground, it was obvious that the man was missing the tip of his pinkie finger, so he had no fingernail. It was a clean healed wound, just part of the landscape of his body, not something that had occurred as part of the trauma of his death or his immersion.

The chief met Akal's eyes and nodded sombrely.

'But Parkins told us he went off to fight in the war.'

'I had not heard that. Mr Parkins doesn't confide very much in me,' the chief responded with a wry smile. 'I had not seen Mr Brown for a few weeks, but there is nothing unusual about that. We do not mix with the plantation people. Too much sadness there.'

So, had Brown lied to Parkins, or had Parkins lied to Akal?

Chief Sukuna agreed to transport the bodies back to the plantation, eager to get the corpses off his land. The doctor and the chief had conducted most of these conversations and had concluded that Kunti would go back to her family for cremation, but the final resting place for Brown remained undecided. Whatever was to be done with him, it would need to be done quickly. They assumed Parkins would have a view on what to do with Brown's remains.

The doctor had decided against an autopsy of Brown, as there wasn't much more to be learned from his body. He did want to examine Kunti's body further, to at least learn how far along her pregnancy was. But given the state of her body after her time in the river, and with the lack of facilities, a proper autopsy was going to be difficult to conduct.

Akal was almost hoping that the autopsy of Kunti's body would not happen at all, or at least that he wouldn't have to assist. He did not think his stomach would handle it very well. He wondered how the doctor could look at a human body so dispassionately, as a mere collection of components. He imagined viscera on display instead of remaining as secret inner workings, private and mysterious. How could the doctor be around people, talk to them, drink with them after seeing all of that?

Akal and Dr Holmes remained at the river while one of the boys ran back to the village and came back with sheets to cover

NILIMA RAO

the bodies, while Timi and the chief worked out how to move the corpses. They then rode slowly back to the plantation, with assurances from Timi that they would have the bodies that day. Occasionally one or the other of them threw out suggestions for the next step, the conversation as disjointed as their thoughts.

'Well, I obviously can't go back to Suva yet,' said Akal.

The doctor distractedly replied, 'No, no ...'

'I will have to tell Parkins about his overseer. I wonder if they were friends,' Akal said, to no response. A little while later, he blurted out his next series of questions. 'Where were they shot? By the river? Did anyone hear the gunshots?'

The doctor didn't respond to any of these questions, and instead muttered, 'I hope I can determine how far along she was.'

Akal cocked his head, curious. 'You said she was four months?'

Frustration made the doctor's tone gruff. 'It's hard to tell with the malnutrition. I would say four months if she was well-fed. She could well be five months with an underdeveloped foetus.'

Akal pushed away a curious mixture of sadness, guilt, and anger – anger at the situation and anger about the guilt he did not want to feel. 'Did her family know? Neither the husband nor the daughter mentioned it. Did Kunti hide the pregnancy? How did she hide it? *Why* did she hide it?'

The doctor was back to his own musings. 'I hope Timi keeps his word and does manage to get Kunti's body back to the plantation today,' he fretted. 'If I'm going to do an examination of any kind, sooner would be better than later.'

'We need to talk to her husband. Surely he must have

known about his wife's pregnancy.' Akal sighed. 'It rather seems like neither of us is going back to Suva yet.'

The doctor grunted his agreement.

They both lapsed into silence, consumed with their private thoughts, and remained that way until they cleared the sugar cane and could see the plantation sprawling out ahead of them once again.

By this time, it was just past noon. For once, storm clouds did not gather with their usual threat of rain, last night's epic storm having temporarily exhausted the supply of water in the heavens. The humidity wasn't letting up, and both men had sweat-soaked shirts. Akal pulled his shirt away from his chest and lifted his arms up, trying to generate a bit of breeze on his overheated armpits.

'We are both starting to smell a bit ripe.' The doctor mimicked Akal's movements, flapping his arms like wings. 'Might see if Susan can do a bit of laundry for us.'

'I don't think she is the type to do laundry.'

The doctor nodded ruefully. 'We'd better find Parkins and ask him what the bloody hell happened to his overseer,' he said, snorting. 'Off to war, he says. In a pig's ear. The bullet in the back of his head says some kind of war found him here in Fiji.'

THE FIJI TIMES,
THURSDAY, OCTOBER 8, 1914.

Chop Chop

At Government House they say there are far too many suicides amongst Indians in Fiji. Planters must really stop this practice. Why not placard the plantation with notices: 'Anyone committing suicide here will be fined!'

CHAPTER SIX

When Akal and Robert arrived back to the plantation, they rode straight to the Parkins house, but Henry Parkins had not yet returned from the fields for lunch. In his absence, they scavenged some lunch for themselves and returned to the overseer's house to eat, Akal's stomach having settled after the trauma of smelling the bodies and now rumbling to be refilled. They were sitting on the balcony, lunch finished, when Akal noticed a disturbance in the cane leaves in the distance and pointed it out to the doctor. They were able to follow the progress of the men bringing the bodies by the ripples spreading through the cane field long before the group emerged. It was sooner than Akal had expected, given the usual slow pace of things in Fiji, but later than the doctor would have preferred, as he fretted over the condition of the corpses in the heat.

It was a sombre procession. For each of the bodies, the villagers had suspended a mat woven from green palm leaves between two wooden poles, two young men carrying an end of a rod on each shoulder. In Kunti's case, she was carried with more reverence and respect than she had probably ever experienced while she was living. She was home, as unhappy as that home may have been.

Timi was leading, with the four young men following, their unfortunate burdens swaying between them as they walked in perfect sync with each other. The doctor and Akal headed down the hill to where Timi and the boys had stopped, waiting for them.

'Here she is,' Timi said quietly. Kunti was nestled peacefully in her hammock. Her clothes and hair had dried, leaving her looking a little more natural, a little less corpse-like, but the pallor of death and the puffiness of her submersion remained. The doctor took charge of the de facto coffin bearers and led them towards a shed where he would conduct his examination.

'Thank you, Timi. I know this can't have been a nice job,' Akal said, shrugging regretfully with open hands. 'I'm sorry I don't have any more tobacco for you.'

'No tobacco needed, Mr Police. Poor woman should be with her family. Good we found her and the other one. If they stayed in the river, problems in the village, for sure,' Timi said, shaking his head. 'You find who killed her? Or him?'

'Not yet. But we will.'

'Good. We don't need any angry *kaivalagi* ghosts.'

When Akal and Timi joined the doctor in the shed, they found Robert clearing tools and garbage from a cluttered, dusty table, muttering to himself while the two men carrying Kunti looked on patiently, rods still on their shoulders. The men carrying Brown's body had put their burden down on the floor at one edge of the shed, wrapped in the palm leaf mat, and were standing by to watch, leaning on their poles.

'Doctor?' Akal asked cautiously.

'I just need to get this cleaned up,' the doctor said with a sigh. 'This is hardly an appropriate place for me to examine a body. Heaping more indignities on this poor woman.'

Akal and Robert tidied the table as best they could, but there was little to be done for the liberal layer of dirt remaining.

Eventually enough of the surface was available for the two boys carrying Kunti to manoeuvre her body onto the table. The boys knelt to lower her down, with the coconut palm mat still below her, protecting her from the dirt. As they stepped away, both boys started massaging and stretching out their necks and shoulders, testament to the fact that it had not been an easy journey for them. They had red impressions where the poles had pressed into their shoulders as they carried Kunti.

'I need the room empty.' Dr Holmes was all business now and had started to unwind the sari, pausing to usher the Fijians out and give Kunti a little dignity in death. 'Not you, Singh.'

Akal reluctantly remained. Robert gently lifted Kunti's shoulder to slip the end of the sari out from under it. The cloth was awkwardly wrapped around her body, covering her completely but gaping and sagging.

'It was nice of the boys to cover her up like that,' Akal said. He wondered whether this was out of respect, or whether the fear of *kaivalagi* ghosts was a motivating factor.

'Nice, perhaps. But bloody annoying.' The doctor didn't look up from his job of unwinding the length of faded threadbare cotton from her body. With some difficulty, he removed the sari cloth from her upper body, to reveal the blouse she wore underneath. Robert paused over Kunti's lower body, clad in a petticoat and the rest of the sari. The material was loosely wrapped around her waist and was not tucked into the petticoat, clearly the work of inexpert hands.

'How does this thing work, Singh?'

Akal flushed a deep red. 'I ... sir, that is ... I don't know exactly. I've never ...'

'Oh. Well. Never mind, then. We'll just blunder our way

through.' The doctor actually looked at Akal for the first time since they had brought the body in. He was standing well back from the table towards the door, acutely aware that he was not doing a good job of hiding his unease. 'Are you quite alright, Akal?'

Akal nodded. How could he explain how disturbing he found this? The doctor was pragmatic and absorbed in his work, handling Kunti's body gently, kindly, but with a detachment that Akal found baffling. For Akal, her nakedness was exposing secrets that he had thought he would learn in marriage, and the doctor's tenderness was a parody of intimacy that left Akal twitchy and ashamed.

The doctor looked at him dubiously and said, 'I'd say you could step out, but I will need you to help me turn her over in a minute. And two sets of eyes are always better than one. You'll probably need to get a bit closer to be any help.'

Akal shuffled closer. The doctor crooked an eyebrow, and Akal sighed and shuffled closer still. 'Close enough?'

The doctor nodded abstractly, attention already back on the job at hand. He slid his fingers under the skirt to release the tucked-in portions of sari. His solid pale fingers with clean, square-cut fingernails were an unsettling contrast against the skin of her stomach, turned a greyish-brown in death. Akal, giving in to the inevitable, went to help the doctor.

Akal shuddered as they turned Kunti on her side, his palms cringing away from her yielding flesh. He pointed out the tie fastening at the back of her skirt, and with some difficulty, they wrestled the petticoat and the rest of the sari off her. Every time she was moved, a smell of the river released from her – Akal couldn't tell whether it was from her clothes, her hair, or her body itself. The smell of silt and rotting vegetation and something else he couldn't name made him want to hold his breath so he wouldn't be contaminated by it.

When they were done, Akal stepped back again and averted his eyes. He heard rustling as the doctor moved about.

'You can look up now,' Robert said with wry sympathy.

The doctor had covered her from her neck to her feet with her sari, like a sheet. She was lying on her back with her hair hanging down on either side of the table, still damp enough that a slow drip had started from each hank to form puddles on the dirty floor. He started his examination with her head, then continued down her neck, moving the sari as he needed, only exposing what he was examining at the time. Akal fidgeted by the door.

'You can go now, Singh. I'll let you know what I find out. And then you'll have the sorry task of informing her husband and daughter.' The doctor did not look up as Akal fled out into the sunlight.

Akal was not looking forward to telling Venkat of his wife's death, but he was keen to get it over with. He waited outside for the doctor to complete his examination, leaning against the shed with his eyes closed, trying to clear his mind of the memory of Kunti's body on the table. Akal was so focused on clearing his mind that he didn't hear Robert leave the shed, and his first indication of the doctor's presence was the disturbance in the sunlight filtering through his eyelids.

'Five months,' the doctor said briskly, once Akal opened his eyes. At Akal's blank look, Robert elaborated, 'I think she was five months along, not four as I said back at the river.'

Akal nodded, pushing himself away from the shed wearily. 'I'll go tell her husband.'

Venkat should have been the first person to hear about Kunti's demise, but in order to find Venkat, they had to talk to Henry Parkins, so they went to the Parkins house to check if he was back for lunch. They found him on the verandah, sprawled back in one of the rattan chairs, hat pulled over his eyes. An occasional soft snore was muffled by the weathered leather.

'Ahem ... Henry,' the doctor said, leaning over Parkins, hand hovering above his shoulder.

Parkins woke with a start, catching the hat as it started to slide down his torso.

'What the ... ? God, Robert, don't sneak up on a man like that.'

'We stomped up the stairs like a herd of elephants, Henry. Can't help it if you were out like a light.'

'The sleep of the righteous, Doctor, the sleep of the righteous. You get worn out when you do actual work instead of running around on wild goose chases.'

The doctor sobered up. 'No goose chase, Henry. Is there somewhere quiet we can talk?'

Henry Parkins sighed. 'I'm not going to like this, am I? It had better be the office, then.'

They followed him through the house, away from the kitchen and into a small room at the front. Parkins took the seat behind the tidy wooden desk and waved a hand at the chair in the corner.

'Sorry, I've only got the one seat to offer you. Nobody comes in here but me. And Brown, before he ran off to get himself killed by the bloody Germans.'

'We won't take too much of your time,' said Akal. He

watched Parkins closely. 'When did your overseer leave the plantation? What ship was he taking to Europe?'

Parkins's eyes narrowed as he looked at Akal suspiciously. 'Brown? Why are you asking about Brown?'

'We are trying to find him. Your wife suggested that Kunti ran off with him. I am trying to figure out whether he has left Fiji yet,' Akal lied easily.

Parkins relaxed as he nodded. 'Oh. Well, that makes sense. Let me think ... Well, he left the afternoon before we realised that the woman was missing.'

'And the ship?'

'No idea.'

'There were no ships due to leave for Europe anytime this month.'

'Yes, yes, I think he might have been going to Australia first. There are always ships going to Australia.'

'Is there any reason he might have decided not to get on the ship?'

Parkins frowned. 'Only the woman. Why do you ask?'

Akal considered Henry Parkins carefully. The man had been somewhere between passively obstructive and mulishly rude since Akal's arrival at the plantation. Akal didn't have a specific reason to suspect Henry; nonetheless, he didn't trust him. The man had secrets. It would be interesting to see how he responded to the truth of the bodies found on his plantation.

'We found both Mr Brown and Kunti this morning. They did not go to Australia.'

'Well, for God's sake man, spit it out. Where are they?' Henry Parkins started to rise from his chair, looking around as though Akal may have been hiding the missing pair behind his back.

Akal stepped closer and said with quiet gravity, 'I am very sorry to have to tell you this, sir, but we found them this morning in the river. They are dead.'

Parkins slid back into his chair and looked from the doctor's serious face to Akal's impassive visage and back again. 'Is this a joke?'

The doctor shook his head.

Parkins asked incredulously, 'What? Where?'

Akal filled him in on the events of the morning.

'Kunti as well? They drowned?' Parkins repeated. 'Well, that's ... awful.'

All three men remained in silence as Parkins absorbed this news, staring down at his hands. Eventually he sighed deeply and looked up.

'I guess that's that. At least we know what happened.' Henry started to move some papers around his desk, as though to end the conversation. Akal's vague suspicions of Henry Parkins were roused again – why didn't the man have any other questions about the death of two employees?

'No, I'm afraid not,' Akal responded. 'They were both shot.'

'Well, perhaps he killed her, then killed himself. A lover's tiff.' Parkins continued to look at his paperwork.

'No,' replied Akal emphatically, wondering what it was going to take for Parkins to stop avoiding his gaze. 'He was shot in the back of the head. He could not have done that to himself. Your overseer was murdered.'

'Well, then maybe *she* shot *him*, and then shot herself out of guilt.'

'Their bodies were weighted down,' Akal countered flatly. 'That is why they were only found after the storm.'

Finally, Henry Parkins looked up.

'Ah, for God's sake!' he exclaimed, shaking his head and pushing back from the desk. 'Can you just leave this alone? At least for now? I've got cane to get in. I've got no overseer. I've got a plantation full of coolies to keep calm. I suppose now I'll have to make some arrangements for the burials, unless you are going to take care of that. No? I didn't think so. And I've got an election coming up. Can't you wait a few weeks? They aren't getting any more dead.'

'No, I can't,' Akal replied, struggling to keep the affront out of his voice. 'Even if I could, do you want a killer to be free on your plantation? With your wife here?'

'Well. I see. I suppose you will do what you want to do,' Parkins replied angrily, his face visibly reddening. 'I will be busy, and so will my coolies, so I don't imagine you will see any of us over the next few days. Good luck figuring it all out.'

'Who has access to firearms on the plantation?' Akal asked, ignoring Parkins's outburst.

'I do, obviously. Brown had his own pistol and a rifle. We used to go wild boar hunting.' Parkins paused, looking like he was trying to conceal a satisfied smile, and then continued in a considering tone. 'Come to think of it, Venkat, Kunti's husband. He is a *sirdar*. Brown may have given him access to guns as well.'

Parkins reluctantly took him to inform Venkat, arguing with him the whole way.

'Why do you have to tell him now?' Parkins asked. 'He is supervising ten men. This is going to distract all of them.'

They were riding single file once more through a cane field, so Parkins had to crane around and argue with Akal over his shoulder.

'The man's wife is dead. I think his work can wait,' Akal shot back at him.

'I don't think it can. And it is my plantation,' Henry growled, facing forward once more.

Akal glared at Parkins's back. He was sufficiently disgusted that he did not remember to maintain his usual diplomatic demeanour, so it was lucky that Parkins couldn't see him.

Parkins shook his head, sighed and said, 'I won't have it said that I blocked you. Fine. Do what you need to do.'

They found the men at the farthest field from the house. They were stripped to their *dhotis*, toiling with wicked-looking machetes to cut down the rows of cane, sweat on their scrawny bare chests. The *dhoti* may not have been the most elegant article of clothing, the loincloth simply wrapped and tucked securely, but it was a cooler option than Akal's uniform trousers.

Akal noticed that the workers who were closer to them had stopped work, laying their machetes on the ground and stretching while keeping an eye on what drama was about to unfold. Unfortunately for them, Parkins noticed as well and started towards them, shouting and making gestures which threatened a walloping. The curious workers all jumped to and got back to their work. Akal suppressed a smile. Clearly, they weren't so cowed that they wouldn't indulge in a little casual eavesdropping.

Akal walked along the edge of the cane field, peering into the gloom underneath. Eventually, he found Venkat harvesting the sugar cane with a group of men. He was focused on his work and didn't see Akal approach at first. The other workers noticed Akal first, stopping work one by one, until finally Venkat looked up to see why they had halted. He jerked when he saw Akal and barked a terse command to his fellow workers, who reluctantly resumed their harvest. Venkat hurried over to Akal, his stride jerky and agitated.

'Sergeant Singh. Do you have news?'

'I do. It is not good.' He paused, casting about for the right words and not finding any good ones. 'I am afraid your wife is dead.'

At this final word, Venkat squeezed his eyes shut. Both men stood motionless by the cane field, Venkat with his shoulders slumped, chin to his chest, Akal leaning towards him, ready to catch Venkat if he dropped. After a few moments, Venkat lifted his head, squared his shoulders, and lifted dry eyes to Akal.

'What happened?' His voice was cracked, hollow, as though he was far away.

Akal told him about their discovery of Kunti's body, skirting over the ravages inflicted by her immersion in the river. For now, he omitted mentioning whom else they had found in the river. Venkat deserved to hear about his wife's death first, before other matters overshadowed it. And if Venkat didn't deserve it, Kunti certainly did.

After all the other facts had been relayed, Akal concluded with a statement, question implied. 'She was pregnant.'

Venkat remained silent, and after a pause, nodded once.

'Why didn't you tell me this before?' Akal kept his voice gentle.

Venkat shook his head and sighed. 'Why would I tell you this? I thought she had run away with her lover. I needed to humiliate myself more by telling you that she did this while she was pregnant?'

'So, the baby was Brown *sahib*'s?'

'I do not know.'

'Kunti did not know either?'

'She said it must have been mine, that he could not have children,' Venkat said bluntly. His tone brooked no further questions, but Akal was not deterred.

'How did she know that he couldn't have children?'

Venkat frowned. 'There was a woman before Kunti, Magamma, and she never had a baby with him. Magamma spoke with Kunti and told her that she didn't have anything to worry about, that she didn't do anything to stop a baby but in three years one never came. Now that she has finished her contract and remarried, she has had one child already with her new husband, and a second on the way. The baby had to be mine, so Kunti said.'

There was that name again: Magamma. Akal decided he would go see her tomorrow, assuming he could follow the old lady's directions.

'So, you were happy about the baby?'

Venkat looked away, leaning on his machete.

'No. I know what Kunti said, but how could I be sure? Maybe we would be lucky. Maybe the baby would look like me, but otherwise ... how would I ever know?' Venkat paused and gestured to the fields. 'Every day I am out here is one day of my indenture completed. But if that baby was fair ... my indenture would never end, Sergeant Singh. Even when we were gone from this place it would be there with us.' Venkat's voice had lost its hollowness and was instead laced with bitter regret.

Parkins was already pointing the finger at Venkat, and every time Venkat spoke, he made the case against him stronger.

Akal hoped he would not have to take Divya's father away from her, so soon after the loss of her mother. He wondered how Venkat would react to his next piece of news.

'We have also found Mr Brown.'

'Found him? Did he kill Kunti? Where is he?' Venkat asked, his fists and jaw clenched, grief giving way to anger.

'He is also dead. With a bullet in his head.' Akal kept a watchful eye on Venkat as he delivered this with dramatic flair. Gratifyingly, Venkat's jaw dropped.

'He was shot?' As he recovered from his shock, a fierce smile grew over Venkat's face. 'Good. Good. I'm glad he was shot. He deserved it. Who shot him?'

Akal decided to abandon subtlety. 'Right now, you seem to be the person with most reason to kill him.'

Venkat scoffed. 'Me? Shoot Brown? With what, my finger?'

'Aren't you a *sirdar*? Don't the *sirdars* have access to guns?'

'He made me a *sirdar* to keep me quiet about the fact that he was bedding my wife. Brown never trusted me with a whip, let alone a gun. And anyway, what *sirdar* has access to a gun?'

Parkins had told Akal that all the *sirdars* had guns. Had he lied or did he really did not know what was going on in his own plantation and what his overseer was up to?

'So only the *sahibs* have guns? Would anyone have noticed the gunshots?'

Venkat shook his head dismissively. 'I don't think anybody would pay attention to gunshots. The *sahibs* go hunting for pigs, and sometimes they'll shoot if they see them near the buildings. Gunshots are fairly common.'

Akal frowned. It seemed that avenue of questioning was not going to be fruitful.

'I need to get back to the coolie line. I will need to make

arrangements for Kunti's cremation,' Venkat said, lifting his machete over his shoulder and looking around. His gaze collided with Henry Parkins's. 'The *sahib* is going to be very angry when I tell him I have to leave.'

'I already told Parkins that this was too important. Your work can wait for a day.'

'Hmph. Easy to say. If I leave with my task not completed, then all the work I have done this day was worthless, and the whole day won't count against my indenture. But it must be done. I will cremate my wife with dignity.'

Venkat started to walk over to Henry Parkins, his gait slow but his posture upright and proud. Akal watched him walk towards the furious plantation owner for a few moments, and then cursed under his breath as he hurried to catch up with Venkat. He really did not want to get involved, did not want to antagonise Parkins any further, but he couldn't leave Venkat to face Parkins's wrath on his own. When Akal reached him, Venkat acknowledged him with a grateful nod.

Parkins did not offer any sympathies or assistance to Venkat for the loss of his wife. He coldly accepted that Venkat was leaving for the day, but, as Venkat had expected, informed him that this day would not count against his contract, despite the fact that the day was almost over.

Akal offered Venkat a lift back to the coolie line, which he accepted after eyeing the big horse with some trepidation. They rode largely in silence. Akal could feel Venkat brooding behind him.

'What are you going to tell Divya?' Akal asked as they approached the coolie line.

'I don't know. I will have to tell her the truth of some sort before other people do. But we don't really know the truth yet, do we? Maybe I will know what to tell her once you figure out who killed her mother, Sergeant Singh.'

The flames popped and cracked, smoke twisting up in jagged swirls into the night. The entire coolie community had come for the funeral, families and small groups arriving to the funeral pyre by the river. All around the fire, small knots of people dressed in white stared mesmerised, the flames flickering a red glow on solemn faces.

Akal scanned the crowd, looking for familiar faces. He found Dev and Zain together, standing towards the back of the mourners. They were whispering to each other, casting cautious glances around as they fidgeted. It was Dev, of course, who laughed a little too loudly, prompting their fathers to come and grab them by the arm and drag them back to their families.

Word had spread quickly through the community about the deaths and the dramatic recovery of both bodies. The news had been met with surprising equanimity. There was probably more quiet conversation by the funeral pyre than would normally be seen at such an occasion. But nobody was shunning Kunti's family. What would have scandalised Akal's village in India was less startling in this disparate community, all of whom had dealt with upheaval and loss of control every day of their indenture.

One older man roamed around the fire, barking commands and scolding the young men who didn't respond quickly enough. He had come from Taveluka that afternoon and offered to officiate – for a modest fee, of course. With no temple and no priests in Fiji, the family had little option but to accept.

Akal was sceptical to say the least. Was he even a Brahmin? Nonetheless, he was making a good show of it, unhesitating as he set up every obscure detail of the event. It was better than nothing – even if he was making it up as he went along, as Akal suspected he was.

Akal and Robert stood apart from the mourners. They had debated whether they should come at all. Neither of them had the white clothes they should really have been wearing for a Hindu funeral. The decision had been made by Venkat, who had warily approached them at Brown's house and asked them to come. He approached them again now, hand in hand with his daughter. Divya was dry-eyed, her chin firmed and high in the air.

'Thank you for coming,' Venkat said, nodding to Akal and Robert.

'Of course,' replied Akal. He looked at Divya as he continued in Hindi. 'I am sorry about your mother.'

'Thank you for finding her.' Divya's young high voice sounded hoarse, her eyes red rimmed.

Akal nodded, humbled by the young girl's dignity.

'I want to know who did this. Who killed her, Sergeant Singh?' Divya asked, her proud features turning fierce.

'I don't know yet, Divya.'

'But you are going to find out?'

'I'm going to keep looking,' Akal said, hoping that the inspector-general would allow it.

'Did you find the photograph? The one the priest took of my mother? Please can I have it back?'

'We didn't find the photograph. I'm sorry, Divya.'

'Promise me you will look for it,' Divya said, and her voice cracked as her strong façade started to crumble.

'I promise I will do my best,' Akal replied, raising his eyebrows at Venkat in mute appeal. Akal didn't want to disappoint this vulnerable young girl with promises he might not be able to fulfil. Venkat knelt down and spoke quietly to a distraught Divya until she nodded reluctantly. She turned to Akal and recited, 'Thank you, Sergeant Singh.' The words were dutiful, but her eyes continued to flash fire at him.

Venkat and Divya took their leave and started to walk back towards the fire.

'What did the daughter have to say?' asked Robert.

'Divya wants me to find out who killed her mother, but I'm not sure that Venkat really wants to know. If he wasn't under suspicion, I think he would prefer for the whole thing to go away.'

'But you don't think he did it?'

Akal shook his head slowly. 'Why now? It seems like Venkat is getting what he wants if Kunti runs away with Brown – a quieter life with an easier wife. Unless he actually did care that she was leaving him, and he is just doing a very good job pretending he didn't.'

As they mulled over the possibilities, the funeral pyre burned on and the crowd of mourners thinned, dispersing family by family, as people returned to the coolie line ahead of another gruelling day in the cane fields. Akal and Robert decided to head back as well.

As they approached Brown's house, Akal smelt the sweet musk smell of a cigar. He looked around and saw the flare of a burning ember some distance from where they were walking, halfway up the hill. There was a silhouette of a man watching the funeral from a vantage point on the hill, where none of the coolies could see him. Nobody else at the plantation would have a cigar: it had to be Parkins. But why would the plantation owner watch the funeral at all, let alone from the shadows?

Robert absently brought the mug in his hand up to his lips and took a sip, grimacing.

'Are you sure there isn't any more whisky in the house?' he asked Akal.

'No, Doctor *sahib*. I checked everywhere.' Akal exaggerated the respectful 'Doctor *sahib*' with a little head bob. Robert grinned in response. The moment of levity was a relief after the grimness of the day.

When they had arrived back to the overseer's house after the funeral, Robert had immediately proposed drinks on the verandah, much to Akal's horror. He knew he couldn't handle a second night of whisky and had been greatly relieved when a bottle could not be found. They had resumed their positions on the verandah from the night before but were drinking tea instead, much to *Robert's* horror.

'What happens now, Akal? You have found the woman, which was what Thurstrom sent you out here for.'

Akal paced over to the verandah railing and stared gloomily out into the darkness.

'I was supposed to find one runaway coolie,' he said. 'Instead, I have found a dead coolie, and her overseer, also dead, in a river, with bullet holes in them. I can't go back without some answers.'

Robert sipped his tea as Akal brooded. He put the cup of tea aside and broke the silence with some unwelcome news.

'I am going to have to go back to Suva soon. I need to get

back to the hospital. And I've seen everyone I need to see here.'

Akal nodded without turning around. It made sense, but he felt the words in the tightness of his throat. Working on this case with the doctor had eased his loneliness in Fiji.

Their quiet, separate contemplations ended abruptly when somebody came pounding out of the dark night and up the verandah steps. It was Satish, the interpreter who had relieved Venkat at the doctor's clinic on their first night at the plantation.

'Doctor, we need you!' he panted. 'Anjali is having the baby.'

'Of course,' Robert replied. 'Let me get my kit and I will come down.'

Akal followed him inside. 'Is this such an emergency?' he asked. 'Surely women must give birth here all the time without a doctor on hand.'

Robert looked up from the kit he was buckling and shook his head. 'No, it is too early for her – she is only about seven months along. And in any case, I am here. Even if she was having the most normal labour in the world, it is wholly appropriate to ask for my assistance.'

Akal nodded, abashed. 'Can I help?'

'No, I doubt she will be comfortable with another man there. But thank you.' Robert straightened and gave Akal a wry, resigned look. 'What you can do is be ready to have a cup of that awful tea with me when I get back. I do not have a good feeling about this.'

Five hours later, Akal was snoozing on the one armchair in the living room when Robert dragged his feet back up the verandah stairs and into the house, startling him out of his restless doze.

'Wake up, son. You can't sleep here all night.'

'Doctor. How is she?' Akal asked, groggily wiping his hand over his face.

'Anjali is fine, at least physically. The labour actually went smoothly.'

Akal looked at him questioningly as he stood. The doctor took his place, collapsing into the armchair.

'The baby did not survive. He was just too small.'

'Oh. I am sorry, Doctor.' Akal knew from his father's letters that one of his sisters had lost a child during labour. His family had grieved the loss together, but far away from them in Hong Kong, Akal had found it difficult to mourn the death of child he had never met.

'Thank you.' Robert looked up at Akal wearily. 'The couple is grieving right now, so I want you to be very careful about how you talk to them. But you *will* need to talk to them.'

Akal groaned. 'It is too late for mysteries, Doctor.'

Robert scowled at him, a genuine look of displeasure, not the teasing version Akal was used to.

'It has been a long damn night, Singh. I just had a baby die in my hands. Do you think you could save your whining for some other time?'

Akal sat up very straight and nodded stiffly.

'That baby had a white father. I don't know how many women Brown was involved with, but it seems like Anjali might be another.'

Police Court Cases

Deceivers Ever

The matrimonial troubles of an elderly Indian couple were next ventilated, Surgi charging her husband Madabadal with desertion.

Mr Crompton, who appeared for the plaintiff, explained that the defendant had forsaken his elderly spouse to take to himself a newer and younger bride. He had turned out his wife who had been with him for over thirty years and refused to keep her.

The Magistrate said the man must take his wife back.

...

The defendant here volubly declared his intention of 'keeping the other young girl', to which he said he had his wife's permission.

Plaintiff interjected that he had nothing of the sort.

CHAPTER SEVEN

'Suva Police Station.'

'Taviti.'

'Akal. How is plantation life? Relaxing?'

'You have no idea.'

'Would you rather be back here dealing with the Night Prowler?'

'Taviti, I honestly think I would. Has he been peeping in any windows lately?'

'No, all quiet. Funny ... He goes quiet when you leave town,' Taviti said, his tone laced with innuendo.

'Oh, is that what you think? Hmph, I wish it were me. I would just turn myself in. Some quiet time in a cell would be very nice right now.'

Taviti chuckled at this, and then got back to business.

'I didn't find anything about your man Brown. Nothing about him arriving in Fiji, nothing about him leaving.'

'Nothing about his arrival? Is the record-keeping not that good? It is in Hong Kong.'

'Ooh, Hong Kong,' Taviti said good-naturedly. 'Everything is better in Hong Kong.'

'Sorry, sorry,' Akal replied. After a few months of listening to Akal wax-lyrical about how much he preferred Hong Kong, Taviti had started to ask why he didn't just go back to

Hong Kong. Given how much he didn't want to answer that question, Akal had learned to keep these thoughts to himself.

'At any rate, the record-keeping is usually good for Europeans. I think it's not so good for the coolies,' Taviti responded. 'I'll take another look.'

'Just for his arrival. As to the leaving part, that I can answer,' Akal said, pausing for dramatic effect. 'He didn't leave. Well, he has left us for heaven – or possibly hell – but his body is still here in Fiji. With a bullet in his brain.'

'What? Are you saying he is dead?'

Akal briefed him on the discovery of Kunti's and Brown's bodies. Taviti was not satisfied with Akal's dry recitation of facts and wouldn't let him move on until Akal promised a more detailed retelling about the retrieval from the river over drinks when he was back in Suva.

'Murder,' Taviti said, hushed and troubled. 'The inspector-general is going to be so angry. Do I have to tell him?'

'If he asks. But don't worry, you can blame me. He will anyway.'

'He has asked for a report as soon as you call, so I will have to tell him. And I'll definitely blame you.'

Akal could hear the grin through the phone line.

'Anything else you want me to look for?' Taviti asked.

'A couple of things. Keep looking into Brown's arrival. Oh, and with him "going off to war", Parkins said he was travelling to Sydney first, then on to Europe. See if he was booked onto any of the ships going to Sydney.'

'I'll do that straightaway. And the other thing?'

'There was a man here this morning, he escorted Mrs Parkins from Suva. Lewis Robinson. Do you know the name?'

'Hmm ... No, I can't place him,' Taviti said slowly.

'Could you find out who he is? He might not be part of this, but I'd still like to know.'

'Sure thing, I'll ask around. What are you going to do now? More relaxing?'

'I'm going to have some breakfast. Then I'm going to find this woman, Magamma, who I'm told was having an affair with Brown before she was replaced by Kunti. See what she has to say. And I'm going to look for Kunti's photograph at Brown's house. It would be nice to give the little girl something to remind her of her mother.'

'Getting soft in your old age. Well, good luck. And try not to find any more bodies.'

'I can't make any promises.'

After hanging up, Akal went in search of Parkins. He found him in his office, with spectacles falling down his nose and papers scattered on the desk in front of him.

'I need to speak with Shiri. The man whose baby was stillborn,' Akal said.

'Why?' Parkins asked, eyeing Akal suspiciously. 'What does Shiri have to do with the missing woman?'

'No, nothing,' Akal hedged. 'The doctor has asked me to talk to him to give him some instructions about how to care for his wife.'

Parkins regarded him with narrowed eyes. 'If Robert has instructions for the woman's care, why would he send you?'

Akal shrugged. 'He is seeing some patients in town, and used me as an interpreter in any case. Shall I wait for you on the verandah?'

Parkins continued to look at him with suspicion. 'Why don't I just tell you where they are?'

'No, no. I'm happy to wait,' Akal replied evenly. He had strong suspicions on how accurate any directions would be.

'Fine. I'll be a while,' Parkins said, waving him out of the office.

Parkins dragged his feet at the house and even tried to leave via the kitchen without collecting Akal. Akal had anticipated this and was waiting outside the house, just a little down the hill, where he would see Parkins no matter which way he left. Parkins stopped suddenly when he saw Akal and growled something under his breath, then jammed his hat on his head and stomped down the hill towards the stables, Akal following closely behind.

They rode out to the field in silence. Akal used the time to ponder how he should approach Shiri. The doctor was right, kid gloves were needed.

They approached a scene identical to when Akal had been searching for Venkat, the men working in the fields. They still paused to look with some curiosity as to Akal's presence, but it was muted in comparison to the first time – he was becoming part of the landscape. Parkins dismounted and went to talk to Venkat without a word to Akal. He was left on his own to find Shiri. It took a few false starts and the help of a couple of the indentured workers to find the man.

'Sergeant Singh? You wanted to talk to me?' Shiri asked, his face both puzzled and concerned.

'Shiri, I am very sorry for your loss.' He paused, casting about for the right words to bring up the topic and not finding any good ones. 'I know it is not a good time for you and your wife, but I have some questions about your baby.'

Shiri crossed his arms and shook his head.

'You know what I need to ask.'

'The baby is dead. Nothing more to say.'

'Was the baby yours?'

'You know it wasn't.'

'The baby was Brown's?'

Shiri paused, looking nervously over Akal's shoulder. Akal turned to see what he was looking at and found Parkins staring intensely at them.

'He can't hear you. And I will not tell him what you say,' Akal promised gravely.

They both stood, frozen in place until Shiri made his decision.

'The baby was Brown *sahib*'s,' Shiri mumbled.

'So, Anjali and Brown ...' Akal let his words trail off suggestively.

Shiri bristled. 'It was not her fault. That man, he won't leave the women alone. He has had every woman on this plantation. What can we do?' His shoulders slumped and Akal saw guilt instead of grief. 'I was going to treat the child as my own.'

Akal put a hand on Shiri's shoulder. Shiri shook it off and stepped backwards.

'Why are you asking about this? Aren't you looking for Kunti's killer? And Brown *sahib*?' Dawning realisation spread across his face. 'Do you think I killed the *sahib*?'

Akal considered Shiri carefully. 'Would you have any reason to kill Kunti?'

'No! No!'

'Then unless I find you had a reason to hurt her, you should be safe.'

Shiri nodded in Parkins's direction. 'That would not have stopped Parkins *sahib* from blaming me.'

'Good thing Parkins *sahib* is not in charge of this investigation. But if I don't find who did this, my inspector-general is going to send somebody else who won't be as concerned with the truth. Then you or Venkat might be in trouble.'

Shiri looked alarmed anew. 'Please find who did this. My wife needs me.'

'I'll do my best,' Akal replied, echoing what he had said to Divya.

Shiri saluted him with his hoe before going back to his position in the field and resuming his rhythmic motions.

Akal returned to his horse and remounted, pondering what he had learned. If Brown was having relations with all of the women on the plantation, why did the old lady at the market talk about him being obsessed with Kunti? Why run away with her? The old woman had mentioned another target of Brown's obsessions, the ex-coolie Magamma. Akal needed to find her.

Akal paced in Brown's sitting room, waiting for the doctor. He wanted to get out to find Magamma and ask her about her experience of Brown's attentions, but he was wary of heading out on his own. Akal had been doing alright navigating around the plantation, but he wasn't confident about finding the township again. Once he got to the town, he knew how to find Magamma's house. He had written down the very thorough instructions from the old lady at the market. In the meantime, he continued to pace.

Akal stopped in the middle of Brown's sitting room when he remembered that he had been intending to have a good look around the house. He had committed to finding the photograph of Kunti for Divya, the photograph that Brown might have kept here. Looking for the photograph would keep him busy until the doctor returned from his final follow-ups with his patients.

He stood with his hands on his hips and did a quick survey. The house was small. Akal had stayed here a couple of nights already, but he was looking at it differently now. The photograph he was searching for would hardly be prominently displayed. He would have to search every nook and cranny. Akal stretched his neck from side to side, sighed, and then got started.

His search commenced in the bedroom where the doctor had been sleeping. The doctor's fastidious nature was evident in the neatly made bed, the simple coarse linens made taut against the uneven single mattress with crisp hospital corners. Despite the lumps in the mattress and the simple cot-like bed frame, this was luxurious compared to the rooms in the coolie line. This bedroom for one person was only a little smaller than one of those rooms, the living, cooking, eating, and sleeping area for an entire family.

Akal started at the chest of drawers, opening each in turn and methodically removing all the contents onto the bed before checking them, then placing them back as he had found them. The drawers contained only yellowing linens and indifferently laundered rough work clothing, similar to the clothes the doctor had found for them to wear the night of the storm. This was not particularly illuminating. It seemed unlikely that Brown would leave these clothes behind, but not impossible.

They were not particularly good quality and would not have been of much use to a man in uniform.

He checked the bed, inside the pillowcases, feeling under the mattress, patting it down to check that the lumps were just cotton. The table by the bedside revealed a Bible with its spine barely cracked. On the inside of the front cover, in loopy, extravagant handwriting was the admonition:

John, Keep this Bible with you always and read from it every day. It will keep your soul safe. Know that I'm praying for you always. With all my love, Mother.

Akal wondered, if Brown had read the good book more often, would it have kept him safer? Now surely this he would have taken with him, no matter how short on space he was in his luggage. Akal knew from his colleagues in Hong Kong, many of whom had served in the military, that every soldier kept mementos from his family close, and one with the power to save your soul would have been treasured.

Underneath the Bible, shoved without care to the back of the bedside table drawer, were two letters. They were addressed to a John Chalmers. Akal hadn't heard this name before. Could it be that Parkins had had two overseers, both named John? Akal knew that John was a common English name, so perhaps, but something about this name had his spine tingling with anticipation.

Akal scanned the first letter, full of stories of family members in Australia. This didn't shed any light on the identity of the mysterious John Chalmers. The second letter started the same way, but had a startling ending.

Please, John, be very careful of your cousin. I know you say he has taken you in when you needed him, but he has always been such a bad influence on you. And Henry is bad enough, but that wife of his! I worry about you, John. It has been four years, surely whatever the problem in Australia was, it has blown over by now. I wish you could come home.

So, Brown's real name must have been Chalmers. And he and Henry Parkins were cousins.

Akal sat heavily on the bed, staring sightlessly at the wall, letters in his hand. He moved this information around in his head, trying to see where it fit with the rest of the puzzle. The letter was dated January 1913, which meant that Brown must have arrived in Fiji in 1909. With the timing and with his real name, perhaps Taviti could now trace Brown's steps properly.

Eventually Akal decided to leave it alone for a while, see if it came to him while he thought about something else. Still sitting on the bed, he looked around to see if there was anything he had missed. The afternoon sunlight entered through the glassless window, sneaking around the wooden shutter that the doctor must have propped open that morning. Seeing it in daylight and knowing the fate of the former occupant, the room seemed forlorn, lonely, and abandoned.

There was nothing personal here, barely a trace of the existence of a man whose mother had given him a Bible to protect him, who did not yet know that he was dead. Kunti had become real to Akal when he'd caught glimpses of her daughter in her features, and when he had seen her body lying on the riverbank. Brown remained somehow just a name, his body too misshapen to generate any sense of connection.

Akal moved into the equally small sitting room to continue

his search, satisfied that there was no photograph and nothing more to be gleaned from the bedroom. The sitting room only revealed Brown's collection of fading editions of the *Fiji Times*. He had heard that outside of Suva, the newspaper was highly valued and would be read over and over again. On a plantation such as this, they would receive a few weeks' worth of papers in a batch when somebody, probably Parkins, would visit Suva and return with them. The newspaper would regale the reader with stories of weddings, cricket matches, government administration meetings, and court cases, all luridly described down to trimmings on dresses, wines consumed, and word-for-word renditions of judges delivering chastisements to unruly witnesses and hapless solicitors. And the ever-popular Chop Chop column, savagely cutting down the colonial administration, plantation owners, and that monolith of power, the Colonial Sugar Refining Company. After seeing the drab, brutal life on the plantation, Akal could understand why the newspaper was so coveted here. Still, there was nothing to be learned from these old newspapers, so he set them aside and continued his investigation.

Searching the kitchen proved a bigger job, with more nooks and crannies and pots and pans to search. There was a rust-spotted mirror haphazardly hung above the sink. Akal caught a glimpse of his face and winced. His skin looked dusty and ashy, and he had failed to get all the sleep out of his eyes that morning. A smear of something streaked across his limp, bedraggled turban. He mourned the lack of crisp creases as he tucked a wayward curl of hair off his forehead and back into the turban. Nobody in Suva would recognise him right now.

Previously, Akal and the doctor had found hard biscuits and tinned fish and had presumed these meagre rations constituted all the food to be had. But searching top to bottom in the daylight, Akal found another stash of the same at the back of the top shelf of the pantry, where the doctor would not have been able to reach. He groaned but placed them on the table anyway. If they didn't manage anything else, at least they were not going to starve.

Eventually the methodical search paid off. Tucked away under the sink, behind all the other crockery and newer pots and pans, he found a largeish battered pot, its outside scratched and dented, blackened from time spent over a fire. The lid seemed to be jammed shut and it took some strength and a lot of twisting and turning to get it off. Sitting on the floor of the kitchen, Akal worked at it, determined for no reason other than stubbornness, until finally it gave with a screech of metal against metal. Inside, wrapped up in a pillowcase, he found wads of paper money.

The next couple of hours of waiting were torturous for Akal. He paced the small house continuously, pausing only to snatch a quick lunch of torturously dry crackers. Finally, the doctor returned from his makeshift clinic in town. Akal rushed outside to see Robert leaning heavily on the banister as he pulled himself up the stairs of the overseer's house.

When Robert moved to one of the chairs on the verandah, Akal shook his head urgently and ushered the doctor inside instead, much to Robert's annoyance. Once the doctor had lowered himself into a chair inside, Akal wordlessly showed him the pot full of money.

'What on earth is all this about?' Robert asked, leaning

forward to peer more closely inside the pot, weariness forgotten.

'I have no idea, Doctor,' Akal replied, shrugging helplessly.

'This is a lot of money, Akal. A *lot* of money.'

'I know. I just don't know what it means.'

They counted the money, coming to two hundred pounds, which would happily keep a man for many years in Sydney. Akal rolled it back into its yellowing pillowcase and hid it in his bag. He and the doctor agreed to keep this information to themselves for now.

'I have more news, Doctor.'

'I don't know if I can take any more. It has been a long few days.' The doctor groaned, wiping his hand over his eyes. 'Go on, tell me.'

'Brown is Henry Parkins's cousin,' Akal revealed with relish. 'And his real name is Chalmers. At least, that is the name his mother uses for him.'

Akal showed the doctor the letters addressed to John Chalmers. After he was done, they were both silent as they thought through the implications.

The doctor looked at Akal with a frown. 'So ... I don't know what to make of all of this. None of this explains how both Kunti and Brown – or Chalmers, or whatever his name actually is – ended up in the river. Give me a diseased limb any day.'

'I have to call Suva. See if they have any information on John Chalmers. And then I need a quiet moment to think this all through.'

On the walk up to the big house, they agreed on a plan that the doctor would keep Mrs Parkins occupied so that Akal could make the phone call in private. The doctor was sweating over how to distract her, grumbling the whole way. Akal thought that if the doctor used a fraction of the creativity he was using to curse Akal, he wouldn't have any problems with Susan.

They knocked on the front door to the Parkins house and Susan opened the door a few interminable minutes later. She was impeccably dressed, incongruous against the faded and haphazardly furnished house.

'Dr Holmes,' she said, nodding coolly to him.

'Hello, Susan. How lovely to see you,' Robert said heartily. Akal wondered if perhaps the doctor's concerns about his acting abilities were warranted after all.

'How can I help you?' Susan asked, her tone not warming at all to the doctor's overtures.

'Oh, no, we don't need anything, really. Just here to let you know that we will be heading back to Suva tomorrow. Nothing more to do out here.'

'Well, that is good news,' Susan responded, finally thawing enough to smile prettily at Robert.

'Yes. I've seen all the patients nearby and the sergeant here has found the missing woman, sorry state of affairs that it is, so he will be heading back as well.'

Susan Parkins's eyes flickered over Akal dispassionately before landing back on the doctor. It seemed clear that she no longer saw Akal as a threat, merely an annoyance.

'How about a nice cup of tea and a chat, Susan?' Robert asked, again sounding a little too eager for Akal, but Susan smiled and nodded. 'Akal, be a good chap and make us some tea, would you?'

Susan Parkins's smile broadened as Akal nodded stiffly and went inside. Once inside, he got the water boiling and then made his phone call, speaking softly as he kept some of his attention on ensuring the rumble of conversation on the verandah continued.

The call back to Suva yielded immediate results. 'John Chalmers. Yes, I remember that name. Hold on.' Akal heard Taviti muttering the name a few times as he rustled some papers. 'Yes, here it is, on the regular bulletin from Australia, saying to be on the alert for one John Chalmers. He raped and killed a girl in Sydney a few years ago. Never caught. Never found his accomplice either.'

Akal shook his head to restart his brain. 'Rape and murder,' he said. 'No wonder he changed his name. The accomplice. Who was it?'

'Not named.'

'Ask around, would you? See if anybody has heard anything else.'

'Will do. I looked into Lewis Robinson, by the way. Nothing interesting to report. British, came to Fiji a year ago. Does odd jobs here and there. Keeps to himself, nobody seems to know why he's here. Do you want me to keep looking into it?'

'Interesting. Thanks, Taviti. No, leave that one, focus on finding out more about John Chalmers.'

'Sure thing. Anything to report to the inspector-general?'

'Taviti, I just don't know. It is all a bit too complicated. Can you keep this Chalmers thing away from the inspector-general for now? If he asks for an update, just tell him ... we are interviewing the locals. I need to figure all of this out first before we let him know that Australia is now involved as well, and he blows his top.'

'Better you than me, Akal.'

'Hmph.'

Akal hung up, heart racing as the magnitude of the new information started to sink in. He then made the tea, spilling water everywhere in his haste, and rejoined the doctor and Mrs Parkins on the verandah. The doctor had clearly decided that he couldn't sustain any more complicated cover stories and was just going to rely on a charm offensive to keep her from overhearing the conversation. They were laughing and exchanging gossip about Suva society when Akal entered the room.

'Ah, excellent, the tea,' Robert said, as Akal set the tray on the table between them. 'And you won't be joining us, will you, Akal? I think you have some errands to run, don't you?'

Mrs Parkins was busily pouring tea, but Akal could still see a small smile playing around her lips at Robert's seemingly condescending dismissal of him.

'Yes, Doctor *sahib*. Mrs Parkins.' He nodded politely to both of them and quickly left the house. It was time to speak to Magamma. Akal felt that he was missing something important, and he was going to keep going until he found it.

◀▮▶ ◀▮▶ ◀▮▶

'*Namaskaram*. I am Sergeant Akal Singh of the Fijian Constabulary, Suva Division. Are you Magamma?'

Suspicion narrowed the woman's face. 'Police. What do the police want with us? We have not done anything wrong.'

Magamma – at least he assumed she was Magamma, given her response – had cracked the door just enough to put her face and one shoulder through. Akal was glad the doctor wasn't there. Magamma was already alarmed enough by an Indian police officer; a white man accompanying him would not have helped. The fact that they could at least converse in Hindi might help ease matters, assuming he could get her to talk to him at all. She looked over at his horse and then scanned his uniform. Her gaze snagged on his sidearm. Fear flashed across her face, and she pulled back, preparing to slam the door shut again.

'No, I just want to ask you some questions about somebody you know. You are not in any trouble. Nobody is in trouble. I just need some information,' Akal assured her, holding his hands up, well away from his weapon. A child poked his head through the door down below and Akal smiled and waved at him. The boy grinned and waved back. This seemed to reassure Magamma more than Akal's words had, and her wariness faded a little.

'Questions about who?'

'Kunti.'

On hearing this name, Magamma's face relaxed as understanding replaced the suspicion.

'Well ... come around the back.'

Magamma opened the front door and came outside rather than letting him in. She hauled the small boy, who continued to smile at Akal, up onto her hip, and led Akal around the house. They passed a sprawling kitchen garden with tomatoes ripening on the vine next to sporadic clumps of coriander growing wherever there was space. This led to a cooking area, a little corrugated iron shed containing an open wood stove with a blackened pot sitting above it ready to cook the evening meal. There was a solitary wooden chair with a metal dish full of beans, half still in their pods sitting on the seat. She hastily snatched the bowl up and dusted the seat off, then ushered Akal towards it.

'No, no, I am happy to sit over here,' Akal protested, gesturing towards a tree stump that was obviously the other seat.

Before she could respond, a shout echoed from the distance. They turned towards the field of sugar cane, which started immediately behind the cooking area. The cane was waist high, and Akal could see a man in the distance, waving for his wife to come over.

'*Acha, theek se hai*, very well. You sit here. I had better go talk to my husband,' she said.

'My questions are just for you,' Akal said quickly.

'*Acha bhaiya*, don't worry. I know what you want to talk about. I will make sure he stays out there while we talk,' she said over her shoulder as she started out towards her husband. Her boy wriggled out of her arms and started running towards his father as quickly as his little legs would let him, his mother following behind.

Akal made himself comfortable on the tree stump and waited. The whole scene transported him back home, to his village in the Punjab. A rooster strutted under a tree nearby, feathers glossing black and iridescent green as he moved in and out of the shade. He was followed closely by a harem of chickens jostling for a position near him between frenetic pecks at the ground. Sheets flapped in the breeze, a noise which soothed Akal and brought a wistful smile to his face. The sheets were hung precariously low on an improvised clothesline strung loosely between two posts which were pushed into the ground with a drunken lean.

Magamma returned, jolting Akal out of his nostalgic reverie.

'My husband apologises that he can't leave his work, and he has agreed that I should answer your questions,' she said without inflection.

Akal had a strong sense that her husband had merely bowed to her force of will.

'Let me get you a drink,' Magamma said, ducking inside before Akal had a chance to object. But he didn't have to wait long; she soon emerged from the back door of her wooden shack with a tin cup in her hand. Magamma handed the cup to Akal with an expectant smile.

The tangy smell energised him before he even tasted the pips of lime floating in the cloudy water. '*Nimbu pani!*' Akal cried out, face exploding into a smile. 'I have not had homemade *nimbu pani* in a long time. This is wonderful!'

'Our lime tree has started to give us fruit this year. The first time I made a glass for my husband he nearly cried. It is such a small thing, but it is something from home that we could not get while we were indentured.'

'It is something I did not even realise I missed,' Akal replied.

They were quiet for a moment while Akal enjoyed his drink, the tartness refreshing, crunching coarse grains of sugar between his teeth. Reluctantly, he broke their moment of quiet bonding with a sigh.

'I wish I could just sit here with the chickens and drink *nimbu pani*, but I have to ask you some questions for my investigation.'

Magamma chuckled, her face illuminating as she laughed. '*Acha bhaiya*. Ask.'

'Have you heard about Kunti's disappearance from the Parkins plantation?'

She nodded. 'Yes, I had heard about this. She ran away,

didn't she?' Magamma said, her tone a little scornful at this last sentence.

So perhaps she had not heard about the discovery of the body. Akal preferred it that way. Murder tended to make people quiet.

'That is what I am here to investigate. A priest in Suva is saying she must have been kidnapped, if you can believe it. So, I got sent out to see what is what.'

'Oh, *bicharra*. Poor Mr Police Officer, having to come out to the sticks to deal with the peasants like us.' There was a warm mirth in her eyes.

'I was in the middle of a big investigation in Suva,' Akal protested. 'The Night Prowler case. You must have heard about it, even out here in the sticks?' At her amused nod, he continued. 'It was going to be my big break. If I can solve that one, my boss might get off my back and give me some decent work. I might even be promoted.'

'Oh, well, in that case, I had better help you. I would not want to stop you from being promoted. But what can I tell you?'

'Somebody mentioned that you knew Kunti. They said she had taken over some of your duties at the plantation ...' Akal carefully kept his face neutral.

'Is that what they said?' she asked, a little bitterness creeping into her voice. 'I am sure they said plenty more.'

'It does not matter to me what choices you made. I need ...'

'Choices?' Magamma interrupted, looking at him with incredulity. 'I did not have any choices, not at first. I did not have a choice on who my first husband would be. The *arkathi* made that choice for me in India in order to get me on the ship. I did not have a choice on what the *sahib* did to me when I got here. I did not have a choice on the beatings my first husband gave me.' She spat out the word 'husband' like it was poison.

'He beat me for what he called my "infidelity". Oh, he knew that was what got us lighter tasks. That weak man knew that my "infidelity" was the only way he was going to get through his indenture, and he hated it.'

Magamma paused, looking down at her lap and taking a deep breath. When she looked up, it was with dry eyes. She continued with a quiet determination, the fire in her voice banked but still burning.

'My choice was to cry or to use what I had to try and have some control over my life, so I could make choices later. Like deciding who my second husband would be, so I could have a kind man who does not beat me.'

Akal did not want to ask, but he pushed the words out past the boulder in his throat. 'The *sahib* forced you?'

She nodded, tired now after her emotional outburst. 'He forced me the first few times. Then I came to accept it. I started to think of it as part of my indenture. I thought, five years. It will be my job for five years. Then the hardest part was dealing with my husband. So, I got the *sahib* to get rid of him. He sent him to a different plantation.' She smiled with cold triumph. 'See, I started to make choices then.'

'Did he force Kunti as well?' Akal asked, in the way of confirmation. He was fairly sure he already knew the answer, given what he had just learned about Chalmers's offences in Australia.

'Of course he forced her. You really do not know anything, do you, Mr Police Officer? Disgust dripped from her words. 'I tried to tell her to use this like I did, but Kunti found it harder. She already had a real family. I think that was the difference.'

Akal winced at her assertion that he knew nothing but didn't refute it. How could he protest, when he was only now starting to learn about the degradations the Indian women suffered on the plantations? How could he, when he had stayed as far away from the coolies as he could, until he was forced to witness it himself? 'Did you have his baby? Kunti was pregnant when she went missing.'

Magamma's smile was full of malicious delight. 'No. At least that did not happen. I believe he cannot have babies. The whole time he was making me ... lie with him, I never fell pregnant. But with my current husband, we have had one child already, and another on the way.' She placed her hand over her abdomen.

Akal nodded diplomatically. Magamma may not have fallen pregnant to Brown, but Anjali had just given birth to his baby. It seemed that Brown *could* have children. Perhaps there were other reasons Magamma had not become pregnant during her indenture.

'Her husband thinks she ran away with the *sahib*,' Akal probed. 'So does Mr Parkins. Do you think that is possible?'

'Eh? What do you mean, "so does Mr Parkins"?' She sounded puzzled. 'If he has run away with her then he should know, shouldn't he?'

Like misaligned cogs suddenly clicking into place, Akal realised with painful clarity the mistake he had been making all along. 'The *sahib*. It was Mr Parkins? Not Brown the overseer?' Akal asked, his voice low and urgent.

Magamma looked a little frightened, but she held her nerve and nodded, eyes wide. 'Maybe it seemed like it was Brown *sahib*. It didn't start until Brown *sahib* arrived. He made sure I had the duties that kept me closer to the house, away from the other women so Parkins *sahib* could … well, you know. And Brown *sahib* made sure my husband had easier work. But he never tried to have relations with me. I think he saw me as Parkins *sahib*'s woman. Anyway, Brown *sahib* was too busy with every other woman on the plantation.'

Akal buried his face in his hands and groaned. '*Sahib, sahib, sahib* … and I never thought to ask the old aunty which *sahib* she was talking about! But Venkat also said it was Brown … well, I suppose Kunti did not talk openly to her husband, it would have been an awful thing to talk about. She must have just said *sahib* as well. Parkins! Parkins …'

Magamma looked on in bemusement as Akal composed himself. After a few minutes he raised his head out of his hands and grinned sheepishly at her.

'Thank you,' he said. 'You have solved this case for me.'

She tittered nervously. 'Are you sure you are alright?'

'Yes, I'm sure,' he replied, bounding to his feet and striding quickly back through the garden to the front of the house where his horse was tied up, Magamma struggling to keep up with him. 'I need to get back to the plantation.'

As he was about to mount his horse he stopped and stepped closer to Magamma. 'Are you well now? Do you have choices?'

Magamma laughed, a contented, indulgent sound. 'There are not too many choices to make when you have a husband and children. And chickens. But I am happy with the choices I have made. Nothing for a Suva police officer to fix here.' She gave him a playful push on his shoulder. 'Go on, go find Kunti.'

Akal winced, realising he could not withhold the truth from her any longer. 'We already have. I am sorry to tell you this, Magamma. She is dead.'

She closed her eyes and sighed. 'I see. I suppose I am not too surprised. He was a bit ... obsessed with Kunti. Far more so than he ever was about me.' Magamma opened her eyes and fixed Akal with a fierce stare. 'You will make sure he pays? For Kunti.'

'Yes. And for Venkat and Divya,' Akal promised solemnly. 'And for you.'

Akal could hear his heart pounding in his ears the whole way back to the plantation. He arrived at the stables with his horse well-lathered, and he chafed at the extra time it took him to take care of the beast. Akal rushed through the job, promising his horse an extra-long grooming next time. Finally done, he practically ran back to Brown's house, taking the front steps in two huge strides.

'We've got it all wrong!'

The doctor's caterpillar-like eyebrows jerked upwards.

'That is quite the greeting, Sergeant. What exactly do we have wrong?' he said from his seat.

Akal paced back and forth on the short verandah, having to about-face every four strides.

'Brown wasn't the one taking advantage of Kunti, it was Parkins.'

Akal quickly sketched in the details that Magamma had provided him as a thoughtful frown grew on the doctor's face.

'Well, that changes things,' Robert mused. 'So, Henry was taking advantage of Kunti, but is probably not her baby's father.'

Akal gave the doctor a puzzled look.

'Brown is Anjali's baby's father. Shiri confirmed that when you spoke with him, correct?' Robert asked. After Akal nodded, Robert continued, 'Magamma never fell pregnant the whole time Henry was similarly molesting her but had no problems conceiving with her second husband. Susan Parkins doesn't have any children. My guess is that Henry is infertile.'

'So even though Parkins and Brown were both taking advantage of women here, the only women to fall pregnant were those who Brown was with. It sounds like he stayed away from Kunti, though,' Akal said. He focused on the facts, ignoring the sick feeling in his stomach at the thought of what the women on the plantation suffered.

The doctor nodded and said, 'I can't say for certain, but I believe that Kunti was pregnant with her husband's child.'

Akal sighed. Venkat would be devastated. 'If it was Mr Parkins who was abusing Kunti, it would explain why I couldn't find the photograph here at Mr Brown's house,' he said.

'No photograph, just all that money. I still can't see how that ties in.'

'Oh, I completely forgot to tell you!' Akal exclaimed. 'Brown, or rather John Chalmers, is wanted for rape and murder in Australia.'

The doctor exhaled sharply. 'I suppose I shouldn't be surprised, given what has been going on at this plantation.'

'Indeed. If we hadn't found him in the river next to Kunti, I would have said he was our murderer. He has done it before.'

'So, Brown ... Chalmers, rather, was in Fiji as a fugitive?'

'Yes. Henry Parkins helped him hide, given they are cousins. Or perhaps there is another reason. They never figured out who Chalmers's accomplice was. Maybe it was Henry Parkins? We know that neither of them has any qualms about raping women,' Akal said.

They both contemplated all of the new information until Robert shook his head.

'Well, where does this leave us, Akal?'

'Doctor, how do you feel about using some of that charm of yours again to get Mrs Parkins out of the house while I do a little snooping?'

THE FIJI TIMES,
FRIDAY, OCTOBER 9, 1914.

New Housing Provisions Enacted for Coolies

3. No dwelling assigned to an indentured servant shall be deemed a suitable dwelling unless the internal dimensions provide not less than 50 superficial feet space for each adult.

...

8. Inner partition walls shall be continued from the top of the wall-plate to the roof, by strong battens two inches apart, or by strong wire netting.

CHAPTER EIGHT

Akal watched from a sheltered spot halfway up the hill as the doctor and Mrs Parkins walked towards Brown's house. They had devised a plan that the doctor should ask Susan Parkins to help him do an inventory of Brown's goods. Akal had suggested that if she refused, the doctor play on Mrs Parkins's dislike of Akal by suggesting that Akal couldn't be trusted to do the inventory. He wondered if the doctor had had to resort to the manipulation. In any case, it looked like the plan had worked.

Once they were safely inside Brown's house, Akal sauntered up the hill, attempting to maintain a casual demeanour. He did not know how successful he would have been if anybody was watching, as it felt like his knees were knocking into each other, wanting to break into a run. He knocked on the front door and waited a minute, hoping fervently that Henry Parkins was out working as he should have been at this time of day. When nobody answered the door, he boldly walked down the front steps as though he was leaving, in case anyone was watching, then disappeared around the side of the house and entered from the back, through the kitchen.

Akal moved through the house with purpose. He treaded gently on the wooden boards in the corridor, grateful for the worn carpets muffling his footfalls as he headed for the office. That was Henry Parkins's domain, and the only place

Mrs Parkins would not see something like a photograph of a beautiful Indian woman with whom her husband was obsessed. He hoped it was there, because he did not know how long the doctor's ploy would keep her out of the house and he did not know where else to look.

After what felt like an age, Akal arrived at the office. He inched the door open, grateful that the hinges didn't squeal, and stepped inside. The only time Akal had been here before was with both the doctor and Parkins in attendance. Without Parkins's presence, Akal could see the room as it was. The furniture consisted of a desk and chair, one filing cabinet, and a bookshelf, all teak and all showing evidence of their long journey to Fiji. The only things saving the office from sparseness were the framed family photographs on the wall. Otherwise, it was painfully neat, lacking the comfortable clutter that Akal associated with a busy man's office. Not a single piece of paper lay on the desk. The matching chair was tucked under the table, precisely in the middle. One pen was placed on the desk to the right-hand side of the chair, perpendicular to the tabletop's edge. Every book on the shelf was lined up so that the spines made a perfect line, one inch back from the edge. He would have to be careful to put everything back exactly as it was – this was going to make the search infinitely more difficult.

The desk was graced with three drawers built into each side. Akal tried to pull open the first drawer on the left, surprised when it stuck. It did not feel like a problem with the drawer; it seemed like the drawer would glide on its tracks, but was recoiling due to some impediment. He wiggled it up and down while pulling, initially gently, but with gradually increasing force the longer it resisted. The drawer finally gave way and burst open. Papers, cards, pens all exploded out of the overstuffed drawer with velocity and went clattering onto the floor. Akal dropped to his knees behind the desk, heart thundering in his ears.

Once he'd gathered up the various bits and pieces from the floor, Akal stood and placed them on the desk. He looked in the drawer hanging open and shook his head. What was this? In this ruthlessly neat office, why was the drawer full of ... everything? He eased and bullied the rest of the drawers open one by one, finding the same story repeated to various degrees. All six of the drawers had crumpled pieces of paper, pens, business cards, such a variety of detritus that Akal had to rummage around to see what was in there. But it did not take too long to satisfy himself that there were no photographs crammed in among the debris.

Akal took a moment to scan the papers, which were mostly the sorts of receipts one would expect for a plantation: invoices from Morris Hedstrom, the premier store in Suva, for food and clothing, receipts from the CSR Company for the sugar the plantation produced. Akal crammed the items back into the drawers and closed them with some difficulty. He did not worry about putting things back where they came from here. There was no way Parkins was monitoring the mess that closely.

He then walked over to the filing cabinet. It consisted of two drawers, each containing a series of folders. Akal pulled out each folder and flipped through the contents. The folders all seemed anaemic, thin, and sad. Why weren't the papers filed in here? Why were they all crammed into the drawers? The papers that were in the folders looked like they were crumpled then smoothed flat, evidence of their time in the drawers.

The chaos belied the façade that Parkins was portraying of a successful businessman, of a man in control of his workers, of a future leader of the Planters' Association. Akal closed the filing cabinet door. No photographs here either.

The only place left to look was the bookshelf. Akal sighed. There were quite a few books to get through and he had already been there longer than he had hoped he would be. He scanned the bookshelf and his eye landed on something that looked like a leather-bound album. He extracted it from its place on the bookshelf, careful not to disturb the other immaculately arranged books, and placed it on the desk.

Akal unwound the leather tie holding the album closed and started turning the pages. Evidence of happier times for the Parkinses flipped past in sepia tones, pictures of Mrs Parkins with a smile etched in shades of brown for perpetuity, throwing into stark relief the angry calculating face that Akal had seen for the past few days. Unsurprisingly, there was no photograph of Kunti featuring next to the pictures of Susan.

As Akal gingerly eased the album back onto the shelf, he heard a slithering sound from behind the bookshelf, as though something had dislodged. He stepped back to satisfy himself that the album was positioned exactly as it had been, with no disturbance in the faint dust layer, before going to investigate. The corner of an envelope was resting against the wall, peeking out from behind the bookshelf.

Akal squatted down and put his thumb on the corner of the envelope, being careful not to push it entirely behind the heavy piece of furniture. He slowly wiggled it out, biting his lip in fierce concentration. When he finally liberated it and opened the envelope, Akal found what he was looking for: the photograph of Kunti, a copy of the one he had seen at the priest's house in Suva, the same mysterious almond eyes smiling up at him.

The doctor was dragging a case from the bedroom into the living room when Akal arrived back at the overseer's house. Robert had both hands on the handle of the case and was scuttling backwards while Mrs Parkins looked on, fidgeting with the buttons on her gloves.

'How is the inventory going, Doctor?' Akal asked from the doorway.

'Oh, Singh.' The doctor dropped the end of the case in the middle of the room with a thump of dust and turned around, stretching his back. 'It's getting there. Bedroom is done. How were your interviews?'

'Um ... Yes ... Just routine, you know.' Akal tilted his head towards Mrs Parkins and widened his eyes, hoping the doctor would get the hint.

Susan Parkins was, as usual, ignoring his presence, and did not notice Akal's expression. Instead, she asked the doctor, 'What sort of interviews? I thought you said there was nothing more to do now that you have found that woman's body.'

The doctor looked at Akal, panic in his eyes. 'Ahem, I don't quite know. Akal?'

'Well, yes. I was speaking with some of your Indians,' Akal hastily dissembled. 'Last time I spoke with Suva, they asked me to check on the conditions in the lines. Nothing serious. The administration is just being very cautious, what with the delegation here. Just a few more questions for your husband and we can be on our way.'

'Susan.' The doctor moved to hover his hand over the base of her back, shepherding her towards the door. 'I think this inventory is going to take a few more hours and I know you have to be attending to dinner. Sergeant Singh will want to take over, anyway. Why don't you head on back to the house?'

She looked at them both disbelievingly. 'Do you think I'm a fool? Clearly something more is going on here. I'm not going to be ushered back to the house like some empty-headed little girl. Tell me what you are up to.'

The doctor spluttered some denials while Akal looked at Susan Parkins and considered his options. He couldn't tell her the complete truth. It was difficult to tell how deep her loyalties to her husband ran. Largely, Akal thought that her main loyalty was to herself and to her drive for power. But she clearly wouldn't be satisfied with the bland lies they were telling her. Perhaps if he gave her a little more information, it would shake out some truth from her.

'Mrs Parkins, you are correct, there is more to the situation,' he said, cutting short the doctor's ramblings. 'There is some concern in Suva about the treatment of women on the plantation, particularly by your former overseer. I have learned that he was forcing himself on Kunti, and it seems Kunti was not his only victim. We need to know how much your husband knew about this. I'm afraid he might bear some responsibility for Brown's actions, if Mr Parkins knew about the many women Brown was ... interfering with.'

Susan Parkins paled. It was the first time since Akal had met her that she looked alarmed. 'I'm sure Henry won't know anything about it,' she said quietly, without any of her usual venom. 'I'd better get back home and look into dinner, as you said, Doctor.'

Susan turned and fled the house without another word.

Robert turned to Akal and said with urgency, 'Well?'

Akal nodded and handed over the photograph.

'Damn. Poor Susan,' the doctor said, a sentiment Akal didn't agree with. 'So now what?'

'Will you come talk to Henry Parkins with me? I think I might need a witness.'

Akal waited in Venkat and Divya's room in the deserted coolie lines. It was late afternoon, and the Indians were still working in the field, their children no doubt running wild by the river. Akal had found one man drowsing under a tree by the rows of rooms. He was ill, but had grudgingly agreed to go and fetch Parkins, after Akal had given him the remaining tins of fish found in Brown's kitchen.

The first time Akal had been in one of these rooms, he had felt the walls closing in on him. The atmosphere was still oppressive, stifling, and airless. However, he could now see evidence of Venkat's and Divya's lives being lived out here: the rag doll resting on Divya's bunk, and a small, tattered picture of Ganesh in the corner, with a single flower before it. It was a dreadful home, but a home nonetheless.

Akal was jittery. Adrenaline had him moving restlessly around the room until he heard footsteps. Henry Parkins slammed the door open and entered, angry energy crackling off him. Akal met his eyes but didn't say a word.

'What is this all about, Singh? What have you got me down here for? Where is Robert?'

Maintaining his silence, Akal handed over the photograph

of Kunti and, with his breath caught in his throat, waited for Parkins's response. Parkins squinted at it in the gloom of the room and started when he recognised what he held. He thrust the photograph back at Akal, who clasped his hands behind his back, refusing to take it. Parkins's hand dropped by his side, still clutching the damning picture.

'That's a photograph of Kunti, is it? Why are you showing me that?' Parkins asked. He had stopped meeting Akal's gaze.

'Have you seen that picture before?'

'Well ... maybe ... I don't know. It's just a photograph.'

'I think you have seen it. I found it in your office. Hidden behind the bookshelf. How did it end up there?' Akal kept a level tone.

'In my office! What the hell were you doing in my office?' In his surprise at Akal's effrontery, Henry forgot to avoid Akal's gaze. Akal saw equal measures of surprise and anger on Parkins's face. Did the man really think his privacy was somehow inviolate?

'Investigating a murder, sir. In fact, investigating two murders. I'll go where I need to.'

'You dare to presume that you can "investigate" your betters? You don't know your place, but I will be happy to teach you,' Parkins snarled. 'Maybe in Suva they gave you a badge and called you a police officer, but on my plantation,' he said, thumping his chest, 'you are just another coolie.'

The slight bounced off Akal without impact. He was too focused on his prize. He leaned towards Parkins and asked again, 'Why was this photograph in your office?'

'I'm not answering any of your questions. I'm calling the inspector-general.'

Parkins stormed towards the door. Akal's next words froze him in his tracks.

'You said that Brown was Kunti's lover. *I* say it was you, and you were her rapist, not her lover. You believed you were her baby's father. And you killed her. What I don't know ...'

Parkins whirled around and advanced on him. 'Ridiculous. Where are you getting this from? And where the hell is Robert?'

'. . . is why?' Akal continued without acknowledging the interruption. 'Oh, did I say Brown? I meant John Chalmers, of course.'

Parkins lost all the blood from his face, sun-marked cheeks stark in comparison to the pallor around them.

Akal moved in closer and fired questions at Parkins, his voice harsh to his own ears. 'He is your cousin, correct? Did he ask you to hide him after the murder in Australia? Were you his accomplice? Did you know we found a large amount of cash in his house? Was he blackmailing you?'

Akal could see that the first few questions fell like landed blows on Henry Parkins, as he progressively reared up during the questioning, but the questions about the money seemed to puzzle him. They were the only questions he chose to answer.

'What money? I didn't give him any money.'

'We found two hundred pounds hidden in a pot in your cousin's kitchen.'

'Where would John get that much money? You must believe me. I do not know anything about it.'

'What about the murder in Sydney?' Akal asked, giving Henry Parkins a look that said his guilt was a foregone conclusion.

Parkins leaned against the bench and said again quietly, desperately, 'Where is Robert?'

For the first time in the conversation, Akal looked away and hesitated before admitting, 'He has gone to do final rounds with some patients. He didn't agree with my suspicions and said he would not have anything to do with the arrest.'

Parkins seemed to gain strength from this and stood back upright, lip curling in a sneer.

'Arrest? Go ahead and arrest me. What evidence do you have? A photo? That's nothing. Even Robert doesn't believe you, and I've seen how cosy the two of you have become. If he doesn't believe you, who will?'

Akal needed to shrug off his uncertainty. 'Why did you kill your cousin?' Akal asked, back on the offensive.

'Cousin!' Parkins spat. 'I treated him like a brother.'

Akal waited, letting the silence fill the room. Parkins paced the room, shaking his head, starting to mutter to himself.

'He is the one who killed that woman in Sydney. He tried to say I was part of it, but I knew how to restrain myself. She didn't die when *I* was with her. He's the one who got me banished to Fiji. And even then, I hid him here when he showed up, desperate. Then what do I find him doing? Trying to rape Kunti. She thought he was going to kill her. So yes, I shot him. I let him have every other woman on the plantation. He deserved what he got.'

Akal felt every muscle in his body exhale at this confession. But he couldn't let the pressure off; his job was not done yet. 'Tell me why you killed Kunti.'

'Kunti ...' Her name fell from Parkins's lips like a benediction. 'I promised her that she would be safe. I couldn't kill her.'

'But you did,' Akal said implacably.

'Susan ... couldn't let it go. She just did not understand. She had her life in Suva, and I had my life here with Kunti. But she kept saying I had to end it. Said it was going to ruin my chances at the Planters' Association.'

'And that is why you killed her?'

'I loved her.' Parkins was shaking his head, voice breaking.

Akal placed a heavy hand on Parkins's shoulder. 'We will sort out the details in Suva.'

'Like hell you will.' Parkins pushed Akal's hand off and barked a scornful laugh. 'You have no evidence. I will deny I said any of this. Who will believe you over me?'

The doctor's disembodied voice came through the chicken wire mesh at the top of the wall between Venkat's room and his neighbour's. 'They will believe him, Henry. And if they do not believe Sergeant Singh, they will believe me.'

Parkins whirled to face the wall, and with a snarl, he shoved Akal out of the way and ran towards the door. Akal fell back and cracked his head against the edge of the bunk bed on his way to the floor. His last thought as his head thudded to the dirt was that Parkins was stronger than he looked.

'Wake up, for God's sake, man!'

Keeping his eyes closed, Akal swatted away the hand that was grasping his shoulder and shaking him vigorously. But when the same hand slapped him gently on the face, Akal opened his eyes. He immediately closed them again as his head swam, and his stomach revolted against this rude awakening. Taking some deep breaths, he blinked until the blurred features of the object hovering above him resolved into the doctor's concerned face. Akal levered his way up into a seated position with a groan.

'Where is Parkins?' Akal asked.

'I don't ...' Robert's response was interrupted by the unmistakable sound of a gunshot.

'Shit,' muttered Akal.

Robert helped him up and they left the oppressive room, Akal stumbling at the entrance. His head cleared and the world stopped swimming as he stepped out into the fresh air.

'I can't be sure, but I think that came from the Parkins house,' the doctor said grimly. 'What the hell has Henry done now?'

They made their way to the house, the doctor supporting Akal, half-dragging him up the hill. Akal grasped the railing with some relief as they climbed the stairs to the verandah. He drew his sidearm with a shaking hand. The doctor took one look at this and said, 'Akal, if you shoot yourself and I have to patch you up, I'm not going to be best pleased.'

Akal shook his head and immediately regretted it, as the verandah swam in front of him.

'No chance, Doctor *sahib*. Well, I might just shoot a toe off.'

They ran through the house, searching for Henry Parkins, Akal taking the lead. The sound of their boots thumping against the wooden boards echoed through the house, obscenely loud. After coming through the kitchen to the back of the house, they found Susan Parkins sitting on the ground by her husband. She was holding his hand as he lay, unmoving, on the grass a few metres from the back steps. His chest was marked with a brooch of blood. It bloomed in the shape of a flower, each petal expanding slowly as she watched, mesmerised. Susan didn't look up as Akal approached with the gun aimed at her, the doctor behind him, but she still seemed to know they were there.

Her lips didn't seem to move as she said, barely louder than a whisper, 'I had to do it. He had gone mad.'

Akal nodded absently, trying to make eye contact with Mrs Parkins while keeping her rifle in his peripheral vision. It was lying on the ground by her left thigh. She seemed oblivious to it. Susan was stroking the hair back from her husband's face now. Akal took a step closer, and then another, when it was clear that she had no further use for the weapon.

Susan finally looked up, dry-eyed, as he approached, and her face hardened when she saw Akal.

'You. This is your fault. You couldn't leave it alone?'

'Mrs Parkins, may I have the gun, please?' Akal kept his tone gentle as he held his hand out. She looked down at the rifle as though surprised it was there.

'Yes, yes, of course,' she responded quietly, the anger draining from her face as awareness of her surroundings seemed to come back to her.

Akal took Susan's gun, then gently helped her to stand, and escorted her a few steps away from her husband as the doctor stepped forward to check on Henry. After checking his pulse and the wound, Robert looked up at Akal and subtly shook his head. The doctor then took charge of Susan, leading her into the living room. She went with him without protest, without looking back at her husband once she stepped away.

Akal holstered his gun and emptied the ammunition from Susan's rifle before following them inside. He found Mrs Parkins sitting on a chair in the living room with the doctor kneeling beside her, patting her hand as she stared blankly into the distance. He and Robert exchanged a quick glance. Robert asked the silent woman, 'Susan, can you tell us what happened? You said Henry had gone mad?'

'Yes. He was raving about killing John and that coolie woman. He said he wouldn't go to jail. He was waving a knife at me. I grabbed my gun and tried to run away, but he was too fast. Then I shot him.' She responded in monotone, the words dropping into the still air like rocks, then looked in horror at the doctor. 'I won't be arrested, will I?'

Akal contemplated the pale woman through narrowed eyes. 'He said that he killed Kunti?'

Susan slowly moved her gaze from the doctor to Akal and nodded with a set jaw.

'He denied it when I spoke with him earlier,' Akal said. 'He admitted to killing Brown but not Kunti. Can you explain that?'

'Can I explain the ravings of a madman? Of course I can't!' she cried, the words sounding as though they were forced out of a tight throat. 'Maybe he didn't want to admit it to himself, but he couldn't lie to me. What do you want me to say?'

Akal continued to contemplate her until the doctor interjected.

'For God's sake, Singh, put the poor woman out of her misery. Do you think she will be charged for killing Henry?'

Akal thought for a moment and concluded, 'Based on what you have said, it seems unlikely. If he threatened you with a knife, then you acted in self-defence. I do not think the inspector-general will want to pursue charges against you.'

Susan Parkins's distressed demeanour seemed to momentarily lift as she looked up sharply and considered Akal through narrowed eyes. The look was over so quickly that

Akal wondered if he had imagined it. The doctor certainly hadn't noticed.

'Thank you, Sergeant Singh, that is reassuring,' she said, her voice shaky.

'Do you know why he might have wanted to kill Kunti and your overseer?' Akal asked, staying back but slowly lowering himself down to be on her level.

Susan stared through him at first as though she hadn't heard the question, but her eyes gradually focused. Akal waited patiently for her reply.

'Well, I suppose ... I know he was obsessed with one of the coolie women. It might have been her. There was always one. I was never enough for him,' she responded, her words sounding as though they were dragged from her chest.

'What about John? His cousin, John Chalmers,' Akal asked, watching carefully to see her reaction to Brown's real name.

'John,' she spat. 'He ruined our lives. Henry would have been Lord Mayor of Sydney if John hadn't come back into his life.'

'He ruined your lives?' Akal probed. He ignored the doctor's disapproving frown. The woman might have been in shock, but this was the most forthcoming she had been since Akal had met her in Suva.

'He was always trouble, was John. That whole side of Henry's family was. The family came from old money, from England. Henry's aunt on his father's side married a wastrel and all the children came out the same way. Well, blood will tell. Henry's parents had nothing to do with them. But for Henry, John was like the brother he didn't have. They became inseparable, but John kept getting Henry into trouble. His parents tried to forbid Henry from the friendship, with no success.

They just started meeting in secret. And Henry was becoming more and more wild. Finally, after they stole gin from the local store, Henry's parents had had enough. They paid off John's family and moved them out to the sticks, out to Taree.'

'And that worked?'

'Yes, of course. Henry is inherently a good man. Away from John's influence, he straightened up, finished high school, and did well at university. He was going to run for a position in the Sydney City Council.'

The phrases had a cadence to them. They were well-rehearsed but performed without feeling, as though they were part of an Italian opera being sung by an English diva who hadn't cared to learn their meaning. But at the next stanza in her personal aria, her brow furrowed, and her voice hardened.

'But John came back into our lives, and something happened. Suddenly, Henry's parents sent us out here to look after the plantation instead of helping Henry with his political career. I don't know what it was. Something with a woman. As I said, there were always other women.'

'John came back into your lives?' Akal echoed. 'When was this?'

'A few years ago, while we were still in Sydney. I don't know how he found us, or how he insinuated himself back into Henry's good graces. The first I knew of it was when Henry invited him over for dinner. He introduced John as a school friend, and at first, I didn't connect the dots. John seemed like a nice enough man, friendly and unassuming. But when I remembered the name, remembered the stories Henry's mother had told us, I was worried. I asked Henry if it was a good idea to resume his friendship with John. He dismissed me. And for a while, I thought he'd been right. As far as I could see, Henry spent a little time with John occasionally, but nothing else had changed.'

'So, he didn't pull Henry back into trouble?'

'No. At least, I didn't think so. But he was clearly still trouble himself. He stopped coming around some time before we left Sydney. I didn't think much of it, he'd never been in steady work. I thought he must have just taken a job somewhere else. Anyway, we were too busy packing up to move here. But when he showed up at the plantation, less than a year after we arrived, with long hair and a beard he had never worn before, I knew he had done something. Henry was furious. But still he let him stay. I begged Henry to send him away, but he wouldn't even talk about it. Then John became our overseer, and we quickly fell into a rhythm, he and Henry here at the plantation and myself in Suva. Everything seemed normal, for years now.'

She paused and looked at Akal with wide, tear-filled eyes. 'Well, *almost* normal. Recently, there seemed to be money going missing. I asked Henry about it, and he got quite angry with me. I think he was giving it to John.'

'Why would your husband be giving his cousin money?' Akal asked, troubled by the inconsistent stories from Mr and Mrs Parkins. Henry had seemed genuinely puzzled when Akal had confronted him about the money.

'I have no idea.'

This last statement was said plaintively, and Susan Parkins turned teary eyes back to the doctor.

'Please, I'd like to rest.'

Robert looked at Akal, who nodded. He didn't have any further questions for the distraught woman. It seemed clear that Henry Parkins and his cousin John Chalmers had been bad men who came to a bad end. Tragically, they had taken Kunti out with them. The doctor resumed patting Susan's hand and lapsed back into soothing nothings as Akal went back outside.

Akal looked around the grass by Henry Parkins's body, searching for the knife that Susan Parkins had claimed she was threatened by, but without success. He squatted down by the body and considered the man who had ruined so many lives with his obsession with Kunti. Henry Parkins had seemed composed – unhappy about the investigation, but in control nonetheless – right up until the last few minutes of his life. Now, in repose, he seemed calm again. Henry's sightless eyes stared up into the azure sky. Akal pressed Parkins's eyelids down and immediately felt some of his unease ebb.

Akal steeled himself to search Henry's body for the knife. He started by rolling Henry up from one side and then the other to look underneath. The body was still warm and pliable, making the job harder and making Akal's skin crawl. He found crushed grass underneath, stained with blood, but no knife. Akal started methodically checking Henry's pockets in case the knife in question was easily concealable. He still didn't find a knife, but in the right pants pocket, thankfully spared the blood that was trickling down Parkins's chest, was the photograph of Kunti.

Akal stood and scanned the area again. There was no knife. He slowly started to walk back to the house, dreading the phone call he would have to make back to the station. This was not the quiet, clean wrap-up that the inspector-general had wanted.

Akal found Venkat and Divya at their room in the coolie lines that night. They were not surprised to see him. It seemed rumours of the day's happenings were running rampant through the community. Akal beckoned for them to join him outside, away from prying ears. He had learned all he needed to know about the lack of privacy in the rooms that afternoon.

The three of them walked, silent and tense, Divya clutching her father's hand. When they were out of earshot of the rest of the coolies, they came to a halt and Venkat asked, 'What has happened, Sergeant?'

Akal knelt until he was eye level with Divya, then pulled out the photo in his breast pocket and handed it to her. She looked at it for a long moment, despite the low light. When she looked up, Akal was relieved to see no tears, but rather a quiet dignity that made the little girl seem much older than her eight years.

'Who had it?' she asked.

'Mr Parkins,' he replied.

'Did he kill my mother?'

Akal nodded. He waited with dread for the question that he did not know how to answer, but it didn't come. It seemed that Divya did not need to ask why the man had killed her mother, which made his heart heavier again for the child. Divya turned and clung to her father, burying her face in his leg. Venkat absently patted her on the back.

'Divya *beti*, go back to the room. I will be there soon.'

Divya came over to Akal and joined her hands in front of her chest, bowing to him. '*Dhanyavaad*, Sergeant Singh.'

Akal met her eyes and said, 'You are welcome, Divya. I am so very sorry I couldn't bring your mother safely back to you.'

The little girl smiled up at him, tears finally welling. She turned and walked back to the coolie lines, spine straight and steps sure, if a little slow.

'What happened to Kunti?' Venkat asked.

Akal stood and filled him in on what they had learned.

'So, she was in a relationship with Parkins *sahib*, not Brown *sahib*?'

Akal glared at the man, infuriated by Venkat's continued refusal to see what had been done to his wife. 'She was not "in a relationship" with Parkins. He was forcing himself on her. You can't tell me you didn't know?'

Venkat folded his arms and replied with a set jaw, 'Kunti never said anything.'

'And what could you have done if she *had* said anything?' Akal asked sharply. 'Perhaps she was trying to spare you.'

'She was trying to spare me?' Venkat repeated scornfully. 'She was pregnant with his baby. How was that sparing me?'

'I don't think so,' Akal shot back, pausing between each word for emphasis. "I spoke with Magamma. She, too, was molested by Parkins, not Brown, like we thought. You already know she never fell pregnant while the *sahib* was forcing himself on her, but she has fallen pregnant with her own husband twice now. Mrs Parkins has not had a child. Henry Parkins could not have gotten Kunti pregnant,' Akal said. When Venkat didn't respond, Akal spelled it out further. 'That child was probably yours.'

They stared at each other in the dim light for a moment. Venkat looked away, and dashed tears from his eyes with the back of his hand, seeming more vulnerable than Akal had seen him thus far.

'I am sorry. I should have ...' Akal trailed off, unsure what he should have done. At a minimum, he should have held onto his temper about Venkat's treatment of his wife and found a gentler way to tell the man that the dead baby was his.

'No, you are right. I did not take care of my wife. I did not protect her. This is my shame.' Venkat rubbed his hand across his face wearily. 'Thank you, Sergeant Singh. You have, in a small way, given me back my wife. And my daughter was able to lay her mother to rest. So, it seems I must thank you. But you will understand why I say that I hope I don't see you again.'

Akal watched as Venkat returned to the coolie lines, shoulders slumped in lines of grief, in stark contrast to the upright posture his daughter had maintained when she had made the same journey. Venkat's bitterness towards Akal had little impact on him; Akal's focus was, as it had been since he arrived at the plantation, on Divya. Giving her some answers felt like the only truly good thing he had done since he left Hong Kong. He would finally be able to write to his father with something that he could be proud of.

Once Venkat had blended in with the other men from the community, Akal turned and walked back up the hill to the overseer's house. He and the doctor were returning to Suva first thing in the morning, and he wanted one more night of peace before the inspector-general took a sledgehammer and finally demolished whatever was remaining of the ruins of his career.

They set out for Suva just before noon the next day, the doctor leading once again, Susan Parkins in the middle, and Akal at the rear. The morning had dawned brightly, belying the tragic events of the previous day, and promising a scorching ride home.

Susan was accompanying them because she had said that she would not feel safe at the plantation on her own, just her and all the Indians. She had been disturbingly efficient in getting her husband buried that morning without any ceremony, a simple rock cairn marking the grave. He was buried next to Brown, the cousins who had been partners in crime together for eternity. Susan said she would have a priest perform a blessing the next time one was passing by.

Mrs Parkins had asked Robert to accompany her as she sought out Venkat and instructed him to keep the plantation going until she could arrange another European overseer to run the place. The doctor had likened her demeanour towards Venkat to that of an army drill sergeant, barking orders and threatening repercussions if everything wasn't in order when the new overseer arrived. Based on his previous experiences with her, Akal was not particularly surprised by this, except for one fact: the woman had killed her husband only yesterday. Riding behind her, he couldn't see her face, but looking at her upright, energetic posture in the saddle, she seemed untouched by grief.

As they passed by the coolie lines, Akal looked over, searching for Divya to give her a last wave goodbye. He didn't see her, but he did notice more movement and life around the two buildings than he had seen the day before. Two heavily pregnant women sat in the shade of a nearby tree, talking and laughing as they picked stones out of lentils, something Akal had seen the women of his village do countless times during his childhood. It seemed that Venkat was going to run the plantation with a little more humanity, giving the indentured servants a brief respite before the next overseer arrived.

They retraced their steps along the same path that had

brought them to the plantation five days ago. The sugar cane on their left farewelled them with a shushing noise as the breeze whispered through the leaves, until the fields ended and nature reasserted herself.

Akal entered the dense forest with a sense of relief, as thoughts of the plantation started to fade. He absently pushed a branch away from his face, an action now second nature, and began fretting about the report he would have to write once he returned to Suva. They were returning to Suva the same way they had come, which had taken the better part of a day, so it would be late when they arrived at their respective homes. Akal knew he would be working long into the night, writing and rewriting his report, trying to balance his need for the truth with his desire to win the inspector-general's approval.

THE FIJI TIMES,
SATURDAY, OCTOBER 10, 1914.

Emigration from India

Report on Conditions in British Colonies

The *Times of India Illustrated Weekly* in its latest edition has a notice of a report on Indian emigration to British Colonies.

'Two large and interesting volumes will be issued,' says this paper, 'containing reports by Messrs J. McNeill and Chiman Lal, who left England on 1st October, 1914. They will visit Trinidad, British Guiana, Jamaica and Fiji, to enquire into the conditions of Indian emigrants in those four British Colonies.'

CHAPTER NINE

Early the next afternoon, still weary from the long journey back to Suva and an even longer night wrestling over his report, Akal knocked on the door of the inspector-general's office. He imagined thunking his head against the door as he waited, but refrained from actually doing so, for fear of adding rumours of madness to his already tarnished reputation. Upon receiving the summons – 'Singh, get in here!' – Akal squared his shoulders once more and marched in. The room was unchanged, paperwork still covering every surface. The one difference this time was that the inspector-general had abandoned his paperwork and was glowering at Akal as soon as he stepped inside. Akal stood to attention before the desk.

'Let me see if I have this straight,' the inspector-general said, as he tapped Akal's case report on top of the other paperwork on his desk. 'I sent you out for a missing woman and you have come back with not one, not two … but *three* dead bodies?' His voice, which had started off quiet and controlled, rose in volume as he counted the bodies.

Akal swallowed and nodded once.

'I asked you to keep this simple, clean. And instead, you have not one, not two … but three coolie women being forced into sex with European men.'

Akal cleared his throat and responded quietly, 'Yes, sir. I

merely investigated the case.' He did not think Thurstrom particularly wanted to hear that Brown had likely forced himself on *all* the Indian women on the plantation.

Thurstrom let out a breath. 'Yes, you did. And nobody is going to thank you for it. Least of all me.'

Akal nodded once, the gesture taut with disappointment. He wasn't surprised by this response, but he had hoped that his superior officer would value justice over politics.

The inspector-general continued: 'I can see that your investigative skills may live up to what I was promised, but your ability to obey orders doesn't.'

Akal opened his mouth to respond but shut it again when the inspector-general glared sharply at him.

'You have one more chance to mitigate this disaster at least to some small degree, Singh. Rewrite this damn report. Leave the other women out of it. Keep it to the dead woman having an affair. A *consensual* affair.' The inspector-general's gaze shifted downwards, and he didn't look at Akal again. With this brief reprieve from Thurstrom's critical stare, Akal's shoulders dropped despondently out of their crisp posture. The room was silent for a moment as both men contemplated the command.

'This is not something I ask lightly, Sergeant,' Thurstrom said gravely, his usual glare missing. 'Those plantations need workers. Even if the native Fijians would work the cane, the governor won't allow it. It seems that preserving their way of life is more important to him than anything the planters have to say.' Thurstrom shook his head and sighed out a gust. 'This colony is not viable without the coolies. Your report, as it stands, adds fuel to the fire of those calling for the program to end. I can't allow a report coming out of this office to be used that way.'

This explanation was delivered without disdain or jibes. For that moment, Akal felt like a trusted colleague again, but he knew it was more likely to be a sign of how important this was, for Thurstrom to have set aside his animosity.

'Dismissed,' the inspector-general said quietly, holding the offending report out to Akal. Akal retrieved the report and left the room without a word, easing the door shut behind him. He stood outside the office staring down at the papers in his hand for a long time, his mind blank.

A few hours later, Akal sat at a table in a small room off the lobby of the Totogo Police Station, his unchanged report in front of him. He had watched the shadows lengthen across the floor and fade as the sun had started to set, but had made no progress. He kept turning the same considerations over and over again in his mind. Was it ethical to disobey orders which themselves seemed unethical? As he restarted the same circular logic once more, he heard Taviti calling out, but his fogged brain did not register that it might have been directed at him until a hand landed on his shoulder.

'Oi, man, are you alright?' Taviti's voice sounded like it came from another world. Akal shook his head and focused on Taviti's face.

'Taviti ... of course, yes, yes. I'm fine.'

'Did the inspector-general thank you for a job well done?' Taviti asked, cheeks bulging out as he suppressed his grin.

Akal rolled his eyes at his friend. 'What do you think?'

'Oh, yes, I think you are probably his favourite now,' Taviti said, nodding with a flourish.

'This sort of humour doesn't suit you,' Akal grumbled.

'So, what happened?' Taviti asked as he ushered Akal back into the lobby and over to the front desk so he could resume his post while they spoke. Akal leaned against the counter with his shoulders slumped.

'He wants me to rewrite the report and leave out the truth about what was happening to the coolie women.'

Taviti's eyebrows shot up. 'Are you sure? That doesn't sound like the inspector-general. He always wants the reports written properly, no detail missed.'

'This is not a normal case. What do I tell Mr Choudry?'

'Do you need to tell him anything?'

'He asked for a copy of the report.'

'He isn't your boss. You don't have to send it to him. What can he do to you?'

'Have you seen how the coolies live? I think I do have to send it to him.'

They stood contemplating the report on the counter between them for a moment. Akal tapped on the papers and said slowly, 'Here is another thing that worries me. What if I submit this report thinking it is the truth and everybody starts shouting here and in England and in India? What happens then, if it turns out I have got something wrong?'

'I thought it was all wrapped up neat and tight?' Taviti asked, puzzled.

'Well, yes. I wrote the report that way. Henry Parkins is dead, and he confessed. It seems pretty final, doesn't it? But, between you and me, there are still some things ... Like Mr Parkins. He didn't actually ever tell me he killed Kunti. He said he couldn't. So why did he tell his wife that he did?'

Taviti shrugged. 'I tell my wife things I don't tell anyone

else. You wouldn't know, bachelor that you are.' He seemed relieved that Akal's argument was so easily defeated.

'Well, then, how about the fact that I didn't find the knife?' Akal warmed to his topic, now invested in talking Taviti around to his point of view.

'What knife?'

'Susan Parkins said her husband was threatening her with a knife, and that is why she shot him. But I didn't find a knife anywhere near his body. And there were no knives missing from the kitchen.'

'Maybe she put it back?'

'You think a woman who just killed her husband is worried about her cutlery?' Akal asked, arching a disbelieving eyebrow at Taviti.

'Okay, okay, bosso. So, you have a missing knife and a husband telling his wife something that he didn't tell you. Anything else?'

'Yes, there is something else,' Akal retorted. 'How about the timing? I just do not know how there was enough time for what she described. Henry Parkins ran up to the house, found a knife, and threatened her. She ran back inside and got a gun and shot him. We were not that far behind Mr Parkins.'

'Are you sure? Hadn't you hit your head?'

'Well … yes, I had. And no, I'm not sure,' Akal replied, his last statement muttered resentfully.

They pondered on it for another moment, and then Taviti slapped his hand down on the documents with a clap.

'Leave it, man. Everyone is dead. There is nothing left to follow up. You are in enough of a mess as it is.'

'Well, actually, there is one thing I didn't get to. Remember Lewis Robinson? I didn't speak with him again.'

'Oh yes, Lewis Robinson. He got into some trouble yesterday. Public drunkenness. The constables didn't bring him in, just cited him and sent him home.'

'Why didn't you tell me?' Akal asked, thumping Taviti on the arm.

'I didn't know you were still interested in him. What do you want to ask him?'

'About his relationship with the oh-so-charming Mrs Parkins. See if he had any knowledge of what was going on at the plantation. Get an outside perspective on it.'

Taviti looked sceptical, but shrugged and said, 'Sure, why not. If it will get you to drop this, let's see if we can find him.'

Taviti dug through the files on the desk and pulled one out.

'Here it is. He was cited outside the Rewa Hotel.'

'Well then, how about we go get a drink?'

'*Gerrroffame!*'

The garbled shout came from a European man who had managed to wedge himself into the front door of the Rewa Hotel. His hands were restrained behind his back and the two Fijian men who were evicting him were pushing him out from behind.

Taviti and Akal joined the small crowd that had gathered to watch the antics. They observed with amusement as the European man continued to hurl slurred expletives in English at his two captors, who responded with insults in Fijian.

Slowly but surely, the burly Fijians pushed him out the door until he gave way and landed cheek-first on the road in a burst of dust. Hands now free, the dishevelled man pushed his way into a seated position, and Akal got a good look at his face once the crowd around them lost interest and cleared.

'Hello, Mr Robinson. I would like to have a word with you about Susan Parkins.'

At hearing that name, Lewis became agitated again, stumbling as he tried to stand. 'That bitch!' He spat out the words. 'Look what she did to me.'

'What did she do to you?' Akal asked, approaching with his hand out in a calming gesture, as Taviti went to help him get on his feet.

'Getting drunk during the day. Fighting. I used to be a good person,' he said, trying half-heartedly to pull his right arm away from Taviti. 'And then I met her. She ruined me,' he ended on a whine.

'Mrs Parkins ruined you?' Akal asked.

'She pretends to be so demure, she looks like an angel,' Lewis sneered. 'If you only knew.'

Akal's nose started to twitch. There was something here. Something that might lay his concerns to rest.

'Why don't we go back to the station and sit down. We can have a nice chat,' he said, laying a comforting hand on the drunk man's shoulder. Akal and Taviti took over on either side of Lewis and supported him as they staggered back to the station.

'You just couldn't leave it, could you?' Taviti asked, turning his nose away from their pungent burden.

'A chat, that's all,' Akal said, straight-faced and innocent. Taviti gave him a disbelieving look, and Akal could hardly blame him.

◀▮▶ ◀▮▶ ◀▮▶

'Could I get a rum?'

The muffled request came from the cavern Lewis had fashioned with his arms on the table, where he was hiding his head. From across the scratched wooden surface, Akal frowned. He wasn't going to get much out of the man in this sorry state.

'How about a coffee?' Taviti suggested. 'I think you could do with one.'

'Rum,' Lewis groaned.

'Coffee it is,' Taviti responded cheerfully as he left the room.

When Akal had met Lewis at the plantation, Lewis had been cordial and polite, much more so than the Parkinses had been. Akal thought that his best strategy here would be to befriend him. 'It looks like you have had a bad day. What has brought you so low, Lewis?' Akal asked sympathetically.

Lewis lifted his head and looked at Akal blearily over his crossed forearms. Blood smeared his right cheek where he had sustained a cut during his scuffle as he was evicted from the hotel.

'Susan Parkins.' The venom in his voice made her name a curse.

'You seemed quite close to her at the plantation,' Akal said, careful to keep the judgement out of his voice.

'I thought we were.' The indignation in Lewis's voice seemed to propel him upright in a moment of clarity. 'I thought she loved me.'

Akal felt a sense of kinship with the heartbroken man and saw an opportunity to increase their connection. 'I knew a woman like that once. I thought she cared for me. But she ruined my life, too.'

Lewis looked a little more at peace – perhaps grateful to

be understood, perhaps just relieved to have told the truth, so Akal gently probed for more information: 'But Susan Parkins, she is a married woman.'

'Pfft,' Lewis snorted, not noticing that he was spraying spittle across the table. 'That was no marriage. They didn't even live together. He had his coolie women on the plantation, she had me in Suva.'

'And you were satisfied with that?'

'No.' Lewis shrugged, causing his head to wobble dangerously. It took him a moment to refocus before he continued between hiccups. 'She said ... she said ... she couldn't leave him. She wanted the Planters' Association leadership. She married him ...' Once more he paused, his eyes closed, then blinking open blearily. 'He was going to be Lord Mayor of Sydney. Power ... all she cares about.'

'That was more important to her than a life with you?'

Lewis nodded, his shoulders starting to shake as he quietly sobbed.

'And now? Her husband is dead. Shouldn't you be by her side?'

A tear ran a path through the blood on Lewis's cheek. 'She won't even see me. I knocked on her front door this morning, now that I can. She tried to have her house girl turn me away, but I wasn't having any of that. I've waited long enough to be with her. I went around the back and let myself in the way I always do.' He snorted in disbelief. 'She seemed surprised. Surprised! That I dared to let myself in against her wishes.'

'What did she say when she saw you?'

'She was packing, going back to Australia. No point staying here, she said.' Lewis closed his eyes tightly as if reliving the moment. His voice was getting progressively louder. 'I said,

"What about me? Aren't I a reason to stay? I could come with you." She just looked at me like I was an idiot. "It has been a pleasant diversion," she said. "But that's all. Just a diversion." Just a diversion! Was it just a diversion when she asked me to kill that woman?' Lewis shouted.

Silence reverberated around the room. The shock of his declaration seemed to have instantly sobered Lewis up. He sat bolt upright now, wide-eyed and ashen.

Akal tried to keep his voice gentle and curious, though his guts were clenched in anticipation. 'You killed Kunti?'

'No. God, no,' Lewis choked out. 'She offered me a lot of money, but I said no. I couldn't believe she had asked me.'

'Of course, you seem like a good man,' Akal said soothingly. His attention had snagged on something else Lewis had said, his mind flashing back to a pillowcase full of money inside a blackened soup pot. 'How much money did she offer you?'

'Two hundred pounds. She thought my soul was worth two hundred pounds.'

And there it was, the same amount of money Akal had found in Brown's kitchen.

'Mrs Parkins must have had a reason. Did she you tell you why?'

'She said her husband needed to clean up his act for the election. But when I said no, she laughed the idea off as a joke. I believed her. I didn't think anything of it when the newspaper report came out. It's only when I saw you at the plantation that I started to wonder. But then I heard a rumour that Brown was in the river as well, and it seemed like something else must have happened. I didn't want to believe it.'

At that moment, Taviti bustled back into the room.

'Coffee. It's not good,' he said placing the mugs on the table.

When neither of them responded, Taviti looked from Lewis to Akal and back again. 'What happened here?'

Both men ignored him, and Akal leaned forward, all pretence of indifference forgotten. 'So, you believe that Mrs Parkins had Kunti killed?'

Taviti gasped audibly, but snapped his mouth shut when Akal glared at him.

Lewis was silent for a few moments, then slowly shook his head. 'I don't know. I think it's possible.' He closed his eyes and slumped towards the table, face starting to look a little green. 'I drank too much.'

'Did she say anything else about this after your first conversation?' Akal asked urgently.

Lewis shook his head, eyes still closed, his chin grazing his chest. 'We hardly saw each other after that. The only time I saw her again was when she asked me to take her out to the plantation.' He harrumphed gently and slumped farther until his head was once again cradled in his arms on the table. The next words came out muffled.

'I was so happy when she asked me. I thought it meant something. It's not like she needed me. Normally she rides out there by herself. Carries her rifle with her. She's pretty handy with it.'

Akal could believe how handy Susan was with her rifle, given she had shot her husband with it. So why had she asked for an escort? It clearly wasn't about a desire to be near her lover, considering that she had thrown him aside so easily. Kunti was already 'missing' when Lewis had escorted Susan to the plantation, so it was not another bid to have Lewis kill Kunti. Could it have been an attempt to hide the fact that she could get to and from the plantation on her own? If so, why would Susan feel the need to hide that fact? It was time for another conversation with the newly widowed Mrs Parkins.

Akal questioned Lewis Robinson for another thirty minutes until the man could no longer keep his eyelids open, but learned little else. Taviti then completed the paperwork to process Lewis's arrest for public drunkenness, which took much longer than usual given Taviti had to keep stopping to wake Lewis back up again. Akal paced in the background, champing at the bit to go question Susan Parkins. Finally, they wrestled Lewis into a cell and left him snoring on his cot.

By the time they left the station, the sun had long departed. The journey up Knolly Street was hazardous in the dark. Taviti trotted along, swerving to avoid the potholes that sprang up under his feet, cursing quietly under his breath. Akal ignored him, forging forward through the inky night. The potholes appeared to be leaping out of his way.

'Bloody hell, man. Slow down!' Taviti exclaimed.

'What?' Akal said, swivelling around. This distraction broke his focus, and he immediately turned his ankle in a small crevice in the ground. 'Damn it.'

'Sorry,' Taviti said, puffing a little as he caught up to Akal. 'Are you alright?'

'No,' Akal said tersely. He awkwardly balanced his injured ankle against his other knee, using Taviti as a support and rubbing his ankle with his other hand. 'Why are you going so slowly? We aren't out for a midnight stroll.'

'What's the rush? She can't go anywhere. The ship to Australia isn't leaving until tomorrow.'

Akal's face creased in frustration. 'I don't know. I just need to get this figured out.'

'What are you going to do, anyway? We don't have any real evidence against her.'

Akal scowled. 'If this was a black man's house we were going to, would it matter?'

'No. But it isn't a black man's house. It is a white woman's house. What are you going to do, change the way the world works on our little trip up the hill?'

'I don't know.' Akal sighed. "Let's just ask her some questions and see what happens.'

'You better hope *nothing* happens. Otherwise, you won't have to worry about getting back to Hong Kong anymore. The inspector-general will kill you himself.'

'I'll be careful,' Akal said, with no idea of how he could possibly fulfil this promise.

'Okay, bosso.' Taviti shrugged, his good nature restored with his breath. 'But do you think we could try to do this without breaking our necks?'

They set out again, forced to a slower pace with Akal limping. Now he was the one cursing under his breath.

The Parkinses' garden was sinister in the dark, the bougainvillea reaching out its spindly branches to scratch and grab at them. Akal brushed away the branches along with his sense of unease. Taviti knocked on the door, the rapping echoing like gunshots in the hush of the night. After a moment, the door was opened. Expecting a house girl, Akal was surprised to see Susan Parkins opening her own door, clad in the homeliest attire Akal had yet seen her wear: a shapeless long nightdress in coarse blue cotton under a thin robe. She stiffened when she saw Akal and Taviti.

'What are you doing here?' Susan asked warily. 'It is the middle of the night. You can't just stop by whenever you want.'

'We are here on official business,' Akal replied sternly. 'May we come in?'

'What official business? It's over.' Mrs Parkins wrapped her arms around herself.

'There are some questions we need answered. It won't take long. May we come in?' Akal repeated.

'Questions that meant you needed to come here at this time of night? No, you may not,' Susan snapped.

'We heard you are leaving tomorrow for Australia,' Akal replied. He felt calmer, more in control now that Susan Parkins was in front of him, and he could ask the questions that had been burning in his mind.

She looked down her nose at Akal, quite a feat given her diminutive height. 'And what of it?'

'It is very sudden.'

Susan stiffened. 'My husband is dead. I can hardly stay in Fiji on my own.'

'You have been living in Suva on your own for quite some time. Why is it different now?'

'These are your questions? What has this got to do with your investigation?'

'Were you in a relationship with Mr Lewis Robinson?'

'Certainly not,' she scoffed.

'He contends that you asked him to kill Kunti.'

She gasped. 'He said what?'

'Mr Robinson said that you asked him to clean up your husband's affairs so it wouldn't embarrass him with the upcoming Planters' Association election. He said you offered him a substantial sum of money to kill Kunti. Now, why would he say these things?'

Susan Parkins took a deep breath. She was visibly composing herself and her next statement was uttered in such a detached tone that it put Akal on edge.

'The man has previously made improper advances. I rejected him. He is obviously jealous. He must have run mad to say such things.'

'That seems to happen to the men you have relationships with,' Akal observed, one eyebrow crooked.

'I said I was not in a relationship with Lewis Robinson,' she replied with a biting tone.

'What about Mr Brown? We found a lot of money in his house. When Mr Robinson refused you, did you approach the overseer instead?'

Susan laughed incredulously. 'You are just making this up as you go along!'

Akal changed the topic a little, trying to keep her guessing. 'Why did you ask Mr Robinson to take you out to the plantation?'

'I needed an escort. He knows the way,' she replied, speaking slowly as though Akal might have trouble understanding.

'You asked a man to take you on a remote journey when he had previously made improper advances?' Akal made no effort to hide his incredulity.

'There were not many options available.'

'Why did you need an escort? Mr Robinson tells us that you were perfectly capable of making the journey on your own.'

The diminutive woman laughed and swept her hands down her body. 'Capable of making it on my own? Look at me. Do you imagine I'm going to traipse through the wilderness without any protection?' She smiled at Taviti, a sweet sort of smile, radiating delicacy and gentleness.

'Mr Robinson says you are very proficient with guns.' Akal considered her with his head tilted to the side. 'Kunti was shot.'

Susan Parkins narrowed her eyes, dropping her helpless façade. 'Mr Robinson seems to have told you all sorts of stories. Who is going to believe a rejected suitor over a well-established member of the community?'

Akal nodded slowly, deciding to change tack again. The Lewis Robinson line of questioning seemed to be exhausted. Perhaps a threat to her reputation would achieve some results. 'You may be right. Did you know, Mrs Parkins, that I've been asked to send a copy of my report to the Indian delegation who were here recently? Mr Choudry was very interested to know what is going on out at the plantations. I think he will find the reports of your husband's dealings with the Indian women under his power fascinating,' Akal said, the menace evident in his voice.

'Hmm ... I met Mr Choudry at the gala at the Grand Pacific,' Mrs Parkins said, another small smile playing on her lips. 'He left with the rest of the delegation, didn't he? What do you imagine he will be able to do?'

She was clearly unimpressed by his threat. Akal, running out of ways to crack Susan Parkins's confidence, put his hands on his hips and stood up as straight as possible to his full imposing height, doubling down on his attempt to intimidate. 'Well, Mrs Parkins, I imagine he has good contacts with the press in London. And you know what the press are like. This will be in the papers in Australia before very long.'

They waited on the verandah, all suspended in place and

time, as Akal's words sunk in. When Susan continued to smile, Akal turned to Taviti and said wearily, 'Let's go. I've got a report to write.'

As he followed Taviti down the stairs, Akal glanced back to see Susan Parkins standing where they had left her, her eyes darting from side to side. Perhaps the questioning had rattled her after all. The two men walked out into the garden before they gave each other a sideways glance, shrugging, wordlessly expressing the same sentiment – there was little more they could do. She was probably right that nobody would listen, and although they now knew the truth, nobody else ever would.

Their silent communication was interrupted by the sound of a gun being cocked behind them. Akal turned back to find Mrs Parkins walking down the verandah stairs, her rifle trained on him.

'I can't let you write that report,' she said, her voice shaking but her hand steady. 'I'm going back to Australia, and I am finding a better husband this time. Who will have me with that police report floating around?'

'How are you going to explain two dead police officers?' Akal asked, maintaining eye contact. The rest of his being was focused on the gun.

'Two black men in my house in the middle of the night?' She gave a little shiver, a little catch of the breath, becoming a parody of a frightened child. 'It's dark. I thought it was the Night Prowler.'

Akal took a step towards Mrs Parkins, putting himself between Taviti and the rifle. A gunshot rang out, and Akal fell blindly forward, Taviti's entire weight crashing into him. Time slowed as Susan Parkins expertly pulled the bolt back to eject the spent cartridge, taking a step back as the bodies toppled at her feet.

As she loaded her next shot, Akal reached out and grabbed her by the ankles, pulling her feet out from under her. The shot she fired discharged harmlessly into the night sky above. She landed on her back, stunned, the rifle falling into the grass beside her.

Akal heaved himself out from under Taviti's weight and scrambled to his feet, kicking the rifle away from Mrs Parkins and retrieving his own sidearm. He aimed at Susan, who was trying to get to her feet, and she froze.

'Susan Parkins, you are under arrest for assaulting an officer of the law.'

Moments ticked by as they remained in this dimly lit tableau – Taviti prostrate at Susan Parkins's feet, Susan glaring venom at Akal, and Akal standing with his gun trained on her body. Akal tried to determine what to do next. He couldn't take his eyes off Susan Parkins for a moment. To his relief he felt, rather than saw, Taviti stir.

'Taviti. Are you alright?' Akal asked, moving around so he could see both Susan Parkins and Taviti.

'Yes … yes, I think so. What happened?' Taviti responded groggily.

'You saved my life.'

'Of course I did. Had to happen eventually, the way you go around annoying women until they decide to shoot you,' Taviti said, his voice still a little thready despite his teasing words.

He took a deep breath and levered himself off the ground

with his good arm. He stood, swaying, and clasped his left hand over his bleeding right shoulder. When he pulled his hand away and looked at his blood-covered palm, Taviti greyed and his sway became more pronounced.

'Come and help me with Mrs Parkins,' Akal said sharply to snap Taviti into action before he could faint.

Taviti looked over and nodded, regaining his colour as he moved over to Akal.

'What are we going to do now?' Taviti asked. He sounded worried, something Akal had never heard in his voice before.

'Let me go before this gets worse for you,' Susan called out.

'We take her to the station, get her in a cell, then we get you patched up,' Akal responded, ignoring Susan. He hoped his matter-of-fact tone would calm Taviti. He hoped that he could fool himself into being calm as well.

Taviti looked at him wide-eyed. 'Are you sure? They won't let her go to jail. Can't we just ...' He trailed off.

'Just what? She shot you, Taviti. She shot a police officer. We don't have any choice at this point.'

Susan Parkins laughed scornfully from her position on the ground.

'Listen to your native friend, Constable Coolie. I won't stand trial. And I promise you, when I get out, I will ensure that your life is ruined.'

Akal laughed derisively at her threat. 'You just shot the nephew of a powerful chief. My life might be ruined, but I don't believe that you are going to walk away from this as easily as you seem to think.'

The gravity of the situation seemed to sink in for Susan Parkins. The defiance drained away from her face, and for the first time, Akal saw fear. Finally, Susan Parkins's presence matched her small stature.

'Come along,' Akal said to Taviti. 'Let's get her to the station and see how much trouble I just got myself into.'

The report didn't take that long to update. In a furious rush which left him with an aching hand, Akal added all the details of the night before to the report, unadulterated. There was little hope for a cover-up now, with Susan Parkins in jail for shooting Taviti. But the chances that she would stand trial for the murders of her husband and Kunti seemed slim. It appeared that nobody in the colonial administration wanted to deal with prosecuting her.

When Akal had returned to the station in the morning, it was to the unwelcome news that Lewis Robinson had been released without charge. Akal had stormed into town, knocking on every door he could think of, until the shipping line's ticketing office had revealed that Lewis had departed that morning on a ship bound for Australia. Further questioning had revealed that he had been accompanied by a uniformed police officer, who had made it clear that Mr Robinson needed to be on the ship regardless of any ticketing processes. It seemed that Thurstrom had ensured that their one witness who could have testified against Susan Parkins would be conveniently unavailable. At this point, Taviti's elevated position in the colony was the only reason she remained in jail.

Setting the report aside, Akal placed a few blank sheets of paper onto the table beside him. He laid the pen down, stood, and walked to the edge of Dr Holmes's verandah, considering the ocean sparkling ahead of him. The doctor had sent a note inviting Taviti and Akal for a sundowner and dinner at his house to celebrate wrapping up the case. With the doctor's consent, Akal had arrived early, affording him a quiet place to complete his report away from the noise of the police barracks and the sphere of the inspector-general's influence. Here, on the doctor's verandah, the decision to be completely honest was easier to make, despite the likely consequences.

The next choice Akal had to make was more troubling. Telling the truth in his police report was his duty, and hiding the abuses was unethical. The morality of the situation was clear, regardless of the personal repercussions for his career. The larger quandary before him now was whether to go further than that and share with Mr Choudry what he had learned about the treatment of the Indian women on the plantations. He was under no legal obligation to tell Mr Choudry anything, but he was contemplating defying his commanding officer and betraying the police service to do something with an impact far beyond putting a murderer in jail.

Akal walked down to the beach and sat under a coconut palm, sifting the warm sand with his fingers. This country was so different from his home, and so different from Hong Kong, but the warmth of it was starting to sink into his bones.

He thought about the cases he had solved in Hong Kong to much acclaim. None of those cases had been as important as this one. None of them had revealed anything that could shatter the foundation of a society, as this case had. None of them had had the potential to save a class of people from the kind of systemic abuse this case had revealed. And none of them had cost Akal anything personally – but this one was going to cost him everything he had worked so hard to regain.

Akal put his hand in his pocket, rubbed the well-worn paper of his father's letter, and thought of his parents. His mother would expect him to follow the rules and not jeopardise his standing in the police force. He had formed an emotional callus when it came to disappointing his mother, but disappointing his father would have had a sharp sting to it. Fortunately, this was unlikely to happen, as his father would understand his predicament. Akal so rarely let his father down; not because Akal was a paragon, but because his father, despite never leaving his village, had a deep understanding of the world. In this situation, his father would expect him to follow his conscience.

Decision made, Akal returned to the house and picked up his pen again to write two letters. One to Mr Choudry, conveying to him the details of the case and his observations on the coolie lines. Akal didn't know what actions Mr Choudry would take with this information. He didn't know when Mr Choudry was due to deliver his report from the visit to Fiji, but this letter's progress to his forwarding address in London was likely to be circuitous.

Akal knew that there were agitations in India to end the indentured servitude program altogether. This letter would almost certainly come to light eventually as part of this political movement, and it would do so with his name on it. Akal could only hope that this would take some time and he would have escaped his exile in Fiji by then. Otherwise, he could not predict the consequence of writing this letter, but they would be more severe than being stuck on the Night Prowler case forever.

Akal wrote the second letter, the one to his father, much more slowly, each word dropping onto the paper like a pebble dropping into his stomach, leaving him heavy with regret. In this letter, he put words to his fears. Acknowledging these to his father, without covering up his feelings with quips and humour, left him feeling wrung out.

He had finished writing his letters and was back to contemplating the beach when the doctor arrived.

'Akal. Did you get your report written?' said Robert as he came up the stairs.

'Yes, Doctor, all done.'

'Excellent. Time for a well-deserved gin, then.' The doctor grinned and moved towards the door.

'Doctor *sahib*, before we relax, can I please ask you to do something for me?' Akal said, his words coming out more hesitantly than usual.

Robert moved back towards him, a curious look on his face. Akal handed him the letter to Mr Choudry.

'Would you please ensure that this letter reaches the forwarding address in London? Perhaps when you send your next reports back to England? It is quite sensitive, and I want to be sure that it reaches its destination.'

Robert nodded, considering the address on the letter. 'So, you are sending a report to the chappie from the delegation, as he requested. Well done, young man. Let's see if this makes any difference for the coolies. I'll make sure it gets there.'

The doctor took the letter inside as Akal leaned back against the banister, tension draining from him and leaving his limbs loose. He had thought he was doing the right thing, but the doctor's approval of his course of action provided a validation that Akal hadn't realised he needed.

Taviti arrived just as the doctor came out with a tray with three drinks on it.

'*Bula*,' all three of them chorused, breaking into grins. It was a word that was impossible to say with anything other than joy.

'Perfect timing, Taviti,' Robert said, handing Taviti a glass. Taviti accepted it awkwardly in his left hand. His right arm was immobilised in a splint, which the doctor himself had fitted. The doctor ushered them towards the mismatched seats he had set up on the balcony and kneeled next to Taviti.

'How is your arm?' he asked as he checked the splint to make sure it was still properly in place.

'Fine, Dr Holmes. Thank you for taking care of me so late in the night.'

'It looks fine, Taviti,' Robert said, pushing himself up from his kneeling position with a groan. 'Now just stop getting yourself shot. Aren't you supposed to be permanently on desk duty? What are you doing following our Akal here into danger?'

Before Akal could protest, Taviti cut in to reply. 'No more behind the desk for me,' he said, puffing his chest out. 'I have proven myself now. I will be speaking with my uncle and making sure I am given proper policing duties.'

'Wonderful,' Akal said ruefully. 'I wonder how many cases you will have solved before I get off this bloody Night Prowler.'

'Oh, yes,' Taviti said, wide-eyed. 'I heard that the inspector-general tore a strip off you.'

Akal filled them in on his conversation with Thurstrom the night before. The news about Susan Parkins's arrest had spread like wildfire. Before Akal could leave the station, the inspector-general had burst in, uniform askew. He had pointed a shaking finger at Akal and stormed into his office, Akal following in his wake. For the subsequent half-hour, Akal stood stoically to attention as Thurstrom shouted at him for his insubordination.

There was little Thurstrom could do officially. Despite his ranted assertions that Akal should have left well enough alone as he had been told to, they both knew that Akal had done his duty. Nonetheless, the inspector-general followed through on his initial promise: Akal was back on the Night Prowler case, which had gone nowhere in his absence.

'So, I will be chasing the Night Prowler until we catch the bugger, or until I'm grey,' Akal concluded gloomily.

'And what did you put in your report?' Taviti asked.

'The truth,' Akal answered with a helpless shrug. 'What would be the point in covering anything up? I don't think I'll get back to Hong Kong anytime soon. At least this way, I can hold my head high.'

'I knew it. I knew you wanted to stay in Fiji. It's because you love me, isn't it?' Taviti's grin covered two-thirds of his face as he reached out with his good arm, ready to hug Akal.

'No, no, I think it's because we thrashed his team at cricket, and he needs to redeem himself,' the doctor quipped.

The two continued in this vein, throwing around increasingly absurd theories on what had motivated Akal to ruin his career. Akal laughed along with them, his heart lightening. While these two men weren't the reason he had told the truth in his report, they were going to make it easier to stay in Fiji. He slipped his hand in his pocket and rubbed the letter from his father between his fingers again. His father had faith that there was a plan to all of this. Akal, in turn, would try to have faith that part of the plan included him staying in Fiji for longer than he had hoped.

Taviti finally gave a sufficiently absurd explanation,

something about a chicken, that the doctor started laughing uncontrollably. And then Taviti started laughing, his booming laughter rolling out past the verandah, down the beach, and over the ocean. Akal looked at his two friends with a smile and surrendered to the laughter. Surrendered to Fiji.

AUTHOR'S NOTE

I am a Fijian Indian Australian, a combination which is reasonably well understood in Oceania, but raises some eyebrows elsewhere in the world. This means I was born in Fiji, am of Indian heritage and grew up in Australia, where we migrated when I was three. My family had strong connections back to Fiji, with much of our extended family back there. I grew up vaguely knowing that sometime in the dim and distant past, my antecedents had gone from India to Fiji to work in the sugar cane plantations. The how and why of this migration was a matter of no interest to me for my childhood and early adulthood, absorbed as I was in modern Australian life.

In my late twenties, I travelled in India and that experience changed my perspective dramatically. I had never really identified as Indian. I wasn't ashamed of my ethnicity; I was just really removed from it. Travelling in India was an emotional experience for me. The depth and breadth of the poverty was confronting. Driving from Delhi to Agra, I witnessed a woman on the side of the road picking up cow dung with her bare hands, likely for fuel. I was in tears. I think for the first time in my life I had a living, breathing, visual representation of what it might have meant if my ancestors hadn't gone to Fiji. It left me wondering – who were these people who came before me, who had made this decision that gave me a life they likely couldn't have imagined?

The Indian indentured servitude program had been established by the Indian government under British rule and came into its own when slavery was abolished in the British Empire. Under this program, Indians were being sent all over the world, to places like Trinidad, Jamaica, and Mauritius. The conditions varied slightly from country to country, but generally involved signing a contract for a fixed period, with fixed work required daily, for a fixed rate of pay, with accommodation and return sea journeys included. To destitute, indigent Indians, it must have seemed like a godsend.

Unfortunately, the system was primed for abuse. Unscrupulous agents in India signed up illiterate workers with a fingerprint or an 'X' on a contract, misrepresenting the contract conditions. Working conditions on the plantations made the daily task difficult to achieve. Ruthless plantation owners had complete control over every element of the lives of the Indians on their plantations, and corporal punishment was de rigueur.

When the sugar plantations of Fiji needed workers and the British governor of Fiji didn't want to interfere with the native population's way of life, the decision was made to import cheap and plentiful labour via the indentured servant program. From 1879 to 1916, over sixty thousand Indians went to Fiji as indentured servants, or *girmityas*. About half of them cashed in their return trip to India, leaving about thirty thousand to start a new life in Fiji. My great-grandparents were part of this thirty thousand.

My research process included a couple of months in Fiji in 2016, spending time at the Sir Alport Barker Library at the National Archives. I also spent some quality time at Births, Deaths and Marriages, trying to track down my great-grandparents. Boy do I know how to have fun. I think I went to the beach once. During this research, as well as the general background on Fiji and the indenture system, I found the inspiration for three people in the book – Akal, Kunti and Chop Chop.

I'm sure you recognise the first two, but you may be wondering – who is Chop Chop? If you look back through the article snippets at the beginning of the chapters, you will see that the byline for several of them is 'Chop Chop'. Chop Chop was an anonymous newspaper columnist, whose biting commentary on the politics of the time really caught my eye.

Akal came to me when I read, also in the *Fiji Times*, about a group of ten Sikh police officers who had come over from Hong Kong and were performing with distinction. This was organised by the governor of Hong Kong, who had previously been the governor of Fiji, to help build out the fledgling police force in Fiji. I've always imagined two moustachioed, grey-haired men sitting in overstuffed leather armchairs in a room full of wood panelling, complaining over the difficulty of getting good staff in these colonial outposts. The good old boys' network in action.

With Kunti, I borrowed the name and have made a nod towards the story of a real woman. Kunti was an indentured labourer who was sent to an isolated place to work as punishment. While she was there, the plantation's overseer came, restrained her, and made 'improper suggestions toward her'. She escaped and threw herself into the river, and was rescued by a boy who was in a dinghy nearby. Her story made it to the newspapers in India and highlighted the degradation of Indian women on colonial plantations, sparking a campaign to end the Indian indenture program altogether.

I also wanted to run through a couple of liberties I have taken with historical accuracy. In the scene towards the beginning of the book, where Akal visits the doctor at the hospital, my descriptions are based on the Colonial War Memorial Hospital which stands to this day. It was not constructed until 1923, but I couldn't find any descriptions of the hospital that existed in 1914.

I've taken a similar liberty with timelines on the descriptions of the coolie lines, as I wanted to show the conditions that the earliest indentured servants would have had to live under, but it didn't quite fit in with the timing I wanted for the novel. The requirements for accommodations for the indentured labourers was heavily regulated. The descriptions I've provided were based on the original requirements, which were changed by 1912. For example, I've got the cooking area being inside the room. By 1912, the regulation stated that 'There shall be provided to each dwelling, for the use of the immigrants to whom such dwelling may be assigned, a kitchen or cooking shed roofed with galvanised iron and of such dimensions as may be necessary. Such kitchen shall be placed at a distance not exceeding thirty feet from the dwelling to which it appertains.'

Finally, a word on the article snippets at the beginning of the chapters. Largely the article snippets are actual articles from the *Fiji Times* from the period, though not necessarily for the dates mentioned. The intention was that each article would illuminate some element of life in Fiji.

Unfortunately, as far as I can tell, the only place to see back copies of the *Fiji Times* is in Suva, on an ancient microfilm machine at the National Archives. I took some copies when I was there in 2016 (with permission) and intended to go back when I was close to finishing to find the perfect articles. The global COVID pandemic put paid to those plans.

As I write, Melbourne, where I live, is in our strictest lockdown, with everything closed and nightly curfews. Fiji, which survived 2020 with barely any cases, now has the highest rates of daily COVID infections per capita in the world. I have made do with the articles that I had and had to be a little creative in filling in some gaps. The main example of this is the article at the beginning of chapter 8. The text is genuinely from the housing provisions of 1912 but the timing and the concept of this as a newspaper article is entirely fictional.

I have sought out whatever information I could about the political and social environment of the time, as well as questions of daily life. My sources of information included government gazettes (sort of like minutes of government meetings discussing legislation under debate and general administration of the colony) and copies of the *Fiji Times* from the time period.

I wasn't always successful in finding answers to my questions, particularly when it came to the daily lives of the Indian indentured labourers. There is virtually nothing available in terms of first-person accounts from the indentured labourers, given that most of them were illiterate. And somehow, it is not a thing that was ever discussed in my family. Since I've started looking into this, I've wondered if there is a lingering sense of shame about that part of the family history.

If you would like to read more on my research process for the book, please take a look at my blog, https://nilimagoes2fiji. wordpress.com/.

If you would like more information on the Indian indenture system, the preeminent scholar on this topic was the late Professor Brij Lal, so any of his publications will provide a thoughtful and nuanced insight into the experience of the indentured labourers.

Thanks again for reading. I hope you've enjoyed the story and learned a little bit about Fiji and the Fijian Indians in the meantime.

Bula Vinaka,
Nilima

ACKNOWLEDGEMENTS

I would like to thank the following people for their contribution to this project, in chronological order.

My cousin Sanjeev, thank you for your help while I was in Fiji, for putting me up, showing me around and introducing me to interesting and lovely people.

My writing buddy Chris Foley, thank you for your steadfast support and your patience with my penchant for starting the scene in the middle and working backwards! And thank you for inviting me to be on Historical Novel Society Australasia's historical crime panel as an emerging writer. That event gave me the confidence to call myself a writer.

Andy, thank you for everything. For your love, for your pride in me and in this project, for giving me the only nickname I've ever liked. For table reads so I could better understand how men talk to each other, for scrawling title ideas all over your coffee table. For introducing me to Colin and making magic happen. For being the wonderful, generous, brilliantly creative person that you are. Love you Comma Man.

My editor, Taz, thank you for your excitement and enthusiasm for this project. Every one of your emails has brought a smile to my face and thank you so much for championing Akal with such passion!

Juliet Grames and the rest of the Soho team, thank you for giving my story a home.

Juliet Rogers and the rest of the Echo team, thank you for giving my story a home at home.

Kelly Smith and the rest of the Zaffre team, thank you for giving my story a home in the UK. London feels like my home away from home so I'm glad it will be on shelves there.